the SHOEMAKER

A Tale of Love, Magic & Unnatural Acts

KATHRYN COTTAM

To my Family

And to dreams. May all of yours come true.

HOUNDSTOOTH
Population ~~879~~
868

Utterly
Peak

the Palace

the Shade

Shoemaker

The
Wolf &
Foxtail

the Mire

Gaol

the Fields

to Ferrybone

PART
ONE

CHAPTER ONE

Wherein a story begins.

Edward Cordwainer is the ordinary son of an extraordinary father. He was born and raised in the small village of Houndstooth, under the magnificent height of Utterly Peak, a mountain so high its top is always hidden by clouds, and the village itself is rarely touched by hot summer sun. Houndstooth owes its existence to its proximity to the King's Summer Palace. For when royalty is in residence, it is the citizens of Houndstooth that keep the King, Queen, Princess and their multitude of servants supplied with fresh crusty breads, deep fried pickles, sweet honey peaches and dry salt pork.

Edward's father, Thomas the Elder, loves Houndstooth because he can name every friend and foe that walks its cobblestone streets. He reminds Edward daily how fortunate they are to reside in a place where no one is a stranger. Little does he know, this is precisely why Edward dislikes the village. For in a place where you know everyone, and everyone knows you, it is difficult to hold secrets. Not that Edward has many, or any, secrets. T'is just that he wishes he could have at least one.

Edward's mother, Marianne, died when he was but seven years young and Thomas did his very best to ensure the boy was not without a mother's love. In fact, he enrolled various women of the village in helping to raise his son. Chicken casseroles, pork pot pies and lamb stews would arrive from the kitchen of the Grocer's wife, Cynthia Hardcastle, each week for Sunday supper. Thus ensuring Edward's belly was full for the week ahead. Jenny Juniper, the tailor's wife, would sew him a new school uniform each September and thus Edward was never teased for wearing pants with cuffs that were well above his ankles. And finally, Betsy Candlewick, the local baker, provided Edward and Thomas with leftover raisin biscuits each day thus ensuring the time honored Houndstooth tradition of afternoon tea-time was maintained in their household. But no matter the meat, bread or suit, Edward was convinced Marianne, had she lived, would have done better.

Local rumor swirled regarding his mother's death on Utterly Peak. The Grocer whispered that Marianne had discovered Thomas's many affairs and so she had climbed high above the clouds and snow and jumped to her death. While the Tailor was equally certain that Thomas had always been faithful, but was wed to a woman with a touch of the brain fever and who, while wandering about the mountain one fateful day, accidentally fell to her death. Regardless, whatever new version of the story reached Edward, he adamantly refused to believe the ones in which his mother took her own life.

Yes, t'was true she was unhappy in Houndstooth. For at night while he lay in bed, and his father was in the shop below cutting leather for tomorrow's shoes, he would hear his mother pace the creaking floorboards of her bedroom, muttering and wailing. He chose to blame her sorrow on his father and not any weakness inherited from her own mad mother. For, Marianne was from the city and coming to live in Houndstooth had broken her heart. If only Thomas had packed their belongings and moved the lot of them back to Ferrybone, where Marianne was happy. Perhaps then she would not have climbed Utterly Peak, would not have accidentally fallen and would not have been dashed to pieces on sharp black rocks.

Edward knows her death was accidental for she would never have chosen to desert her son to his father's care, to the village of Houndstooth, to the meager life of the shoemaking trade. Marianne despised this life. She despaired at the calluses the hard wooden broom handle gave her soft palms as she swept up scrap shoe leather every afternoon in the shop. She hated crawling across the rough wooden floorboards on hand and knee, searching each crack and cranny for the hog hair bristles that fell from her husband's hand as he stitched the leather. And she especially loathed the ugly (yet sturdy) dirt brown boots, Thomas made for the farmers who worked the field and the dull (yet supportive) sandals for the women who ran the local shops. The only reason Marianne stayed, the only reason she tolerated this life, was Edward. But she also decreed that he was to have an education and not a trade. And she made her husband agree that when old enough, Edward would be sent abroad for university so that he could become a man of great importance.

But then Marianne died and everything changed.

Edward, who had been praised by his grade school teachers for his cunning and logic, began to miss more and more of his schooling in order to help his father in the shop. For with Marianne dead, Edward was now required to assist Thomas in his labors. And the more school Edward missed, the more his grades fell and the less inclined he was to apply himself to make up his studies. And while, yes, the hog hair bristles seemed to fall more quickly to the floor than ever before, and his father's hands shook with the threading, and his eyes squinted with the cutting, all these things seemed deliberately acquired in order to sabotage Edward's future promise.

And then the morning of the day before Edward was to graduate, he rose to find the kitchen stove cold. This was unprecedented. All his life, Edward remembered rising to find a pot of lukewarm congealed porridge on the stove from his father's breakfast, eaten hours earlier, so he could take advantage of the morning sun that filtered in through the shop window. But that morning, there was no pot, no porridge. Moreover, his father was not to be found in the shop, the kitchen or in the water closet out back. Edward retraced his steps, upstairs to his father's bedroom above the shop, and knocked on the door. There, Thomas sat on the bed, his bare feet flat on the floor, his once muscular hands, now gnarled like tree roots, settled in his lap. He raised his head to look straight in Edward's eyes and said: "Who's there?"

Perhaps it was the way the morning sun lit his father's face, but for the first time, Edward saw how completely the milky white cataracts had drawn across the old man's eyes like curtains, shutting off all vision.

And with the loss of Thomas the Elder's sight, came the loss of Edward's dream to leave Houndstooth. For being a shoemaker who kept his prices reasonable, Thomas did not have the funds to employ someone to cook, clean or care for him. Moreover, there was no other Shoemaker in the village, and none willing to relocate to so northern a destination, and thus the shop could not be sold. In the end, Thomas refused to close his doors simply because he was blind. Edward became his eyes and hands, constructing shoes under his father's guidance (though they tended to look nothing like what Thomas used to make). At times, Edward doubted his father's blindness. After all, how could his sight be there one day, only to be gone the next?

Edward entertained daily thoughts of running away and leaving the old man to his misery. But his feet rebelled against such action and he would find himself paralyzed, and unable to move. For his mind could not stomach the cruel things the villagers would say about him behind his back should he choose this path.

So like his father, before him, Edward became Houndstooth's Shoemaker.

But the choice to stay was like a fish bone caught in his throat, always threatening to choke him.

CHAPTER TWO

Wherein a small candle
plays a large role.

Anastasia is the daughter of a successful Ferrybone merchant and his beautiful wife. She is younger sister to one older brother and two older sisters. Her father spent her younger years voyaging beyond the Kingdom's borders, crossing the turbulent waters of the Atalantic Ocean by ship, importing shiny copper kettles, golden silk fabrics, and oddly shaped beasts with curving horns and multi-colored hides. Anastasia missed her Papa desperately when he was abroad but her mother and Nanny were ever present, ensuring his void would not be felt too deeply by her and her siblings. And thus, Anastasia's childhood days were a riot of noise and childish chaos. She played polished rocks and spiral shells with her sisters and climbed apple trees and ran along the rooftops with her brother.

When Papa returned home from his journeys he would hold each child in a breath-crushing bear hug, presenting the girls with chunks of chili-flecked chocolate or lengths of pretty pink ribbon and her brother with silver coins with holes in the center or yellow peppers that made the eyes tear up and the tongue burn.

But for Anastasia, he would always bring something extra: a book.

Sometimes they had maps that illustrated the water dragons of the Northern Oceans and the mer-mistresses of the Southern Seas. Sometimes they were filled with plays warning of the political perils of being King. And sometimes the words hinted at the dark danger that befell those who invoked magic; how those tempted to use it for gain, almost always perished. For everyone knew magic demanded balance and what was not rightly earned through toil and effort would decay until dust and rot was all that remained.

Anastasia's love of books was matched by her Nanny. Together, they would spend many an evening snuggled together in bed, reading by candlelight. Nanny would speak aloud the inked words of the pages, weaving tales for Anastasia's ears alone. And while Anastasia never imagined she would leave Ferrybone, (she fully expected that like her older sisters, she would find a husband amongst her friends and settle down in a house not far from her parents), she enjoyed living the exotic journeys and mad-cap adventures found within the crisp linen pages of her books.

And then when Anastasia was ten, her blissful world was interrupted. If what had occurred had happened within the pages of one of her books, Anastasia would have been delighted to partake. For if the book had already been written, she could peek at the end to ensure the heroine lived happily ever after. But it had not…

What happened occurred in the summer preceding her eleventh birthday. Summers in Ferrybone were always an ordeal with temperatures soaring so high the mercurial thermometers threatened to collapse into molten steam. This extreme heat was the reason the Royal family fled Ferrybone each summer for the cooler mountain climes up north.

This particular summer was worse than all others combined. The air was hot, stifling, without a hint of moisture. And the winds were fierce, as though they too protested the heat. The air about one's skin felt as though it had been cooked in a fiery oven. Nanny lay sleeping on the bed as Anastasia, her hair tied back with one of Papa's pink ribbons, curled up in the chair next to the open bedroom window and read her most recent book. She stayed awake deep into the night pouring over the color plates of the book by candlelight. There were birds with plumes of gold and burgundy, Felines with burnt orange manes hanging low to the ground, Elephantines that stood as tall as trees and had enormous curved tusks that twisted together.

Eventually, Anastasia fell asleep with the book still in her lap, and her head tipped back against the chair.

She awakened to an intense heat.

At first she thought it was simply a hot wind blowing in through the open window that was licking at her skin. It was only when she heard her mother's hysterical screams, and then her name *(Anastasia! Run)* being called deep and urgent by Papa that she opened her eyes.

To see the entire room engulfed in flame.

It was weeks or possibly months later when she found out the candle she had been reading by was toppled by the wind. The flame travelled from the table where the candle sat, to the curtains, the wall and ultimately the bed itself. One by one, Nanny, the dresser, the carpet, the ceiling and ultimately the whole of the house, fell to the flames. Papa said, the fact that Anastasia's chair, next to the window was last to catch light, was a miracle.

But it did not feel like one at the time. The noise of the flames as they ate through wood and cloth and gnawed at metal and glass was as frightening as any monster's voice in her books. The smell was nauseating and her lungs felt like she was inhaling the fire itself. Indeed, Anastasia felt as though she were burning from the inside out. And the screams. Her mother's and then others. Alarmed male voices, that all of Ferrybone could become tinder to this one candle.

It seemed an eternity, was probably only seconds, that Papa stood in the doorway blocked from reaching her by a wall of flame and ordered her to jump from the open window *(Now, Anastasia, Now!)*. Her brother and sisters had already dragged her mother outside. So now her world had shrunk to Papa, the flames, herself. Anastasia felt lost in a hell of her own making, quite unable to move, as though the compass of her existence had been broken. Her hair was in flames, her flesh had begun to melt. But she could not move. And then she was hit by a large figure and lifted from the chair. She did not know how Papa crossed the fire, but suddenly he was there. His large hands smothering the flames on her head, and then she was falling, all the while held tightly in his arms.

She landed on the ground two stories below her bedroom window, but did not feel a thing. She only remembered staring up into the darkness and hearing her mother's screams; it was, in fact, the only sound she could recall for days after. Then the boy from down the street, the one whose Papa sold newspapers and whose hands were always black with ink, was standing above her with a bucket of water, pouring it over her head. It was brilliantly cold and she gasped, falling into its current, unafraid to drown and away she drifted under a canopy of stars…

For the next two months Anastasia lived in a cocoon.

It was a dreadful time and Anastasia frequently wondered if it would have been better to have died. For she was completely immobilized. Her entire body from feet to neck was wrapped with mustard poultices designed to draw out the flame that still seemed to burn beneath her skin. Her eyes were bound so they might repair. And healing elixirs were poured into her throat by hands not her own and she struggled to keep down the bitter taste. The only grace was that every evening when Papa returned from work, he would make his way to her room and read aloud from her favorite books. It wasn't the words that made the difference, it was his voice. For in hearing him, she knew she was safe.

Anastasia was eager for the day the bandages would be removed so she could look once again on her Papa, mother, brother and sisters. So she could taste the honey bread from the baker down the street. So she could smell the scent of the lilac tree outside in the garden. They had been staying at a neighbor's house for the past three months while their home was under construction. After the fire, it had to be torn down and rebuilt. It was now even finer than before. Wider windows, taller spires, grander rooms. The grounds had even been replanted. When it was complete, one would never have known a fire had occurred in such a magnificent place as this.

Except for one thing: Anastasia's face.

The scars that had formed there were stubborn creatures and would not fade, preferring to remain puckered, red, shiny. The scars on her arm and leg were naturally less visible and much easier to hide. But the right side of her face caused much consternation. Many medicine women tended the flesh and administered their "never-fail-always-reliable-secret-recipe" lotions and potions, but to no avail. The spiritual men of the Abbey were invited to the house to speak spells of mystery and science, plead for angelic intervention, pray for healing and compassion and still the skin stubbornly resisted their words. One healer, traveling to Ferrybone from lands afar when she heard word of Anastasia's suffering, suggested magic was the only choice in a matter such as this. No sooner were her words spoken, then she was banished from their home, indeed Ferrybone itself, and her suggestion never spoken of again.

As Anastasia grew she noted how the citizens of Ferrybone would stare at the puckered flesh of her right cheek or turn aside in horror. She heard whispers that she was lucky to survive. That she was cursed, and it would have been better had she died, for now her parents were burdened with a deformed daughter. Indeed, Anastasia watched her mother's beautiful ebony hair whiten under the stress of trying to pretend her daughter looked normal.

Anastasia stopped walking to the newspapiary down the road to purchase the daily paper from the boy who ran his father's kiosk. She took her studies at home with an elderly tutor who had poor vision. She stopped visiting the King and Queen at the Palace with her mother (and Papa when he was home), although Anastasia was rather relieved for she had never cared for their daughter. Instead she chose to spend her days alone in the garden, pruning withered leaves from the roses, watering the parched soil, coaxing tulips, daffydils and hollyhocks out of the parched soil. And while the flowers blossomed, as the years passed, Anastasia grew gaunt, pale, invisible. And with all eyes turned away from her, Anastasia, may as well not even have existed. Her father was the one person who would still look her in the eyes, but he was gone most of the year, forced overseas for trade to cover the costs of the new house.

Then one morning while Papa was still away her mother called her in from the garden. In the sitting room sat an old woman so crippled, she could hardly stand upright and was instead forced to look at the ground with each step she took. She had iron grey hair and matching whiskers on her chin. Her hands were bony and stiff with arthritis and a black tattooed swan stained her right wrist. Anastasia knew her on sight. She was the most respected and powerful Matchmaker in Ferrybone, traveling the width and breadth of the Kingdom, creating successful marriages for parents who struggled to find compatible mates for their offspring. Anastasia sat across the table from the old woman as her mother poured out cold rhubarb and strawberry tea with mint leaves Anastasia herself had picked earlier that morning from the garden. An ice cold lump formed in Anastasia's stomach as she listened to the Matchmaker speak of a Shoemaker who lived in the cool mountain region up north and was looking for a city bred wife. He didn't have much coin, but he had a home, a noble profession, a thriving business. Upon meeting him, the Matchmaker immediately recalled Anastasia's plight. For despite her parent's great wealth, what man of the realm would choose to wed a woman whose dowry primarily consisted of a melted face? Therefore, would Anastasia consider the Shoemaker's proposal of marriage?

Anastasia's answer was, no.

The old crone exited the house to profuse apologies from Anastasia's mother.

Anastasia's reason for the refusal was simple (although she was too embarrassed to tell this to her mother), she was terrified. Of this unknown man. Of this unknown place called Houndstooth of all things (what kind of name was that? It had none of the elegance, familiarity and solidity of a name like Ferrybone). Moreover, Anastasia was scared to leave her mother, her Papa, her siblings, the house, her garden. Out there in the world, people in general and a husband in particular, would see her. And Anastasia was not yet certain she wished to be visible. She wasn't ready, it was too soon, she needed more time.

But time was not to be hers.

Every morning at breakfast, over crumpets and potted honey and lavender tea, her mother raised the possibility of Anastasia's marriage to this lonely Shoemaker. She spoke of first opportunity and last chances. She spoke of grandchildren (although she already had two and another on the way). She spoke of a mother's hopes and dreams for a daughter still unwed. And when Papa returned her mother tried to enroll him in the discussion, but he forestalled the conversation, stating it was Anastasia's decision.

Had it been winter when the Matchmaker arrived on their doorstep, Anastasia's life might have taken an entirely different and much less tragic direction. But it was not the final season of the year. It was summer. An especially difficult time for Anastasia as she had come to detest the hot Ferrybone winds. Every night she would lie awake in the dark, soaked in sweat, her skin fevered. Night after night she relived the terror of that awful night ten years before. Night after night, the air was hot and she burned all over again. And then one morning, after a particularly sleepless night, she asked Papa over breakfast if he had ever been to Houndstooth. He had, delivering goods to the summer palace, years before. He didn't remember a Shoemaker, but he did recall the village, a cluster of brightly painted cottages in the shape of a horseshoe nestled in the arms of a towering mountain. He remembered flourishing gardens containing all manner of vegetables and flowers. And humble, cheerful folk who worked the fields and enjoyed the fruits of their hard labor. He spoke of golden fields of grain, forests of thick greenery and a sky so blue one could almost imagine it were an ocean. And then Papa talked of mountain breezes so cool that one's skin never overheated, of long blue shadows that kept the soil moist and arable, of a sun that never truly warmed the cobblestone streets before it tucked its head away for nightfall.

Anastasia fingered the scar on her face and tried to imagine a place where the air was cool and she might not awake screaming and sweaty in the night. She imagined a place where she could work in the garden all day and not have to retreat from the sun's rays at noon. She imagined a place with color, where the earth and grass and shrubs and plants were not burned to a crisp by hot summer heat. She imagined this place everyday for the next three weeks. And at the end of that time she told her parents, yes.

Three days later, she sat once again with the Matchmaker and her mother, and Papa too. This time she signed the marriage certificate and watched as the old woman lit a candle, dripped wax onto the document and marked it with her seal. Later that day, Anastasia walked for the last time through Ferrybone, to the Courthouse with Papa, and filed the certificate with the local judiciary.

Which is why, Anastasia found herself traveling, by horse and carriage with her two suitcases of belongings, to the distant village of Houndstooth, to a husband she had never met and the life of a Shoemaker's wife.

CHAPTER THREE

Wherein drinks
are spilled.

E dward had worked in his father's shop but for one month when he decided his hands were not meant to perform manual labor. Whereas his father's hands had been (until lately) large, muscular, and callused, Edward's fingers were fine-boned and elegant, the hands of a Genteel-man. They lacked the strength to cut through the shoe leather in a seamless motion and thus the edges were left ragged and uneven. Whereas, Thomas could sit at his bench for hours, Edward despised the way his shoulders ached from hunching over his tools. He put twice as much effort into his shoes as did Thomas, and they were of half the quality when complete. His shoes rarely lasted one month of hard labor in the fields. Thomas's shoes would last a full six. For the first three years of Edward's apprenticeship, the citizens of

Houndstooth continued to buy their shoes from Thomas's shop (even though the leather caused blisters to rise with every step). Edward knew this was because they loved the old man and pitied his current state of blindness. And that eventually they would recognize the son had none of the old man's talent, craft or genius when it came to the comfort and fit of a shoe. And it was only a matter of time before they stopped patronizing the store.

Edward also believed the villagers pitied his current state of being. But, if only they knew how much he pitied them. Pity for their sparse houses and thatched roofs, faded paint and overgrown gardens. Pity for their unadorned and threadbare coats. Pity for their folk tales, humble diet and plain women. And indeed, it was the latter item that caused Edward the most consternation. He was now of a marriageable age and Thomas, indeed all of the village, inquired daily on his prospects for a wife. But Edward was determined not to settle for one of the common village girls. The women of Houndstooth had accents which were flat and monotonous and large hands and feet that enabled them to work efficiently in the fields, but left them devoid of femininity. They wore dresses that were brown and tedious, absent of color or grace, frills or fancy. They were hardly the type of woman befitting a Genteel-man. The Matchmaker who had been traveling through Houndstooth when Edward consulted her, warned him that very few girls would willingly trade the city with its elegance and finery for the peasant ways of Houndstooth. Such a girl, she mused, would have to be a remarkable individual.

Edward reminded the old woman he would not be a shoemaker for long. Once Thomas passed (and Edward was convinced this would be any day now due to his father's mounting ailments), Edward would sell the business and begin his studies at university so he could take up his rightful career (what that may be he had not yet determined, for at present all he knew was shoes and even that, he did not know half so well as he thought he did).

And a Genteel-man must have a Genteel-lady. And, much to the dismay of a great many young girls of Houndstooth who thought Edward quite handsome, he refused to marry until a woman who met his criteria for wiving (beautiful, well-bred, genteel, obedient), could be found. Edward expected it might take years to find the right girl. It took the old crone mere weeks. For she returned within a fortnight to bear news that she had found him such a wife. She presented him with the marriage certificate which he signed and she sealed, all the while regaling him with stories of a bewitching Merchant's daughter who hailed from Ferrybone. As she folded the paper and placed it securely within her satchel, she told him she would return in two weeks with his bride.

Houndstooth was abuzz with the news of his wife's (her name was Anastasia, how glorious!) pending arrival. For not since Edward's mother, Marianne, had an outsider claimed Houndstooth as their own. Edward went to great lengths to ensure the villagers knew his wife was a woman of great beauty, breeding and renown. In preparation for her arrival (and despite his father's protests), Edward closed the shop. He hired the butcher's boy to paint the exterior walls a bright welcoming yellow. He hired the local flower-monger to replace the broken ceramic pots that stood outside the front door and fill their replacements with roses that when they bloomed, smelled of lemons. He hired several local charwomen to sweep the cobwebs from the ceiling corners, beat the dust from the old floor rugs and scrub the grime from the windows, so they let in what little sunshine managed to find its way past the mountains and into Houndstooth. He dug out his mother's jewelry (or what remained of it, having sold several pieces over the past few years to cover the bills when business slowed). He had been holding onto her most magnificent piece; a brooch shaped like a peacock with jade and turquoise stones for tail feathers and ruby chips for eyes. He meant to present it to his bride on their wedding night. Not once did Edward wonder why his bride had chosen to be a Shoemaker's wife.

He had no doubt that the Matchmaker spoke well of him and his intentions, and that was enough.

A week before Anastasia was due to arrive, Thomas died unexpectedly in his sleep. Over the past few months his lungs had grown ever more delicate due to the increased number of hours he spent in repose. On the night he died, he failed to latch his bedroom window before retiring and it had blown open during the night. His lungs, already weakened, were unable to fight off the ensuing chill and he was dead by the following evening. Edward decided it was for the best as no bride wanted to be encumbered with a crippled father-in-law. If the suddenness of Thomas's passing raised any curious eyebrows amongst the citizens of Houndstooth, Edward was unaware of such conversations. After a visit by the Sheriff who methodically studied the window latch and, indeed, found it faulty and then consulted the local medical practitioner (Doctor Wintergreen), who confirmed Thomas's lungs were poor, Edward was given leave to bury his father. He had Thomas interred in the pauper's section of the local church graveyard, and held no memorial or funeral. He knew his father would not want him to spend money on such things when he was about to be wed.

And that day came quick upon him.

Anastasia arrived in a gleaming ebony carriage pulled by two magnificent black thoroughbreds with gold ribbon braided in their manes. Their hooves thundered across the ancient cobblestones of Houndstooth's main street, announcing to all the arrival of Edward's wife.

Edward, himself, hovered behind the thin shop window curtains, not wanting to appear too eager, but also wanting to witness the faces of the folk who stopped in awe to watch her carriage. Never before had such magnificent beasts visited Houndstooth. In fact, the horses and livery were matched only in their elegance by the King's own. But even the Royal family circumvented the town that kept them supplied with provisions, choosing instead to use the eastern road to access the Summer Palace. When Anastasia's carriage stopped before the shop, Edward waited twenty seconds before throwing open the door in welcome. The old Matchmaker stepped out first, placing her arthritic hand in that of the coachman's and alighting to the street below.

Then came his bride.

Anastasia.

One foot, then the other. Silver shoes embroidered with

gold stars. A glimpse of dainty ankle before her silver skirts hid them from view. Ermine cuffs circled delicate wrists and a long elegant neck. The skin on her hands was smooth, pale. She wore an elaborately shaped headpiece and veil that obscured her face. A sudden nervous tremor took hold of Edward's body. His palms were sweaty, as was the nape of his neck, where his collar chafed against his skin.

And then his bride was standing before him, her hand still clinging to the old woman's fingers. He reached out for her free hand, took the delicate fingers in his own, and raised it to his lips. She didn't say a word, merely curtsied when he released her.

"Shall we enter?" the old woman rasped.

Edward led the way into the shop, guiding them through the workroom and into the adjoining kitchen area. He had covered the plain wooden table with his mother's white lace tablecloth. Had picked some of the roses from the front steps and placed them in the cream pitcher, thus filling the room with the scent of lemons. He poured out three glasses of mint water thinking she, or rather, they, would be parched from the journey. Anastasia's hands lifted to raise the veil and Edward's heart pounded in his throat as he prepared to catch the first glimpse of his bride. But the old crone intervened.

"The marriage must first be bound," she said and Anastasia stilled.

The Matchmaker drew from her faded carpetbag a glass vial containing a clear liquid, a lump of bread (that more resembled a rock than something edible), a folded purple cloth, a silver bowl, a taper, a tin pillbox and a short sharp blade with an ivory handle.

"Your hands," she wheezed, squeezing out the words as though she were running out of breath.

Edward and Anastasia both held out their right hands, palm side up.

The Matchmaker broke the bread into two pieces, placing a section in each of their hands.

"Bread, so you might never know hunger," she said. Edward popped the bread into his mouth expecting it to be stale but it was surprisingly moist, tasting of rye and honey. He watched for a glimpse of Anastasia, but she was careful to leave the veil in place, drawing her hand up behind the curtain of fabric that kept her hidden from view.

When they had each swallowed the bread, the Matchmaker unscrewed the silver lid from the glass vial and poured the liquid into her silver bowl.

"Water, so you might never know thirst," she said handing the bowl to Edward. He drank and the water was surprisingly cold, as though it were freshly drawn from one of the glacier fed streams of Utterly Peak. When he had finished, the crone took the bowl and handed it to Anastasia. Once again, she was careful to keep the veil in place while she sipped. When the water was drained, the Matchmaker unwrapped the purple cloth to reveal two gold coins. One she placed in Edward's palm. One she placed in Anastasia's.

"Gold, so you might never know want," she rasped. Edward closed his hand over the gold coin, thrilling at the feel of it in his hand. Bridal gold had no monetary value, but was highly prized. It was an acknowledgment of the regard the bride's family had for her future husband. Few of the villagers in Houndstooth were able to afford the real thing, instead painting ordinary iron coins with yellow paint. Even though Edward knew Anastasia came from a wealthy family, he had not expected such a display of familiarity from her parents given they had not yet been introduced. They each held the gold for the required minute while the old crone muttered foreign words over their hands. And then, so the gold would always be near their hearts, they each placed their piece in a grey silk drawstring bag and hung it about each other's necks.

Finally, the Matchmaker gestured for both of them to hold out their hands once more. Once they complied, the old woman drew her blade across the soft skin of Edward's palm. He felt no pain as warm blood pooled in his hand. The Matchmaker curled her bony fingers around his, forming his hand into a fist and squeezed. Her grip was much stronger than Edward expected and she captured all his blood in her silver bowl. When his hand would drip no more, she turned to Anastasia. Edward saw his bride start as the blade struck, but she uttered nothing, remaining silent as the Matchmaker also curled her hand into a fist, and collected the blood in her bowl.

As the old woman swirled their blood together, she muttered more words that Edward did not understand. When she finally finished her incantation she set the bowl on the table before them and lifted the lid of the tin pillbox. Inside was a yellow powder which she emptied into the bowl where it was immediately stained red by their blood. She lit her taper from a nearby candle and held the flame to the bowl's contents. The powder ignited, caught fire, and burned rapidly. When the flame finally extinguished, the bowl's contents had vanished.

The Matchmaker gave a short raspy laugh, which to Edward's ears sounded more like a cackle, and proclaimed: "What was twice, is now once. What was separate, is now combined. What was shattered, is now whole. Until death, your life, your love, your fate are now entwined."

She pressed her dry lips against Edward's forehead and kissed him, then did the same to Anastasia, through the veil.

"My blessing forever. Together endeavor. Your lives always treasure. Love without measure."

And thus, the marriage contract was complete.

The old Matchmaker gathered her wares, placed them into her carpetbag and bade them farewell. Edward rose to walk her out but she muttered an exhortation and waved him away, hobbling out of the kitchen on her own merit. Leaving Edward and Anastasia, alone, sitting across the table from one another.

The silence between them was awkward, heavy and Edward watched Anastasia's fingers twist in her lap. He realized she must be as nervous as he.

"Shall I?" he heard.

At first he didn't realize the soft voice, as clear and delicate as birdsong came from the woman across the table from him. But then she grabbed hold of the veil and lifted.

"No," he shouted, his heart pounding and she dropped her hands, her face still shrouded. He rose from his chair and moved around to her side of the table.

"It's just," he breathed, "allow me."

And so she rose before him, her head reaching his shoulders, the smell of her rose-water perfume filling his nostrils and his blood warmed to the fact that this delicate creature was now his.

Then she folded her hands before her and tipped her face to the right.

Edward's fingers seized the light grey fabric and pulled it up and away from her features.

Her profile was exquisite. Her skin was pale and smooth with a slight pink blush on her cheek. Her eye, the lid partially lowered in shyness, was silver in color, framed by thick sable lashes. Her lip, pink, full. The teeth small, white, perfect. Her hair, thick and bound in the traditional matrimonial plaits of Ferrybone custom, was the color of cherry-wood

Edward cupped her chin in his hand and turned her head so that she faced him.

And then he saw what he really married.

Whereas the left side of her face was perfection, the right side belonged to a monster. The skin of her cheek was not pink, but puckered and ridged with shiny white scars. The flesh of her forehead drooped as though it were melting. The eyebrow and eyelashes were absent, leaving the eyeball naked and accusatory. The lip was twisted as though she were perpetually sad.

He froze, spellbound by the ugliness before him.

Until Anastasia uttered a cry and pulled his fingers away from her chin. Only when he saw the white marks his fingers left on her skin, did he realize how tight his grip had been. A clattering sound like falling knives echoed in his ears. But then he remembered the Matchmaker. And recognized the sound as the hoof steps from her horses.

Edward turned from Anastasia and ran out of the kitchen, through the shop, and into the street. The Coachman had turned the carriage so that it might return to Ferrybone and Edward launched himself in front of the horses so they could not pass. The animals reared back at his sudden appearance before them, with angry whinnies and the Coachman snapped his whip.

"Bloody fool!" he shouted at Edward.

Edward ignored the man and strode past the foaming beasts. He grabbed the handle of the carriage door and threw it open. The old crone was settled back in the seat with her eyes closed, a wool blanket over her legs, her carpetbag in her lap.

"You cheating hag," he snapped.

The old woman's eyes flashed open and looked at him as though he had bade her nothing more than good morning.

"You seem out of joint," she stated, her wrinkles looking even more defined in the shadowy recess of the carriage's interior.

"I most certainly am," Edward snarled.

"And why would that be?" she asked. "I have fulfilled your request and delivered you a wife who is well-bred, genteel, obedient and beautiful."

"Ha!" Edward barked. "You call that thing in there beautiful?"

The old woman's eyes hardened and Edward felt a chill akin to a cold knife scraping down his spine.

"In the days to come you would do well to recall, Mr. Cordwainer, that true beauty has very little to do with the package in which it arrives." Then the Matchmaker reached out, gripped the carriage door and wrenched it from his grasp. As soon as the door slammed shut, the Coachman snapped his whip yet again and the horses bolted forward.

Edward jumped back to avoid being dragged under the carriage. Mud from the horse's hooves splattered across his trousers. The wheels clattered against the cobblestones and then the carriage was gone. Edward shoved his hands into his trouser pockets. Something sharp pricked his right hand, reopening the wound made earlier by the Matchmaker. He yanked out his hand and licked away the blood from his fingers. When the wound had clotted he slipped his hand back into his pocket and pulled out the object. It was his mother's peacock brooch. He studied it for a moment, then returned it to his pocket and stepped back inside closing the door behind him.

Anastasia's two trunks sat on the floor next to his workbench. He stood there staring at the worn brown leather, unable to move, as though his shoes were nailed to the floor. He had wanted to prove to the citizens of Houndstooth that he was more than a motherless boy, more than this shabby shoemaking shop, that he was just more. And now here he was, stuck with Ferrybone's discards. How Houndstooth would laugh at his hubris, his desire to overreach his father's grasp. How they would laugh to see him cut off at the knees. A black rage boiled through his blood and he curled his fingers into fists.

"Excuse me."

He turned to see she was standing at the door that connected the kitchen area to the shop, had moved so softly he had not heard her arrive.

"I meant no trickery, no deceit," she said gesturing to

her face. "I assumed the Matchmaker would have told you. If you will deliver me to the nearest Inn, I will take the evening carriage home. I am most certain my Father will dissolve the marriage."

Edward stared at her for a full minute. At no time did she turn from his gaze and he supposed she must be used to people staring. He had hoped to leverage this marriage for better prospects in the future and now that future was even more uncertain than before. Although—and here an idea took seed in Edward's brain—Anastasia need not bring him disgrace. He could still make this marriage work to his advantage. Houndstooth need not know he was unaware of Anastasia's disability. And how clever, how admired, how esteemed would be the man who chose a woman with such a face, for his wife. Was it possible, after all, that her face could act as currency to better his life? Indeed, even Anastasia's father would be in his debt, because Edward wed his daughter when no other man would have her. Of all men, how could he refuse to assist his son-in-law in obtaining his dreams? If not for himself, at the very least for his daughter?

Yes, this marriage might have value after all.

He shoved his hand back into his pocket, and felt the hard edges of the peacock pin. But he did not pull it from its resting place.

"The Inn?" she repeated.

Edward smiled at her.

Anastasia sat on a corner of the thin mattress. The room was small, no bigger than a pantry. There was only room for a single cot plus a tiny dresser with two drawers wedged beneath an open window. In one of the drawers she found a wax taper, candlestick holder and matches. Otherwise the room was bare of possessions.

"I imagine you are weary from the journey," her husband had said leading her upstairs to a room above the kitchen. "So I think t'is best you recover in here." He had paused to look about the space, "t'is small, but my father always found it most comfortable."

Anastasia had found herself agreeing that the room was sufficient. And yes, she was indeed most tired. He had brought up her trunks which now occupied what little floor space remained and then left, closing the door behind him. Then for the first time since leaving Ferrybone she found herself alone. She turned the key in the door, locking herself in. And then collapsed on the floorboards, burst into tears and cried until no more came. She was tired, scared and wanted her Papa. She opened her trunks hoping her few possessions would provide comfort, but they smelled too much like home and her heart broke all the more.

She had been nervous from the start. At first she thought she was to make the journey alone, but her mother arranged for the Matchmaker to accompany her. Anastasia knew this was because her mother feared she would be stricken with doubt and turn the carriage around mid-journey. Therefore the Matchmaker was hired to distract Anastasia from such thoughts. But the thoughts had come in spite of the old woman's presence. And by the time Anastasia arrived in Houndstooth, it felt as though there were no room in her chest for air. Not even the pretty painted cottages of yellow, green and blue could calm her nerves.

She was a stranger here. Unknown to everyone, even her husband. And yet he had chosen her. As if the old woman could read her thoughts, the Matchmaker had reached out with her bony hand and squeezed Anastasia's fingers in reassurance. It was not long after that, wheel and horse hoof met cobblestone and the carriage drew to a stop.

If it hadn't been for the Matchmaker, Anastasia would have been unable to step down from the carriage. Her hands and feet shook so severely that she could not stand upright alone. Even her stomach was inconsolable, her guts twisting, refusing to calm despite Anastasia's demands that it do so. It was difficult to see through the veil that the Matchmaker insisted she wear. Despite the curtain, however, Edward appeared a most gracious man. He met her at the door, welcomed her with a kind voice and a kiss for her hand, and then led them through the workroom where he practiced his trade and into a clean swept kitchen. A pitcher of roses on the table filled the room with their scent and chased away some of the fears that had travelled these long hours at Anastasia's side. The marriage ceremony, usually performed by a blessings clerk was presided over by the Matchmaker. It passed in a blur and was over before Anastasia realized the rites were complete.

And then she was married.

Anastasia did not remember the Matchmaker leaving. Did not remember Edward removing the veil. All she could recall was the look of horror on her husband's face as he saw her for the first time. In that instance, her stomach dropped to the floor. For she knew the old woman had played Edward for a fool and not told him his wife resembled a monster. He was right to flee. He was right to demand the ceremony be undone.

Anastasia stood in the kitchen listening to Edward's angry voice as he confronted the old woman. But she was not upset by his extreme emotion. She was relieved.

He didn't want her.

She was more than relieved.

He didn't want her! She was elated.

She had fulfilled her commitment. And now she could return home to Ferrybone, her mother, Papa, brother, sisters and beloved gardens. She doubted her mother would try and force another match, given the social ramifications of having a daughter who had already been rejected by one husband.

Anastasia gathered her skirts in her hands, her heart enlivened by the thought of returning home, and made her way from the kitchen into his workshop. Edward was standing there, lost in delirium and she had to clear her throat to awaken him to her presence. At first she was unsure if he had heard her exhortation that no deceit was intended. For he had simply stared at her for the longest period of time. She realized then that he was quite a handsome man. Slim and tall with elegant limbs, soft brown hair in need of a trim falling over his brow, a nose that was slender and graceful, a mouth both wide and pleasant. He had blue eyes that were transforming even now in their color, no longer cold puddles of despair but warm like the turquoise southern seas she visited as a child.

When he spoke, however, his words were like an anvil on her heart. She had expected, nay wanted, him to agree to her plan. But instead he apologized for his harsh words, explaining yes, the Matchmaker had been less than truthful but the circumstances of Anastasia's appearance had merely taken him by surprise. And he had no intention of going back on his word. She was still to be his wife. And then he had taken her hand and once again planted a kiss in her palm. Then in a bit of a whirlwind, he had shown her about her new home. His tiny workshop, the kitchen with its black pot-bellied stove and iron pans, the pantry with a meager store of food, the small overgrown garden in need of a proper weeding. Then he led her upstairs, to the two rooms over the shop. She had assumed the larger one was to be their wedded chamber, given it had been freshly scrubbed and several vases of freshly picked lavender were placed conspicuously on the dresser and side tables. But instead, Edward opened a door on the opposite side of the hallway, ushered her in, and here she remained.

She fingered the soft grey pouch containing the bridal gold and yanked it from about her neck. Given it was very thin, the coin weighed next to nothing and yet it felt heavy and burdensome. Still seated on the floor, Anastasia pressed her head to her knees and wrapped her arms about herself. There was no going back, she had agreed to this, chosen this.

The Matchmaker's words echoed in her head: "Until death, your life, your love, your fate are now entwined."

Until death.

PART
TWO

CHAPTER ONE

Wherein tales are told.

Edward sits across the dinner table from Anastasia.

She has fried the last of the white onions from the garden and serves them over the stale bread she purchases from Betsy's Bakery for half price. There is honey mead to drink and for dessert, a delicacy too expensive for most residents of Houndstooth: papery thin slices of potted pepper cheese. But Margarite Curdsmith, the cheesemaker's wife, feels pity for Anastasia (whether for her burns or her husband, Edward is uncertain, although he has his suspicions about the latter considering how cool Margarite's manner is when he encounters her in the street). And thus Margarite charges Anastasia a mere hay-penny instead of a shilling for the cheese. In return Anastasia shows the woman how to make the most delicate lace Houndstooth has ever seen. Margarite affixes this lace (and there is, by now, copious amounts of it), to the sleeves, neckline and hem of her plain brown dresses. To Edward, it seems a frivolous addition, much akin to dressing the family dog in fancy dress.

It is seven months today that he and Anastasia were married. And in that time he can count the number of shoes he has made on his hands. Each evening when he retires to bed he has every intention of rising in the morning, taking the stairs down to the shop and sitting at the bench with his father's tools in hand. But when he awakes at dawn, he remembers how much he abhors the practice of shoemaking; the smell of the leather, the welts, the cuts, the blisters. All these things paralyze him and he cannot rise. On the very few occasions he does attempt to make a pair of shoes, they fall to pieces in his hands. And apart from the Sheriff who still continues to patronize the shop for the occasional repair, all of his father's customers have abandoned him and now choose to purchase their footwear from Pigsbottom, Fiddletail or one of the other outlying towns in the region.

Given Anastasia's wealth he had expected the first six months of marriage to pass with ease. But it was not the case. He was surprised to learn, aside from the bridal gold, she brought no coin with her. And this past season, Edward has had no income from the shop and the winter has been extremely harsh. He repeatedly instructed Anastasia to request financial support from her family. But each time she refused, reassuring him that, at least for today, all was well. And indeed no matter how often he informs her they are on the edge of starvation, she finds a way to stem their hunger. She has a curious knack for finding the winter potatoes that hide deep in the forest (which she fries on the hot stove with butter, wild mushrooms and the snails she collects from beneath the ramshackle fence out back). She harvests whole crops of violaheads from what Edward had assumed to merely be weeds. And when they run out of candles she arranges to hand letter recipes for Carlotta Oldacre, the butcher's wife (whose memory is starting to fail), and in return receives a pound of pig fat. This, Anastasia turns into candles, using wicks she makes from the braided cotton lining of her trunks. And although the candles provide the requisite light, the stink of burning fat grips Edward's throat with nausea.

He cannot imagine that Anastasia is happy with her current circumstance in life and yet she never complains. He wishes she would, for then he could be the one to admonish her against such thoughts. But no, she never raises her tongue against him, the house or Houndstooth. And how a family as wealthy as hers can allow their daughter to live in such poverty, is a mystery to Edward.

The Matchmaker had made it clear to him that Anastasia came from the merchant class, and indeed the carriage, her clothes, manners and stories supported this fact. However, Edward was still blind to the extent of that wealth until they made their first visit to her family as a married couple. They chose to travel to Ferrybone the month before winter set in, for once the Decemberal snows arrived in Houndstooth, the village was effectively cut off from the Kingdom. The family carriage that originally brought Anastasia to Edward had been sent to to fetch them to Ferrybone. For Edward, it was the first time he had travelled in such luxury. And although he still required a rug to keep his legs and lap warm, the carriage was so tightly sealed it permitted no draft to enter the interior, and its steel elliptical springs added much needed stability and mitigated the jostling caused by the incredibly rutted road that led out of Houndstooth.

The journey to Ferrybone was the first time he and Anastasia had spent a long period of time together in such tight quarters. They had not spoken much, Anastasia preferring to lean her head against the right hand side of the carriage and slumber. Edward, however, was gripped with a fevered excitement to be leaving Houndstooth, even if only for a fortnight, and could not sleep. He had many questions for her but did not want to appear too eager and therefore he matched her silence in tone and length. It was much too cold to have the windows open and so he was forced to look at the wife who sat across from him. Edward found if he squeezed himself against the carriage on his far right, Anastasia's marred face disappeared completely into the shadows and once again he was struck by her beauty. T'was such a pity she had been disabled in such a manner. Her parents must truly be grateful that he had elected to keep her as his bride. In the silence that followed, he daydreamed about how different his marriage would be if the other side of Anastasia's face matched the one that was now on view (that she might not have been his to marry without the incident of the fire in the night-time did not, of course, even occur once to Edward).

Anastasia awoke when they were but two leagues from the village. As they approached, the air grew warmer and so they parted the sashes and opened the windows. It seemed to Edward that the warmth did much to revive his wife. She appeared to enliven upon the approach to Ferrybone, pointing out which of the many magnificent homes he saw were occupied by the Mayoral, the Judiciary, the head of the Merchant Guild. The town itself was much grander than Edward had even imagined. The buildings were primarily wood and very tall, some of them having four or five levels to them. They towered over cobblestones that were smooth and swept clean of their debris at dusk each night. The shops along High Street had large windows in which the merchants displayed their wares and the exterior walls were devoid of the spray of mud from horse hooves that seemed to mark every building along the main street in Houndstooth.

Anastasia's home was perched at the end of a long winding lane that bisected the High Street. It was by far the most expensive home in the area, painted a bright ocean blue (or at least a color Edward thought the ocean would be, having never seen one), with contrasting red shutters. The door opened under a portcullis that led onto the street. There were no gardens out front, but Edward could see that the lot extended quite far back and there were flowering firs that dwarfed the house by at least fifty feet. Edward stepped down from the carriage first, brushing aside the driver, so that he might assist Anastasia himself. He took her hand and his guts knotted briefly as he wondered if she might divulge to her parents, the lack of intimacy in their relationship.

But this thought disintegrated in his brain with the arrival of said individuals. Anastasia's mother - Caroline - was a handsome woman, pleasingly plump which reassured Edward they would not want for food while under this roof. The skin of her face and hands was smooth indicating she did not partake in labor and her hair was a vivid white. She had bright eyes, a wide smile and enveloped Edward in a doughy hug, right there on the cobblestones, cushioning him against her bosom and welcoming him to their home.

Anastasia's mother then bustled him into the house, leaving the footman to bring in their cases. Caroline presented him to Anastasia's father - John - who was almost the exact opposite of his wife. Tall, thin, with a hard face and a firm grip, Anastasia's father had examining eyes. Ones that were not inclined to quick judgment, but instead weighed and measured everything before him (including himself, Edward thought), to see if its quality measured up to its price.

Whereas, Caroline had squeezed her daughter in a hug similar to the one he had received, John merely folded his daughter into his arms and held her there. The grip that was so hard and firm when shaking Edward's hand, was now as soft and gentle around Anastasia as a pair of wings. From the movement of her shoulders, Edward suspected Anastasia was crying and after a moment of uncomfortable silence, John instructed the day-maid to escort Edward to their rooms so that he might freshen up from the long journey.

Edward patted Anastasia's shoulder twice in reassurance and then left her to her parents. He was led through the house to the rooms they were to occupy. Strangely, and quite against the fashion of the day, the bedroom, powder room and sitting area, were located on the first floor, at the rear of the home, overlooking an expansive and abundant garden. The furnishings in the two main rooms were luxuriously appointed, a combination of scents suggesting the chairs, table, bed frame were of cedar, sandalwood, balsam. The elegant curves of the porcelain fixtures in the powder room were amazing to behold and specially designed pipes brought running water (both cold and hot!) into a basin. Edward washed his face and hands while the day-maid unpacked the trunks that the footman had delivered. When she had finished and departed, Edward changed into a shirt that did not carry the stink of their journey. He despaired of its quality for neither this shirt, nor any of his other clothes, were a match for the elegance of this home. It was important for him to be respected by Anastasia's father, after all, he had a proposition for the man and needed to be taken seriously.

Anastasia had obviously freshened up elsewhere, for when the maid guided him to the dining room upon the dinner hour, his wife was present. Her face and hands were scrubbed clean, her hair washed and newly bound and she wore a gown of spring green that Caroline had bought for her daughter just that morning. The table was set with silver utensils, jugs and serving platters. The King's crest marked each porcelain plate and bowl ("a gift from the Regent himself", Caroline whispered). They ate sweet orange potatoes and leafy bitter greens. There was dried pork with sour plums and salted fish with lemon crust. And for dessert, there were small brown fruits with prickly skins that had sweet green seeds on the inside. Throughout the meal, Edward had laughed at her mother's jokes (although he did not understand them in the slightest), and asked John a great many questions about his work. In fact, he seemed unable to stop asking questions. He wanted to stay his tongue, but his nerves were unresponsive. That is until he felt a hand on his own and realized it was Anastasia's. He pulled away with a jerk, unsure why she was touching him. When he met her eyes, she smiled and he felt something in him thaw. She was simply being kind. And so he reached out and resumed contact with her. The skin of her hand was smooth, warm and he felt blood rush to his penis, and was immediately grateful for the cover of the table and its cloth.

Thoughts jumbled through his head as he held her slim delicate fingers in his own. He couldn't possibly be attracted to Anastasia. She was far too monstrous in appearance. Yes, society would naturally assume he bedded his wife (as was his husbandly duty), but what would they think of him should they know he lusted for her? Perhaps they would think he harbored a fetish towards the ugly when, in fact, his brain protested, it was quite the opposite. It was easy enough in Houndstooth for him to have his desires met elsewhere; the girls who thought him handsome before he was married, still thought similarly now. The fact that he had a wife was no impediment and he was more than happy to oblige. Regardless, he found he did not release her hand (compensating rather awkwardly by using his left hand for his utensils). And only when they had all eaten their fill, did they retire to the evening room.

As they settled, the butler brought cigars made of sweet tobacco leaf for John and Edward and port so thick it looked like golden syrup for Caroline and Anastasia. John asked a great many questions of their life in Houndstooth but Edward now found his tongue quite paralyzed and unable to respond to the questions regarding his trade, their home, and plans of children. Anastasia, however, seized the conversation and answered each question in a way Edward thought was truly remarkable. Yes, their house was small, but it was cozy and she enjoyed the process of turning it into a home. No, the garden was not large but it backed out onto the Shade, Houndstooth's forest, and there Anastasia had planted bunches of beans, beds of beets and bushels of berries. And yes, the business of shoes was slow but it was winter when the citizens of Houndstooth stayed indoors and there was little requirement for footwear. Theirs was a seasonal life with spring, summer, and fall spent out of doors planting, growing and reaping. Once winter came, neighbors were seldom seen for months on end. And so no, Edward had not been making many shoes but he was using the time to study with one of the local wine merchants and learn the business of import and export. And yes, children would be nice (and here his wife's unscarred cheek colored quite prettily), but they were still getting to know one another and children could wait another season. Edward was relieved that Anastasia did not share with her parents the long, cold nights where they sat shivering together in the kitchen, next to the stove which burned what little remained of their peat fuel. Or the long days of hunger when she was unable to harvest anything but bitter roots, from the plants she so carefully tended. He appreciated her support and resolved that when they returned to Houndstooth he would make more of an effort to assist her in the garden. And, although he never looked at her with longing, she would of course want children.

He realized he would have to lay with her tonight and, indeed, this would be the first time they would sleep in the same bed. Of course, he tried to initiate himself with her in the past, usually on nights when he had drank too much apple wine, but her face always got between them. When he would knock on her door and enter the room, she insisted the candle remain lit. And when she removed her nightclothes, he saw how the scars on her face had matching brethren on her arms and legs. And as he couldn't imagine touching such deformities, he had always demurred, albeit with profuse apologies, claiming a headache, lack of sleep or a need to study. He wondered if tonight would be different given his response to her at dinner. Perhaps he could overlook his previous apprehensions, if his body were keen to engage with hers.

He supposed he might be able to convince Anastasia to keep her face turned to the right as they lay together. But he knew in his heart that even if she were to oblige, the image of her scars would rise up between them like some ghostly spectral. Nonetheless, when they returned home he determined it would be something he would address. If she wanted children they would have to surmount this hurdle. Even if it meant she had to hide her face with a handkerchief, pillow or other cover. Or he would simply insist she douse the candle. In the dark, Edward resolved, he needn't even see her and she could, quite simply, be any woman he imagined her to be. He watched her sip the last of her port, hand her empty glass to the butler and bid her parents, goodnight (a kiss for each on the cheek and a long lingering look at Edward). Yes, when they returned home things would be much different.

And then Edward turned his attention to her father and his stories of distant kings, courts and cultures.

Edward's time in Ferrybone passed quickly as a chaotic

jumble of dinners, teas and luncheons. Edward had no idea Anastasia had a brother and two sisters. For some reason, he thought her an only child much like himself. It was only in Ferrybone that he discovered, in addition to her immediate family, there was an endless succession of cousins, aunts and uncles. He felt as though he had put on two stone, partaking of every port, wine, brandy and gin fizz offered to him. Anastasia had resisted the invitations at first, claiming exhaustion from the journey, and wanting to spend her time in her father's library or in the garden. But eventually, he determined she could no longer claim exertion from their travels, and insisted they partake in the invitations being offered their way.

Edward found himself generously welcomed by each and every member of Anastasia's family. Her sisters had presented the couple with fine gifts for their home; down pillows for their bed, cut crystal glasses for their dining room (or kitchen, Edward supposed), and even a set of the porcelain dishes with the King's crest. He himself was given a velvet smoking jacket by Anastasia's brother, and he resolved to wear it as often as he could upon return to Houndstooth. And it might have taken him a few days, but Edward finally found his voice and was able to regale his wife's family with amusing anecdotes about the folk traditions of the people of the north. He told her sisters how the Houndstoothians would place a bowl of milk outside under the first full moon in spring for the Moon Queen to drink. And if it were sweet and pleasing to her taste, she would grant a good harvest. And that, although no one spoke of this, the good citizens of Houndstooth were known to add heaping teaspoons of sugar to the milk in order to ensure a bountiful harvest. He told her brother how the children at school were taught flowers do not grow from seeds, but from the fallen teeth of garden sprites. And finally, he told her nieces, cousins, aunts and uncles that in Houndstooth people did not believe honey was made from bees (it was in fact fairy dust), that silk was made by man (cave spiders spun merrily away in realms to the south), and that the world was flat (the local spirit doctor claimed that given the movements of the sun it must be round). With these and other tales he regaled her family for many an evening.

It was on the last night of their stay Anastasia retired to bed early to prepare for the long journey ahead. Edward bade her good night, kissed the cheek that was smooth and untouched by the flame and stated he would join her shortly. Although they had now been here a fortnight, they still had not shared the same bed. Edward told himself that because Anastasia went to bed far earlier, he opted for the divan on the opposite side of the room so as not to awake her upon retiring. He was always quite careful, though, to replace the blanket and pillow on the bed each morning so that the servants would not gossip. And while, yes, Edward had every intention of engaging bodily with his wife at some point, he felt it far more crucial to sit with her father drinking brandy and smoking cigars, talking about his dreams and imagining a home for himself and Anastasia that was similar to this one.

It was on this last evening, that Edward broached the idea of he and Anastasia moving to Ferrybone. John asked whether he had discussed this with his daughter and Edward had been forced to admit, not as yet. But it was definitely something he intended to do upon their return to Houndstooth. John then inquired as to the shop and Edward had stated that he had bigger aspirations for his life, ones that did not see him making shoes.

"What is your plan?" John had inquired and Edward stated he was, as of yet, still undecided. But if Anastasia's father would provide him with the capital to establish himself in Ferrybone, it would only be a matter of time before Edward found a suitable profession among the Genteel class. Perhaps he would become an estate agent, a money lender or a merchant himself.

"What training have you?" Anastasia's father had asked and Edward was yet again forced to admit he had none, but that he was willing, nay, eager to learn whatever trade with which he would find himself compatible.

"Sir, your enthusiasm is to be appreciated," his father-in-law stated, "but prove yourself successful in running what t'is already at hand - your father's shop - and I shall then consider your proposal."

"For how long?" Edward asked.

"Five years," John said, "should give you the experience necessary to seek a better prospect."

Edward stared at Anastasia's father with astonishment. Five years? Why that t'was a lifetime. He could no sooner imagine giving the shop five more days of his life, let alone five years.

"Sir, I beg of you," Edward said, "allow me the means to pursue this venture now, and I will prove myself worthy of any investment you make in me."

"In my time," John stated sipping his brandy, "I have heard a great many men extol their virtues, promise their commitment, and implore me to trust them with my money. Only to then watch their passion fade to lethargy and cynicism as the money drains away. Prosperity is not founded on promises, but the daily grind of living. It is achieved by building your dream brick by brick in the hope that it will outperform anything you thought possible, and by that virtue outlive not only yourself, but your children and their children as well."

Although the brandy was warm in his belly, Edward felt a cold chill spill across his skull as though a nest of spiders had broken open upon his head. This conversation was not evolving according to the way it played out in his head, and he seemed powerless to refocus its direction.

"I am thinking of your daughter, Sir," Edward said when at last he was able to form a thought, "I worry a shoesmith's life is not a fit life for her."

"My daughter, you will come to discover, is extremely adaptable," Anastasia's father said swirling the last of his brandy in his snifter, before he swallowed and placed his empty crystal glass on the butler's tray which sat before him on the table. "Life has thrown much mud in her direction, and still she shines so very bright. Would you not agree?"

In truth, Edward had no idea what John was talking about with regards to Anastasia, but he knew enough to agree with the old man.

"Now," John said rising from his seat and consulting his pocket watch, "while you may not like the business of shoes, the skills you learned from your dead father and the experience of running the shop will be extremely valuable and can be applied equally in other areas. In five years, we will have this conversation once more."

"Sir, I beg you, five years is an eternity —"

"Enough!" John stated and the steel in his voice was enough to wither a far stronger man than he. Edward shrunk back against the divan on which he was seated, clutching his snifter so tight, he feared the glass might shatter.

"As you are my daughter's husband, I prefer we part in friendship and resume this conversation in five years. Agreed?"

Edward examined John's outstretched hand, then took it in his own.

"Agreed," he said at last and as far as he could tell, none of the hostility from their conversation was present in his father-in-law's grip.

"I must retire," John said, "but please stay, enjoy the brandy, the cigars." And then he released Edward's hand and exited the room.

Edward slumped back onto the divan and swallowed the remainder of the brandy in his glass. The bell pull for the butler was on the other side of the room, so Edward grabbed the bottle himself from the table, and restored the contents of his glass.

It was Thomas's fault he was in this current predicament. If his father had not taken so keenly to blindness, Edward would have continued with his schooling, been accepted to a university and would by now have been partially trained in his chosen career. Five years! It was an absolute lifetime. Five more years of Houndstooth? Five more years of making shoes? That couldn't possibly be the life his mother had mapped out for him. He wished that she were here now. At times he felt she was the only one who understood him.

Edward sat up the remainder of the night, unable to

move from the divan except to locate a fresh bottle when his had emptied. He felt tired, old. As though the fragile dream he had proposed to Anastasia's father (he was trying to give his daughter a better life, why couldn't the old man see that?), had been smashed to smithereens on the hard wood floor.

They departed Ferrybone the next morning.

In saying goodbye, John reminded Edward that if he worked diligently in honing the craft of shoemaking and devoted himself to the shop, he may be surprised by the results. And although Edward nodded and agreed that yes, this was the correct course of action, he had no intention of pursuing it. He bade each of her parents goodbye, thanked them for their hospitality and clambered into the carriage. He sank back against the cushions, his eyes closed, and bemoaned the sweet brandy headache that pounded between his ears. He could hear Anastasia crying outside of the carriage and listened as her father tried to convince her, then ultimately order her, to join her husband. As soon as she had climbed aboard, Edward tapped the ceiling and instructed the driver to be away.

It had been a very solemn journey home. Neither had talked to the other. Although, this time, it was Edward who pretended to sleep. The shop looked the same as when they had departed, and indeed, Edward thought, would probably look the same in five years. He left Anastasia to assist the driver with their trunks and hid himself away in his room. On the table at the side of the bed sat three books of financial studies. He had purchased them through the local book seller and had thought to ask Mr. Hawkheart, the local wine importer, for training (although Anastasia had thought this already accomplished). Edward supposed he could work in the shop during the morning and then study in the evenings. But it seemed a tiresome existence.

He could hear Anastasia walk past the bedroom door and enter her room. How could she leave behind her life in Ferrybone for an existence such as this? He had experienced her world for only a fortnight and yet he yearned with every aspect of his being, to return to its embrace. He ran his fingers down the sleeve of the velvet smoking jacket her brother had given him and again felt the thrill of owning such a luxurious possession. Anastasia grew up there, it was all she had ever known and yet here she was.

"Edward?"

Edward jerks his eyes away from the fire to look across the table. He has half-forgotten that Anastasia is here. The right side of her face is embraced by the evening shadow, and if it were not for the pitiful state of her dress she would look almost beautiful.

Two weeks after they returned from Ferrybone the snows began, and they were plentiful and unrelenting. Unable to brave the punishing winds and razor like ice to clear roofs and pathways, the snow level increased with a vigor Houndstooth had not before experienced. A great many roofs collapsed under the weight of the snow including the one above the shop. And when the snows finally abated (and with no money to make repairs), Anastasia had been forced to sell her sumptuous wedding gown to a traveling tinker in order to raise the funds necessary to restore the roof. She had also sold her other fine dresses in order to find enough coin to purchase a side of cow to keep them in winter meat.

Now, they have hardly been home two months, and she no longer resembles the daughter of a wealthy merchant from Ferrybone. She wears a plain yellow wool dress with a red apron, black wool stockings and ugly brown boots he himself made her. Soot from the fire is smudged across her forehead and cheeks and her shiny hair is greasy from the smoke of the fatty candles. The skin on her hands is chapped and red from gathering snow to melt for their tea and thin broth soups. She looks no different than any other Houndstooth woman. Nay, with those scars upon her face, she is even uglier than the plainest girl he eschewed in favor of marrying a merchant's daughter from Ferrybone.

"Are you well?" Anastasia asks, and he wonders if the concern in her voice is at all genuine.

"I'm fine, my love," he states and the words feel as empty on his tongue as they do in the air. He yanks out his pocket watch and consults the time.

"I best be off to meet Hawkheart," he says. The three books on finance which have become his constant companions over the past two months are stacked next to his elbow on the table. He pushes away his bowl which contains the remains of the beet soup they have been eating for the past week. His tongue and stomach still long for the tasty victuals, warm brandies and exotic treats of Ferrybone.

If only he could touch that life again.

If only.

CHAPTER TWO

Wherein a shivermouse
is found in the pantry.

Anastasia sits alone at the wood table in the kitchen. She shivers in the cold air as she has not stoked the coals since Edward departed. She knows he has no intention of meeting Hawkheart for studies, that instead his feet are carrying him towards the Wolf & Foxtail Inn and the barmaid known as Sophia.

For the first few months of marriage, Anastasia lived with the hope that Edward would agree to dissolve the marriage and send her home. After all, he had not taken to her bed, seemed to find it difficult to hold conversation with her, and seldom looked her way unless he could manage to avoid the right side of her face. When he failed to raise the topic, she had done so herself. But Edward was adamant that she stay and that he truly wanted this marriage; he protested that he was simply shy and

54

until he became more comfortable, the time they spent together might be tinged with an awkward flavor. And true to his word, Edward tried his best to make her arrival in Houndstooth a smooth affair. He introduced her to the villagers and certainly seemed proud to do so, saying he was delighted her family (wealthy merchants), had selected him to wed their daughter. But dressed in the finery of Ferrybone fashion - impractical creations of lace, corset and long skirts - Anastasia felt very out of place, like a museum piece on tour. She wanted to divest herself of these dresses and wear ones that were more suited to Houndstooth. Jenny, the tailor's wife, made gowns that ended at the ankle so that the hems were not swallowing up the mud that frequently ran through the cobblestone streets from the heavy rains. Yes, they were made of thick shapeless wool but that was to combat the cool air. And yes, they were brown, yellow, and beige in color but this served to camouflage what dirt and dust managed to cling to the fabric. Edward, however, had insisted at least for the first while, that she remain in the costume of Ferrybone and so Anastasia obliged, settling into Houndstooth and all the while feeling that she didn't belong.

Life was challenging. Despite the excellent post service, she missed Papa and mother quite desperately and wrote to them daily. Until finally, Papa told her to desist writing (sometimes she would take to the pen two, three, four times a day), and start attending to her household. Having never done so before, and having none of her mother's resources, Anastasia was overwhelmed at having to establish a home. However, Edward was accepting of her recommendations: to add a rug to the kitchen floor to keep their feet warm in the winter, to lay wooden planks across the backyard to save themselves from trudging through mud when needing to use the water closet and to create a space in the kitchen to store wood so that it would dry to a tinder and provide more warmth and less smoke when it was required for fuel.

Although, there were nights when Anastasia did not know how to keep poverty at bay, and she would lie awake in bed, the cold wind blowing in from the broken window and wonder where she was going to find food to keep their bellies full. And then one day, while hanging laundry to dry on the line in the backyard, she saw a cluster of violaheads. She recognized them from one of Papa's books *(The Kingdom's Edible Plants, Both Wild & Tame: A Brief Treatise for Connoisseurs, 2nd edition)*, which contained color plates of each plant and instructions on how to cook them. Anastasia wrote to Papa, stating she required use of the book and he posted it to her the very next week. With treatise in hand, she scoured Houndstooth's countryside, locating secret patches of grumble-berries which could be made into pies, syrups and juices. She harvested crops of sticky nettles which they ate boiled with salt or baked to a crisp in the oven. She found whole swaths of rosehearts which could be used to flavor the well water or add extra sweetness to one's tea.

She eventually informed Edward that she could only continue with her gardening endeavors if she had a dress more suited for that purpose. And so she wrote to her mother for the money. Edward could not argue against her decision, if he hoped to stay fed and thus he agreed yes, a new dress was in order. Once purchased, Anastasia took to wearing her hair in a fashion similar to the other women of Houndstooth, one long braid down the back instead of the fussy, continental combination of curls, braids and bows that was the style back home.

In the subsequent months, Anastasia found ways to barter with the local women whom she found to be forthright, strong and friendly (albeit somewhat shy to newcomers). She reintroduced herself to Betsy, the baker's wife, who taught her which grains made the best bread and offered to grind them in exchange for the lavender Anastasia grew in her garden. It was the finest in Houndstooth Betsy affirmed, and she only used the best ingredients in her lavender honey bread. Anastasia supplied Cynthia, the Grocer's wife, with higgelty-figs from a grove of trees she found hidden in the forest. In exchange, Cynthia provided her with wandermelons and every time Anastasia bit into one, it tasted of late summer evenings. Jenny, the tailor's wife, was exceedingly terrified of catching the red fever (though the only documented outbreak was a continent away), and so she took a nightly dose of alcohol made from june-pip berries provided by Anastasia. Although june-pip was not scientifically documented to prevent the disease, if it should ever arrive at Houndstooth's borders, Jenny would be well prepared. In return for the berries, Anastasia received a thick wool coat and blanket to help her through the cold Houndstooth winters. Even the Sheriff, whom Anastasia had met when he stopped by to have his boot resoled, had shown her how to make a snare that would snap the neck of the foxtails that invaded her patch of carotines and parsnipians out back, thereby both saving her garden and providing her and Edward with meat (although she had not yet hardened her heart enough against the lovely creatures to set about killing one).

Soon Anastasia realized she enjoyed very much the citizens of Houndstooth. They did not shun her because she was not born amongst them or because her skin was scarred and frightful or because her manners (polite, reserved), her way of speaking (an accent that was soft and well spoken), her laugh (not so hearty or expressive), were different than their own. They were perfectly inclined to tease her about the differences, but were always careful to be kind with their words. She was just starting to feel settled when Edward insisted he meet her family. She had promised to write her parents and invite them for a visit, but he forestalled her saying he had already taken the liberty of writing them and they themselves were to visit Ferrybone come Friday hence. Anastasia felt a moment of panic, an unwillingness to have the two halves of her life meet for fear they should contaminate one another. But she could provide no reasonable protest to Edward as to why they could not go (she considered feigning illness but did not wish to lie to her husband). And so she had offered her consent and they had gone to Ferrybone.

Edward was welcomed with great fanfare by her mother who declared to Anastasia immediately upon meeting him, that she loved him on sight. For Anastasia, however, standing in the hallway of her home, all she could think about was that she was married to a man she did not love. She had, of course, thought love would come eventually; through companionship, amiable company, kind conversation. But it had been three months since their wedding and she had not thawed towards him, nor he to her. It was not as though she disliked Edward, rather she felt indifferent to him. Yes, he was handsome but she felt no attraction. She remembered when she was young and Papa returned from overseas, smelling of sea salt, his hands dirty from working the cargo of the ships in which he travelled (for at that time he was too poor to pay the transport fees). His hands would be covered in blisters, black with soot and strong from securing ropes and containers. They were hands that made her feel safe and loved and protected. He used to say as she examined each new scrape and cut on his palms that it was a man's job to get his hands dirty, so his wife could keep hers clean.

The men of Ferrybone were not like her Papa. They prided themselves on their wealth, the fact they had never been required to put in a day's labor to feed their families. Their hands were thin and small, almost like a lady's and did not make Anastasia feel safe. She supposed Edward reminded her too much of Ferrybone society; where acquaintances were reserved and guarded, as though the polished surface were more important than the freedom to express oneself with openness. And thus, Edward became more like a brother, friend or child than a husband. A feeling of such abject loneliness swept over her that she collapsed into Papa's arms and not until he had taken her to his study, shut the door on her mother's flutterings and forced spiced rum down her throat, had she been able to recover. And then her life in Houndstooth poured from her lips, like water from a rain spout. She shared the hunger, the cold, the indifference to Edward (and him to her), her longing for home. Papa did not interrupt, did not judge or reassure. He simply listened. And when she finished speaking, he made her drink more of the rum, then dried the tears from her eyes with his large handkerchief.

"You have done well, my daughter," he said placing a warm hand on her head for comfort, "and you are very brave."

"I am not, Papa" she countered, "I am scared all the time."

"And still you wake each day with determination. You may be hungry but you find a way to feed yourself and your husband. You may be lonely and yet you have found friends among the villagers. You may be uncertain of Edward, but you will find a way to connect to him, if you desire such a connection. Give it time. "

"I am tired of the struggle," she said.

"Yes," he said, "and you will go on being tired until you accept that even when times are difficult, life can be effortless."

"How?" she asked.

"Surrender," had been his response.

She wanted to ask more, but her mother ordered her husband to unlock the study so that she might obtain her daughter. Dinner was to be served in an hour, she chided and Anastasia had yet to wash, dress and do her hair ("the wretched state of it la, la, la!" her mother exclaimed and refused to believe Anastasia that Houndstooth did not have access to the latest hair potions to keep one's locks silky smooth). Her mother purchased Anastasia a new gown, of the latest season, knowing they were probably not yet available in Houndstooth salons (that there were no salons would have also been beyond her mother's comprehension).

Edward had been most pleasant and agreeable at the

dinner table, laughing heartily at her mother's jokes, asking about Papa's business trips overseas. He had been most attentive to her, ensuring the butler kept her glasses filled with both water and wine. He talked incessantly and she knew in that moment that he was nervous. So she reached out and squeezed his hand in reassurance. He immediately jerked away, as though surprised by the contact, but then having seen only understanding in her eyes, he joined their fingers once again.

That night in the evening room, she sat next to him on the divan (to his right, of course), and she felt the most connected to him that she ever had. Perhaps Papa was correct; a connection between them simply required time. At dinner, it was the first time since their wedding that their skin had touched and her own flesh now felt electrified. His fingers had been warm and her skin responded to that warmth. So she retired early to the bed, glancing at him as she left the room, expecting him to follow. Upon her return to the chamber, the maid helped her out of the green gown and into the lace nightdress laid out by her mother. Once the maid left, Anastasia tied her hair in such a way that it covered most of her right cheek. Then she climbed into bed, pulled up the covers and buried her hand between her legs, stroking herself, and waited for her husband.

Before, in Houndstooth, when Edward approached her smelling of drink, she had not welcomed his advances, insisting the candles remain lit in the hopes that upon seeing her scars, they would drive him away. And indeed they had. But tonight, she determined, when he arrived in the room she would snuff the candle.

But he did not come.

The candle remained lit until it melted and the wick sputtered and spit when the flame met the wax. As the light extinguished, her hand eventually stilled, her eyes closed and she slept. She awoke the next morning, still alone in the bed, to see him stretched out on the divan on the other side of the room. He had obtained a pillow and quilt from the bed and made himself quite comfortable on the awkward bit of furniture. He, was awake and greeted her with a smile.

"I sat up late with your father," he stated, "and when I returned to the room you were peacefully sleeping and I had not the heart to wake you."

Anastasia felt a prick of tears in her eyes and blinked them away.

Nothing had changed between them at all. The spark she felt the previous night was no more than indigestion from the richness of the meal. Anastasia thanked Edward for his consideration and then as the breakfast bell reverberated throughout the house, he gathered his clothes, and stepped through to the water chamber to change, leaving Anastasia to dress alone in the room.

At first she had been apprehensive to rejoin her family; after all how could she keep hidden from them the fact that her marriage was false? That her husband did not love her, nor she, him? So she hid away in the library. Papa had rebuilt an even grander version than its predecessor and all her favorites were replaced: the french fairy-tales written by the woman known only to the world as Madame LeStrange. The book of color plates illustrating the exotic beasts of Gondwanaland. The scandalous English novel, *The Pirate's Mistress: A True Account of a Noble Woman's Captivity at Sea by that Dastardly Buccaneer Rochester Black* (at first it was banned and then burned, with only three copies known to be in existence). She rejoiced in the smell of the sand on the ancient leather volumes Papa brought from the eastern deserts of Kashpuri and the scent of the sea on those that were purchased from the island kingdom of Finlandia. And there were the many varied volumes which contained pages made from sheepskin, papyrus, bamboo strips, bone and silk.

But she was not permitted to hide for long.

Although Edward was content to remain within their home in Houndstooth, the same could not be said of his time in Ferrybone and he was eager to meet her family (extensions and all) and explore the city. As his wife, it was proper custom for Anastasia to accompany him. She walked with Edward through the streets of Ferrybone, showing him the places of her childhood. The stone church with its colored glass windows depicting the dove, raven, and hawk.The sumptuous rose, lilac and jasmine gardens of the King's castle where the Regent was currently in residence, albeit bed-ridden, struck down by some foreign illness. She showed him the newspapiary at the end of the street where she always bought her father's morning paper. She had not been here since before the fire, and the once bustling shop was now no more than a ramshackle collection of discarded boards covered in dust and cobweb. Mr. Blackbond, from the stationary shop next door, informed Anastasia that the boy's father had died years ago, weakened by the smoke he inhaled the night of the fire. The boy remained at the Ferrybone orphanage until he was of age, then left to join the King's army for the wars in the Asiantine. Whether he survived those infernal trenches, no one knew.

As she walked around the city, it looked very different to Anastasia. Perhaps it was the distance that created the shift in her thinking. In Houndstooth, she watched as the villagers greeted one another each morning with eager handshakes and ready smiles. If one were cranky and cross with one's neighbor, an apology was immediately demanded and then the offender was treated to a cup of bitter coffee and a jam truffle biscuit at Betsy's husband's shop and ordered to speak truth to their troubles so assistance could be rendered. In walking about Ferrybone, one was seldom greeted with words or a smile. Instead, citizens brushed past, in too much of a hurry to connect with anyone else. When someone did stop, their words and accompanying actions had little authenticity. This past friend claimed she was fine and all was well with her parents' health, when in fact worry lines creased both of her eyes and her teeth gnawed her lower lip to the point of blood. That former acquaintance professed business was booming, when it was quite evident the knees and elbows of his suit were almost worn through, his shoes had holes in each toe and there was no hat upon his head. Anastasia's own family was not immune to this practice. Her younger sister Helena smiled and laughed louder than all the rest of her family and yet she had gained two stone in weight since they had last met. And though she denied it, Anastasia knew this was because her sister had discovered her husband's affair with the seamstress who tailored his trousers. Meanwhile, her brother continued to bestow expensive presents on her parents, nieces and cousins, repeatedly stating that nothing was out of reach for him. And yet one night after he had fallen to the bottom of a bottle of whisky, he confided to Anastasia that his gambling debts were now more than he could hope to repay in his lifetime.

Anastasia smooths a hand across the small leather bound volume on the folk-tales of Houndstooth. The book belongs to the Sheriff. He brought it with him the last time he came to the shop to have his boots resoled. She had expressed interest and so he left it behind for her to read. In fact, she has read it seven times in this past month. Not because it is well written (and, indeed, it is), but because she has nothing else to read. But now it is too dark to make words out of the ink on the page. There are no spare candles for reading, and she cannot fathom how she will survive the long shadowy evenings without books to provide a semblance of comfort. She thought to ask her father for money for proper candles but with the death of the King two months past and the coronation of the Princess, she did not want to pester Papa when she knew he was still grieving. For the two men had been friends since boyhood and his death was not an easy one for her Papa to bear.

And now Edward makes his way to the Wolf & Foxtail. Excepting the time they spent in Ferrybone, Edward has gone to see Sophia every Friday night (and the occasional other night), for the past three months. There are no secrets in Houndstooth and the women with whom Anastasia trades gathered her up one day when they finished their transactions and took her to Betsy's husband's bakery. As Cynthia, Jenny, and Betsy ingested butternut biscuits with apricandle jam and blackberry tea, Margarite informed Anastasia that Edward was betraying her with Sophia.

Margarite's husband discovered this one evening quite by accident, promised not to speak of it to poor panicked Edward, but kept nothing from Margarite, as he found her to be a most wise and straight thinking woman who thought only of other people's happiness and how best it might be achieved.

"The lying bastard," Cynthia said picking the butternut from her biscuit in spite of Betsy's critical eye.

"Not good enough for the likes of you, Anastasia," Jenny concurred, pouring into her tea a little of the june-pip berry juice that she carried around in a flask she kept hidden in her basket.

"I ne'er trusted 'im," said Betsy poking her finger at each woman as she spoke.

"By the look on Anastasia's face," Margarite said, "I can see she already knows."

And know she did. She supposed she always knew from the very beginning. One evening Edward forgot the leather case with his abaci, and so Anastasia walked over to Hawkheart's. But the old man said he knew nothing of Edward's plan to study with him, although he would be most willing to have him as a pupil. Anastasia apologized, said she must have misunderstood. On the way home, she passed the Wolf & Foxtail and saw her husband enter the Pub. She thought, albeit momentarily, to join him but did not want him to think she was following him. Perhaps when he returned, he would tell her he changed his mind about pursuing studies. But he did not; instead advising that he was progressing very well in his lessons with Hawkheart and was looking forward to many more. That would have been the moment for Anastasia to confront Edward, to say she had seen Edward herself, enter the

Wolf & Foxtail. But she remained quiet and discovered she was quite content to have him out of the house on Friday nights. That he was seeing another woman and not strictly drowning his sorrows in drink or darts did not occur to her. Until one night, when she awoke to the sound of a woman's giggles. Thinking the voice came from downstairs and wondering if the shop had been compromised, she donned her night-coat and went to check. Edward met her at the door that led from the steps into the shop. He kept it half closed so she could not see in. He smelled of drink and his hair was rumpled, his tie askew.

"I am sorry, my love," he said, "I was talking through my sums, trying to organize my thoughts by speaking aloud. I will quiet my tongue so you are not disturbed."

Anastasia could have insisted he open the door, demand she be allowed to enter the shop but she did not. She was relieved to know Edward found company elsewhere, for now it was certain he would not look to her for companionship.

After all, Anastasia thinks, *I do not mind not being loved.*

At least that is what she tells herself.

CHAPTER
THREE

Wherein a fox tail
is hunted.

Edward steps out of the house and ensures that he has his abaci, pencils and stack of texts. He heads towards Hawkheart's home, then ducks past the bakery to the Shade beyond and reverses direction. He wishes to avoid the cobblestone road that runs like a horseshoe through the centre of town. Instead, he prefers to walk through the Shade, the thick forest that encroaches onto the town like some kind of invading army. Even fingers of moonlight cannot reach between the thick branches to illuminate the forest floor.

It is dark in here, but Edward does not require light. By now, his feet know the path to the pub. When he first began to use the woods he was startled by every shriek-owl hoot, every flame-fly click, every shivermouse that scurried under foot. Now he is as used to their presence, as they are to him. He prefers this route to the Wolf &

Foxtail, because he can avoid the prying eyes and idle tongues of his Houndstooth neighbors. It also means he comes upon the Pub from the back, can slip in through the delivery door, down the short expanse of hall which is located at the end of the bar where no one sits because it is farthest away from the stone fireplace. Here he can sit in a secluded corner of the stairwell and wait for Sophia to join him before they head upstairs to her rooms.

While Edward waits, sipping the golden ale Sophia has left there for him, he wishes not for the first time that his life were different. T'is not that he dislikes Anastasia, he simply does not wish to be her husband. He can see now he made a mistake, for they are very different people with little to bind them together. His mother would have supported his desire for a city wife, but would have admonished him against taking the first one offered. But he had felt desperate, not wanting to let this opportunity slip through his fingers. He wonders what his mother would have thought of Anastasia. He is not certain she would have liked the girl. Though they hailed from the same region, they were opposite in temperament with Anastasia seeming to care very little for the customs, graces and manners that his mother respected so dearly. Edward knows he is not living the life his mother hoped. But he feels as though he is too late to pursue his dream of joining the Genteel class and that all his opportunities have turned to dust. His life is now a pale imitation of what it was meant to be.

Edward is suddenly struck by how quiet it is in the Pub. Yes, the Spring has been cruel so perhaps the threat of a late frost has kept the villagers home. Or perhaps, it is something else entirely. The air feels heavy, thick, as though it were made of sassafras syrup. Edward consults his pocket watch and sees that Sophia has kept him waiting for over ten minutes. He walks over to the door which leads into the Pub. Sophia stands immobilized at the bar and stares unseeing into the room, as though she is lost in a dream. Edward pokes his head around the doorjamb and sees a scattering of folk, three or four at the most, seated in front of the fireplace. They, too, appear half frozen. Cynthia's husband holds a pint of ale in his hand, half raised to his mouth. Betsy's husband's mouth is parted wide as though he were in conversation. But no words come from his lips.

Edward does not believe in magic.

Superstition and nonsense, his mother always said. For if magic were real, would not each and every person seek out and obtain what they most desired? Nay, Edward does not believe in magic, and the laws that govern such arts are antiquated and foolish. But it appears (and Edward shivers), as though some mischief has taken hold of the folks within the walls of the Wolf & Foxtail. He resolves he wants no part of what is occuring and so he makes his way to the back door.

As he passes the stairwell, a figure looms out of the dark, startling him.

"My apologies, good Sir," comes a woman's voice as smooth and silky as though she has been swallowing honey, "I did not mean to cause alarm."

Edward peers into the dark, but can barely make out a form. There is the scrape of a match and the smell of sulphur as she lights a lantern which she then holds aloft.

The woman who stands before him on the stairs is possibly the most beautiful creature he has ever seen. Far lovelier than Anastasia's better half and most definitely superior to the comely country charms of Sophia with her sagging breasts and pockmarked thighs.

"Oh, I have startled you, so," the creature says, placing her hand against his heart as though to listen to it flutter. Then she is taking his arm, guiding him to the stairs.

"Please rest a moment so that you might recover." Edward, incapable of speech, does as she requests and sits on the bottom most step. She joins him there, placing the lantern on the stair above in such a manner that she is illuminated by a halo of light.

It is now that Edward can truly see what she looks like and his eyes devour her golden hair, pale skin, large blue eyes, pink cheeks. Her rose colored dress is cut low revealing a long slender neck, elegant collarbones and high round breasts. She holds out a dainty hand to him, "You must be Edward."

Edward looks down at his own hand. He did not wash before leaving the house and his fingertips are stained purple from the beet-root soup. He spits into his palm and rubs his fingers against the worn fabric of his trouser leg in an attempt to clean them.

"Please do not worry," she says, taking the stained fingers in her own, "I am not afraid of getting dirty." Unlike his wife's flesh which (on the very few times he has touched her), is as cool as ice, this woman is warm. Almost hot.He is captivated by the blue of her eyes. T'is a color he has never quite seen before. Like the color of stormy skies.

"You know my name," Edward says at last. Although it does not sound like his voice. It shakes as though he is a mere schoolboy in the presence of a delicate maid.

"Sophia told me," she says, drawing back her hand and proceeding to wind her long golden braid around her wrist.

For a moment Edward wonders who Sophia is. The vision before him smiles and gestures towards the bar, whereupon Edward turns his head to look.

"Oh, Sophia," he states upon seeing the barmaid still frozen in position. He does not think to comment upon this. It somehow no longer seems the least bit important or out of the ordinary.

"She is my cousin," the goddess says.

Edward stares at the girl; can't possibly imagine how the delicate creature before him could be related to Sophia.

"You look nothing alike," he says, taking advantage of that statement to once again examine her.

"I know," she says with a sigh and wiggles beside him on the stair so that their arms press together, "and t'is a pity, would you not agree, that I am not blessed with Sophia's beauty?"

Edward stares at her, his mouth agape.

"But you are quite lovely," he argues. "In fact you are by far the most enchanting creature I have ever met." And he takes both her bare arms in his hands and squeezes, before releasing her, "you must believe me."

"You are very kind, Edward," she says and a lovely blush spreads across her cheeks and throat and pale breasts, "because unlike Sophia, I have not inherited the wide hips and ample bosom that are necessary for child-rearing."

She cups both her breasts in her hands and look down at them with lowered lashes, "I believe they are considered much too small. Do you not agree?"

Edward's penis is hot and hard in his trousers and he is suddenly struck by the feeling that she is going to disappear on him and he can not bear to be parted from her company.

"What is your name?" he demands, snatching her right hand from her breast and clenching her hot fingers in his own. "I must know." He feels as though he is crushing her fingers, but he cannot loosen his grip. He is terrified she will slip away.

"Rosemary," she breathes and Edward thinks he has never heard a name more lovely.

"I must have you," he says and is alarmed to hear that he has spoken the words aloud.

But she does not chastise him.

"Follow me," she whispers and rises, claiming the lantern from the step and raising it high to light the way upstairs.

She keeps her hand in his and leads him up to the second floor. They stop at the third door on the left and Edward balks, as he and Sophia have lain together aplenty in this space. But Rosemary presses her slender body against him, snaking one leg around his calf, pulling him closer, nestling his erection in her soft skirts.

Her sharp teeth snap at his ear, "I promise you, we won't be disturbed."

And then, although he does not remember entering the room, they are through the door. He tries to kiss her lips, but she deposits the lantern on the bureau and pushes against his chest with both hands. And with more strength than he would have thought possible in such a delicate frame. He stumbles backward and his calves slam against the hard wood frame of Sophia's bed. Then Rosemary launches forward and this time when she strikes him, he falls onto the bed and she is on him. Her hands snag the drawstring of his trousers, yanking loose the knot and her hot fingers dive inside the cloth barrier, grabbing his penis. Edward groans and reaches for her hands, but she swats him away and he is forced to grab the quilt instead. Her fingers are hard and swift as they work him, only now her fingers seem longer, like snakes slithering and curling against him.

She releases him for a moment and he cries out with the loss, only to recognize that she is stripping him of his trousers so that her mouth may follow the path of her fingers. He closes his eyes so that he may capture each lick, each tug, each sensation. Against his skin, her hot tongue seems longer than any creature's ought to be. He tries to open his eyes because she doesn't feel right. But he cannot move. He is caught in a spell, and now her mouth has captured his penis. That her tongue feels as though it is coated in barbs does not matter because the pain somehow contributes to the rush of each pull. And as her teeth scrape against his delicate flesh, he feels the onset of his orgasm. But it isn't until she racks her long claws along each of his inner thighs, that he yelps out that he can hold fast no longer and he allows himself the oblivion of release.

Edward lies gasping on the bed, his skin coated in sweat, his hands covering his eyes. He realizes with shame, that he wants to cry. Why this is, he has no idea. But he wishes his mother were here so that he could climb into her arms and be comforted.

"Edward," Rosemary says, "come back to me."

He feels something warm and soft swallow the length of his penis and he opens his eyes.

Rosemary sits naked straddling him, holding his flesh inside of her as she rocks back and forth. Her golden hair frames her ethereal face, falls about her breasts and cushions the juncture of her thighs.

Edward stares as though seeing her for the first time.

"What are you?" he asks.

"Why Edward," she smiles clenching her muscles around him, "you know who I am. I am Rosemary."

Although he cannot name it, there is something off about her, something … almost evil. A sense of anger engulfs Edward. He knows Rosemary is not her name. How dare she lie to him? She looks him in the eyes and laughs, pinching her nipples between her fingers as she continues to tighten her pelvic muscles. Edward knows she is laughing at him. He launches up from his back, and grabs her right nipple between his teeth. He bears down, biting at the skin, chewing the hard nub. He wants to devour it, devour her. She laughs again as he draws blood and she bucks against him, striking his back with her hands as though he were nothing more than an animal. Then she twists her hands in his hair, yanking as though to pull it from his flesh. He releases his teeth from her nipple and uses his hands to pull hers free from his hair. Then with a great heave he turns them so she is now beneath him. He maintains his hold on her arms so that she is immobilized and pushes her deep into the mattress with his hips. With each thrust, her head slams against the hard oak of the headboard but again she does not cry out. Instead, a wide smile splits her mouth open and her eyes are alight with fire.

Again and again, he takes her and still that chilling smile never leaves her mouth. His hands release hers and find their way to her throat where they wrap around the delicate column, depriving her of oxygen. Her large blue eyes bulge under the pressure of his fingers and she gasps for air. But he does not lessen his hold. At the last possible moment, Edward releases his grip and allows her to draw air. T'is only then that he finishes and with a hoarse cry, drops onto her bruised body, completely spent.

And then he can no longer fight the compulsion to cry and he bursts into tears, his shoulders shaking with heaving sobs.

"T'is all right, beloved Edward," Rosemary says, still cradling him within her as she strokes her long fingers along his sweaty back, "You rest now." Edward feels lethargy creeping once more along his bones and he knows that he must return home before he falls asleep.

"Home," Edward mumbles, trying to push her away although his arms seem to have lost all strength, "Anastasia."

"Not now," Rosemary says, holding him with her hands, "rest awhile."

Edward decides he will rest. Just for a moment or two. And so he closes his eyes. And finds himself in an empty place. He is not in a dream, nor is he awake. It is an in-between place where there is just darkness.

And a voice.

Her voice.

Edward.

Rosemary?

He hears her, but he knows she is not speaking At least not out loud. Somehow, the voice, her voice, is within his own head.

Can you hear me, Edward?

Yes, he answers. Though how she can hear his thoughts in return, he does not know.

Thank you for this special evening, she says and suddenly he is back in that place on the stairs where he first met her and she seemed so innocent and beautiful.

Not at all, he tells her, *t'is I who should be thanking you.* After all, that such a beauty as herself would condescend to be with a lowly shoemaker as him is—

Edward, she interrupts, although there is no edge to her doing so, *in order to complete this contract, you must ask something of me. Anything at all.*

Edward wonders what he can ask. She has already given him a most memorable night. One he will remember the rest of his life. And again, he is hit with the panic that she is about to disappear on him. He wants to grab hold of her but he can longer feel his body, let alone hers.

I want you, he states.

A sound erupts over his skin. She is laughing. But t'is not her harsh laughter of earlier. This is sweet and pure, like the sound of the marigolds in the summer.

Oh Edward, this I gladly give. But tell me, there must be something you want even more than I. Something you want more than anything else in the world.

A feeling akin to bliss envelops Edward and he realizes magic does indeed exist, for he is in the midst of it right now. In the sanctity of this bed, in the confusion of this haze, he understands he is the luckiest man alive. For magic has sought him out and wants to grant him his dreams. If only his father could see him now. Anastasia. The entire village.

I want to be wealthy, he says, *the wealthiest man who ever lived.*

Oh Edward, Rosemary sighs, *this I would gladly give. But I do not deal in needs and wants. In my deck of cards, there is only desires and dreams.*

Then I wish to be the most famous man in all the Kingdom, Edward breathes out, and only upon uttering the words is he aware this is truly what he has always desired.

He grins in the darkness and his heart feels lightened, his head clearer, his strength recouped. With such renown, he thinks, he will no longer be pitied, no longer have to prove himself. Why he'd be adored, worshipped, idolized.

Edward, Rosemary whispers, her hot breath warming his skin, *t'would be my greatest pleasure to make it so.*

And then she is gone.

Vanished.

Disappeared.

Edward feels cold, alone, abandoned. Like he is seven years old again, standing over his mother's coffin while his father tries to comfort him by saying she is just sleeping.

The feelings of elation that he felt moments ago are quickly turning to dread. The kind he last felt when his mother's coffin was lowered into the ground and he cried out to all that she was simply sleeping and they mustn't bury her alive. His heart struggles inside his chest like a foxtail caught in a leg snare. He can't breathe, he can't —

Sleep, darling Edward.

A soft hand touches his brow and he is comforted by Rosemary's presence once more.

Sleep.

And so he does.

CHAPTER FOUR

Wherein a web holds fast.

Anastasia wakes.

Her room is in darkness and she is uncertain what has woken her. Perhaps Edward returns from the Wolf & Foxtail. She listens for a moment but can hear no footfalls on the stairs to indicate his arrival.

She strikes a match and lights the candle on her bedside table. The clock names the hour; it is nigh on three in the morning.

Anastasia rises, wrapping herself in her night-coat. Taking up the candle, she slips her feet into the woolen slippers made by Jenny and walks down the hallway to Edward's room. She taps on the door before opening it, in case he is asleep. But his bed is still empty.

She takes the stairs down to the shop and peers in. The workroom is empty, dark and when she checks the door to the street, it is locked tight. The kitchen, too, is unoccupied with the door that leads into the yard still secure. She shivers in the cold room and opens the stove. There are a few coals still nestled in its belly. She takes the poker and stirs the embers, releasing one last tornado of orange sparks.

Edward has never been this late before and she pictures him lost to the oblivion of sleep in Sophia's arms.

Anastasia retraces her steps and makes her way back to the workshop. Edward's tools, covered in dust, are scattered across the workbench like the discarded bones of some long forgotten creature. She touches the various items, unsure of their use, and wishes that Edward would embrace their purpose. In the larder, there are only five potatoes (two of them half black with mould), one turnip and three salted sardines. The Princess has banned common folk from the Shade and thus Anastasia has lost access to nearly all of her food sources. Moreover, late spring frosts have killed off the majority of her seedlings in the garden. And while she is certain she can replant, the harvest will be delayed. Bartering with her friends will not stave off the hunger this time. For the Princess has increased taxes one hundred fold, and each household in Houndstooth now struggles to make their payments. There are simply no extras to spare.

Anastasia sits on Edward's bench, arms wrapped about her legs, her forehead pressed to her knees. Perhaps she would not mind the hunger, the cold, the want, if she were not so lonely. But with such a wide chasm between her and Edward, there is no sense of solidarity in this poverty. To be deprived of necessities and companionship is almost too much to bear. She pulls up her night-coat and examines her legs. The scars that mar her skin are near invisible in the evening shadows. She runs her hands along her flesh and wishes that, like Edward, she had the courage to find comfort elsewhere.

But even if she does not have the courage to take that step, what harm is there in imagining her hands belong to someone else?

The question simply remains: who? There are not many in Houndstooth Anastasia would choose to touch her. Certainly not Woodspike, the local carpenter. His hands are red and chapped, with scaling skin covered in cuts and embedded with splinters. Nor Pennyeaves, Houndstooth's roofer. His hands are swollen like bloated fish belly, covered in boils, obviously diseased.

She glances again at the tools on Edward's workbench. There is a scrap of leather that looks like the wings of a desiccated flutter-fly. T'is a remnant from when Edward last resoled the Sheriff's boots.

The Sheriff.

Edward's last remaining client.

He is a tall man with broad shoulders, large hands and feet. He has high cheekbones and his forehead and the skin about his eyes are deeply creased as though he has experienced many horrors and shared them with no one. His eyes are amber like the sassafras syrup Anastasia makes in the fall and his nose has been broken several times over. He rarely speaks when he visits, and when he does, his words tend to stutter. His uniform is well worn with holes in the elbows that he has patched himself. Every two weeks, he brings his boots for repair. And while Edward grumbles they are in fine condition and not in need of attention, Anastasia counsels him to be grateful of the few pennies the work brings in to their household.

Last Friday, the Sheriff was late in arriving and Edward had already departed for the Wolf & Foxtail. It was pouring heavily, and the Sheriff was soaked to the skin by the time he arrived. So Anastasia invited him to stay and warm up with a cup of peppermint tea. He agreed and so she led him into the kitchen, placing a chair next to the stove so that his clothes might dry.

At that time she had noticed his large hands, for he struggled to hold the pink peony china tea cup in his hands. His fingers were too large to fit through the handle and so he was forced to hold the cup in his palms in order to drink. She laughed and offered him one of Edward's mugs but he declined and said, like her, he preferred the china. He finished off his tea in two swallows. But he stayed, drinking the entire contents of the tea kettle, not once, but twice. And it was during their conversation that she discovered he liked to read.

Anastasia was not sure how the topic arose, she only knew that it did. Of course, he was unable to afford books on a Sheriff's wage, but a friend of his from his days in the army, forwarded his books when he had no more use for them. As a result, the Sheriff now had a small unimportant collection of thirteen volumes of fairy-tales and folk-myths. He spoke slowly so that his stutter did not impede him, saying he would be delighted to share these books with Anastasia. She in return, promised to write her father and borrow several rarer tomes the Sheriff had not yet read. He thanked her and rose, stating the rains had abated, his clothes were sufficiently dry and he must be off. Anastasia realized she kept him talking about books for over two hours and she apologized for delaying his supper hour. He brushed off her concern, took her hands in his, pressed them in thanks, and departed.

When Edward returned, Anastasia meant to tell him the Sheriff stayed for tea but the next morning it slipped her mind. And when she finally did remember, she realized she did not want to tell Edward, lest he think something duplicitous occurred. And so she maintained her silence.

The Sheriff's hands were very different than her husband's. The fingers were thick and strong with dirt lodged under the broken nails. His knuckles were scuffed as though he had been in a fight. And additional cuts and scrapes indicated he did household labor himself, as indeed a Sheriff's wage would not permit the hiring of help.

Anastasia wonders what it would be like to be touched by those hands. Whether they would be gentle or leave bruises? She shivers, and clutches a handful of her nightgown, pressing it between her thighs. She wishes the nightgown were his body. She would like to wrap herself around the strength she perceives in him. Anastasia disentangles her fingers from the fabric so they can search out the flesh between her legs. She finds her clitoris and rubs at it roughly, as though demanding it respond to her touch.

But only when she spits into her fingers, and begins to coax herself with soft slow strokes, does her flesh swell and heat. She closes her eyes and imagines the Sheriff's hands where hers are now. Her fingers, knuckles, palm are dancing together, bringing her closer to orgasm. Nay, not her fingers. The Sheriff's. T'is *his* hands that pinch the skin around that nub of sensitive flesh, and twist, rub and pull. It does not take Anastasia long, for she is longing for touch.

The orgasm is sudden, fast, and over far too soon.

She wants to reclaim the moment but t'is already gone.

She opens her eyes and her hands drop away.

She is still in the empty workroom.

She is still alone.

Anastasia turns and drops her head to the workbench. She cries until she drops into a restless slumber.

There is a loud rap. Followed by another and another. Anastasia lifts her head to see that she is in the shop and not her own bed. She stretches her stiff neck and shakes off the cold which has slipped through her skin and into her bones. Fragile morning light peeks in through the thick glass window and she is astonished to find it is already dawn.

The events of the prior evening, awakening in the night, Edward's absence, her foray into the shop, all tumble into consciousness as she stumbles towards the door. It must be Edward; he is not lost at all, merely delayed.

She swings the door wide.

But t'is not Edward who stands in the street, but rather the Sheriff. He nods his head and removes his hat to reveal disheveled hair. His amber eyes meet hers but this morning they seem almost shy.

"Ma'am."

"Is it Edward?" Anastasia breathes.

"Edward?" the Sheriff asks.

"You have come to tell me he has been found?"

"I beg your pardon, Ma'am, but I was not aware he was missing."

"He didn't come home last night," Anastasia says, and her stomach tightens with worry. The Sheriff takes her by the elbow and leads her back into the shop, sits her on the workbench once more and crouches before her.

"When did you see him last?" the Sheriff asks.

"At the supper hour. He left a few minutes past seven for the Wolf & Foxtail," Anastasia says.

"Alone?"

"Yes," Anastasia says, "he usually visits on Friday night but he's never been this late before. What if he has met with mischief?" There are no lanterns to illuminate the cobblestone streets of Houndstooth. Could he have taken a misstep in the dark?

"Was he meeting anyone there?" The Sheriff asks.

Anastasia is quiet for a long minute.

"I believe he has a friend there," she says, and places her hands over her cheeks.

The Sheriff pats her knee, "I will stop by the Wolf & Foxtail, see if anyone there has had word of him."

"I should have gone looking for him last night. If something has happened to him —" While her feelings may not have shifted towards Edward, she would certainly not wish him ill.

"Please do not alarm yourself, Mrs Cordwainer. T'would be a rare occurrence in Houndstooth if harm were to have befallen him"

"He often walks the path through the woods," she says, "what if he has been mauled? There have been scrywolves sighted in the Shade these past weeks." With last winter being so harsh, the scrywolves were hungry, coming down further into the valley than ever before. How could she have failed to consider this possibility last night? Edward may have been in mortal danger while she was —

Her cheeks redden further.

The Sheriff touches her arm, "I am sure he is well. Possibly drank too much of Frederick's ale and fell unconscious." He smiles at her, "T'is been known to have happened."

"Yes, of course," Anastasia says.

"I'll find him now," he says, "and he will be home shortly."

"Thank you, Sheriff." He rises then and she follows him over to the door, opening it for him to leave. He turns towards her, gives a bow and restores his hat to his head.

"Ma'am."

Which is when she is struck by a thought.

"Why did you come, if not for Edward?" Anastasia asks.

"Apologies, Ma'am. I forget my mission." He reaches into his pocket and pulls out a small cloth satchel, "Betsy has a handful of extra grain. She wanted to pass it along before the Princess's taxmen arrive."

Of course, wonderful Betsy who was determined not to let the new taxes cause hardship for the village. And so she had had the blacksmith fix her scales to indicate they held more than what was being weighed. What was left over she distributed to those in need.

"Thank you," she says, taking the grain.

He squeezes her arm in reassurance, "I promise I shall be swift in my inquiries."

Anastasia nods. There is nothing more she can do.

She turns to head back into the shop but the Sheriff still has hold of her arm. She looks at him to see that he is staring at the right side of her face. As has become habit, Anastasia turns her head so that he does not have to face the unpleasantness.

"Nay" he says, releasing his grip on her arm and taking her chin in his hand.

She freezes, like a flutter-fly caught in a spiderweave's web. With his thumb he strokes her scarred cheek and Anastasia rears back, yanking her head away, as though his touch were as hot as a poker.

The Sheriff steps back, dropping both hands to his sides, "I beg of you Ma'am, a thousand apologies. I am truly sorry and meant no offense." He spins on his feet and strides along the cobblestones in the direction of the Wolf & Foxtail while Anastasia's heart pounds in her chest. No one, aside from herself, has ever touched her face. No one. She watches him disappear around the curve in the street, then turns back into the house.

As she does so she sees two footprints in the small patch of grass beneath the shop window. Large, like the Sheriff's. And she wonders how long he was standing there in the dark watching her.

The Sheriff walks north towards the Pub. He did not mean to alarm Anastasia by touching her, but nor will he condemn himself for doing so. Every time he sees her on the streets of Houndstooth he is angered by her need to accommodate others by turning her head to the side so her scars will not be visible. He wants her to recognize she has the face of a warrior. For no man or woman bears scars like hers if they haven't fought and won the battle. He wants to tell her this but his tongue has the miserable habit of seizing up and causing him to stumble every time he speaks to her.

It is not something that afflicts him with others, just Anastasia.

The Sheriff has lived in Houndstooth just shy of one year. It is the longest he has remained stationary in a great many years. And he would have moved on if it wasn't for Anastasia. She is blessed with a kind strength seldom seen or appreciated. Indeed, it is most evident her husband does not value this quality in her.

Unlike others in the village who grew up with pity for Edward's circumstances, the Sheriff feels nothing. Yes, Edward's mother died when he was but a child (so had the Sheriff's). And yes Edward had been forced to cast of his schooling and dreams, but the Sheriff is a man of faith. He believes if you play the cards the Goddess deals, she will reward your effort. For only in surrendering to the game, can you ultimately achieve the win. What the Sheriff has seen of Edward on his visits to the shoe shop, is that he is a man who resists the challenge before him and, therefore, neither progresses nor regresses.

He is stuck, trapped in sap like some dreaded insect.

Moreover, the Sheriff has long suspected the Shoemaker's hand in Thomas's death. But there is simply no proof. He made it a priority to frequent the shop as a client in the hopes that in befriending Edward, the Shoemaker might let something slip. But the man had no interest in social graces, nor in befriending him. And slowly, the Sheriff's visit became less about patricide and more about Anastasia.

Anastasia.

The Sheriff is fully aware that Edward slips away to the Wolf & Foxtail on Friday nights to take comfort with Sophia. Margarite informed him of the affair upon her husband's discovery of it, for she was afeared that Edward may intend to dispatch Anastasia in favor of a new wife. So the Sheriff continued his biweekly visits to the shop in order to ensure Anastasia's safety (or so he tells himself). It did not take long to determine, that Edward was too much of a coward to raise a hand against his wife, for the shadow of his father-in-law's might reached all the way to Houndstooth.

The Sheriff thinks back to watching Anastasia last night. He had not meant to. He was simply returning home after retrieving Margarite's cat from a particularly high tree. Betsy had stopped and given him grain (which now rests with Anastasia), for his larder. And then, as he passed the shop, he was stopped by the faint glow of the candle and looked in through the window. He had expected to see Edward, not Anastasia.

But there she sat huddled in her night-coat, head resting on her husband's workbench, fast asleep.

He stood outside watching over her until the dawn light began to crack across the horizon. She looked so lonely and vulnerable. Tears stained on a reddened cheek. He wanted to stand vigil, lest the night unleash a fury against such innocence.

The Sheriff's faith was strong, and after years spent in purgatory, he trusted the Goddess to lead him to what was good and right. That Anastasia is here, in Houndstooth, is nothing short of miraculous. That she is married to a conniving weasel of a man, is nothing short of torturous.

The Sheriff approaches The Wolf & Foxtail. All appears quiet and the wooden front door is locked and bolted. He pounds on the heavy oak with his fist, hoping he does not find Edward here. Nor in the woods. Or if he does, then he hopes he finds what little remains of him, for Anastasia is quite correct about the scrywolves.

A full minute passes before the Sheriff knocks again upon the oaken door. When there is still no response, he walks to the window, strips the ivy from the glass and peers inside. A figure shuffles forward through the gloom and so he returns to the door in time to hear the lock tumble open. And still, it takes several long moments for the door to swing open.

Sophia stands blinking in the morning light. Her skin is a sickly yellow tinge, her eyes unfocused, and foam stains the corners of her lips. As she exhales, a pungent smell like sulphur fills the air between them.

"Sophia?"

The Sheriff takes hold of her arm in case she requires support. She blinks at him like a heifer who has been woken from sleep. He waves his hand in front of her face until finally her eyes focus on his.

"Sheriff?" she asks, as though bewildered to see him.

"Are you ill?" he says.

"Dunno," she answers, then turns to look inside the gloomy belly of the Wolf & Foxtail, "the others."

"Come," he says, and leads her to the trough where the horses drink and sits her on its edge. "Wait here."

The Sheriff enters the Pub. The air itself seems a yellow haze and it carries the same wretched sulphuric smell that accompanied Sophia. The morning light makes only a weak attempt to invade the dark interior, so the Sheriff pauses to light a lantern. Stretched out before the cold embers of the fireplace are the husbands of Carlotta, Margarite, Cynthia and Jenny. They are fast asleep, or at least it is the semblance of sleep. The Sheriff holds the lantern high and sees they have the same yellow tinge to their skin as Sophia. He gives each a shake, pinches their cheeks, but not a one responds. He checks each pulse; the heartbeat is regular, strong, unaffected by whatever ails them. The floor beneath them is sticky from fallen pints of ale.

The Sheriff crosses to the front door, and out into the yard where Sophia has not moved from the trough. She starts when he touches her arm.

He lifts her to her feet.

"Is there anyone else in the Pub?"

"The Pub?" she asks, peering at him.

The Sheriff points to the open door of the Wolf & Foxtail.

"Oh, I should get to work" she says, lurching towards the building, "Father will be most displeased." The Sheriff grabs her arm.

"Sophia. We need Doctor Wintergreen. Are you well enough to fetch him?"

"Are you ill?" she asks, blinking.

"Get the Doctor, Sophia."

"Yes," she says. But it is not until he gives her a little push that she turns and stumbles down the cobblestones in the direction of Doctor Wintergreen's surgery.

The Sheriff retraces his steps into the Wolf & Foxtail, hoping the Goddess will guide Sophia's feet to the right address. He checks the pulse of each man again; there has been no change. He searches the main floor of the Pub to ensure no one has been missed; behind the bar, the storage rooms, the water closet, the kitchen.

All are empty.

He takes the stairs to the second floor. The first bedroom is empty except for a few barrels of beer. The second room is jammed with broken chairs, a cracked mirror, an old marble sideboard.

The third room belongs to Sophia.

It looks like the dressing room of a fan-dancer. The walls are stained red, there are feather wraps and hats tossed here and there amongst a nest of cheap silk dressing gowns. The glass pots and vials that cover the vanity hold creams, tinctures, oils. A large bed heaped with handmade quilts and sagging rose colored curtains stands at the centre of the room.

The Sheriff is about to close the door and continue his search when he spies a foot in amongst the quilts. He crosses the room, yanks aside the top blankets. A man lays naked, face-down on the mattress his head buried under one the pillows. The same yellow tinge infects his skin and the back of his torso, neck, and thighs are crisscrossed with scratches, marred by bruises.

The Sheriff flips the pillow away from the man's head.

Edward.

CHAPTER
FIVE

Wherein a sole
must prove its quality.

dward bats away the hands at his shoulders. He is being shaken, and the movement makes him nauseous. He hears voices, and although whoever is in the room speaks in whispers, the words thunder in his head. He knows they are spoken in Houndstooth's tongue but he seems incapable of deciphering their meaning. A new pair of stronger, larger hands grasp his shoulders to shake him awake.

His bones ache and his skin feels sore, tender and he wants to sleep. Edward strikes out with his fists, makes contact with the interlopers. Ah, bliss. The hands disappear and sweet oblivion claims him.

Until something cold and wet is thrown in his face.

Water fills his mouth and nose.

Edward gasps and opens his eyes.

The room is filled with the cold pale light of morning.

Standing above him is Doctor Wintergreen and the Sheriff who holds a tin ewer, the lip still dripping with water.

What are they doing here?

And then Edward looks around.

Where is he?

He is not at home or in the shop. The room is unfamiliar to him. He opens his mouth to ask why they have brought him here, but his throat is raw as though he has swallowed metal filings.

Doctor Wintergreen holds out a tankard into which the Sheriff pours a good measure of water. Edward's hands shake too much to take the vessel, so the Doctor holds it to Edward's mouth so that he might drink.

When his throat no longer feels parched, Edward wipes away the excess liquid that spills from his mouth.

"Where am I?" he asks. He sees he is naked, covered in bruises. He pulls a quilt over his body. "What happened? Was I assaulted?"

The Sheriff blinks down at him, "You do not remember?"

Edward may not remember how he came to be in this present state, but he does remember how much he detests the Sheriff. The man is constantly hovering about him as though waiting to catch Edward in some criminal act. And the way the man watches Anastasia (who is still his wife!), as though she is prey and he, predator, is most disconcerting.

Anastasia.

Edward scrunches his eyes. The last he remembers is being seated across the table from her at the supper hour. Then he left for the Wolf & Foxtail for —

Sophia.

He lurches up from the bed and looks around the room. He is in Sophia's room.

He now recognizes the feathers and silks and red walls.

However, he cannot reveal to these men, that he knows this room.

"Where am I?" he asks again, not looking at either of them in case they discern his deception.

"At the Wolf & Foxtail," Doctor Wintergreen says, "t'was a bad batch of ale. You and a few others took ill."

"Then I was brought here to recover?" Edward asks, gesturing to the bed. But as to this, he is guessing. For although he remembers walking through the doors and down the hall to the stairs to wait for Sophia, nothing further comes to mind. Whatever happened next, is perched there on the edge of his consciousness, if only he could grab hold of it. But it fades away, like a dream upon awakening.

"I should returns home," Edward says, "Anastasia will be worried."

"Now, just wait, son," Doctor Wintergreen says placing a hand on his shoulder, "you've been ill and need rest."

"I can do that at home," Edward argues searcing the bed for his clothes. The room is starting to feel claustrophobic and Edward wants to get out from under the prying eyes of these men.

The Sheriff walks over to a bureau and collects a shirt, and then from the floor, trousers. He drops both on the bed and Edward grabs the items, uncaring whether both men watch.

"You are certain you remember nothing of last night?" the Sheriff reiterates.

Edward pulls his shirt over his head. Then yanks up his trousers.

"I recall nothing," Edward says. A convulsion seizes his brain and he stumbles, grabbing onto the mattress to stay upright. He hears the Doctor shout. Hands grab him, hold him steady. A woman's voice teases the corner of his mind, *Edward, Edward* and each call of his name is a moment of blinding pain and panic. Only when the voice ceases, does his heart rate calm.

"You are not well, son," Doctor Wintergreen says, taking Edward's pulse.

"I assure you, Doctor, just a bit of nausea." Edward finds his feet once again. He is still absent socks and shoes but the need to get out of this room presses on his chest. "I promise to go straight home to bed."

Doctor Wintergreen does not look pleased as he releases Edward's hand, "Let Anastasia know I will be stopping by tonight to check on you."

"I will. Thank you, Doctor. Sheriff," Edward says, as he staggers toward the door. And then he is out of the stifling room with its sickly sweet smell of Sophia's scent. He is struck again by a bout of nausea and places a hand on each wall as he descends the stairs. When he can breathe again he finds himself on the bottom step, where his books and leather pouch sit.

The feeling that some important memory is just out of his reach returns to torment him yet again. Teasing at the corner of his brain like a flutter-fly skirting a spiderweave's web. But just as quickly, whatever is there disappears. Edward grabs hold of his books and pouch and bursts through the back door of the Pub, just as a staggering cramp seizes his stomach.

He falls to his knees outside in the courtyard.

He is dying.

His insides are ripping apart.

His whole body shudders and he vomits. Again and again. A yellow noxious liquid spills from his mouth and nose, staining the ground before him.

When he finishes vomiting, he lies on the ground gasping in the cold morning air.

Now that he has expelled whatever it was he ate or drank, each breath feels like salvation. Each cell in his body feels reborn.

He rolls onto his back, staring up at the cloudless sky, wipes his mouth and laughs. He feels completely different, like a new man.

He jumps to his feet and pushes up the arms of his shirt. The bruises have vanished. He checks his legs. Gone there as well. He laughs again and looks up at the Wolf & Foxtail.

A man stands at the window of Sophia's bedroom watching him. The Sheriff. Edward gives him a wave, collects his books and begins walking home.

Reborn.

Magically.

The Sheriff hands Doctor Wintergreen a small glass vial of yellow fluid that he collected from Edward's vomit in the courtyard.

"Tell me what it is."

The Doctor gives the vial a shake, holds it up to the sun.

"I've already told you, Sheriff."

"I know. Bad ale. Humor me."

The Doctor shakes his head and gives the Sheriff a pat on his shoulder.

"I'll be in touch. In the meantime, I must get my patients to bed."

The Sheriff nods and watches the Doctor escort the husbands of Cynthia, Carlotta, Betsy and Jenny out the door. Sophia is already tucked upstairs in bed, resting comfortably. Like the others, she too, was restored once she had expelled the contents of her stomach. And she too, like the others, could recall nothing of the events of the past evening.

Bad ale and its affect on the stomach, the Sheriff understood. But the side effect of amnesia was something else all together. Once upon a time, one might have thought magic was involved. But magic was supposed to have been extinct for generations. Or at least that was what most people believed. The Sheriff? Well he wasn't certain of that. He had seen some strange sights in his time, events that defied easy explanations.

He steps out and closes the door to the pub. He needs answers.

And for that, he'll have to wait for Doctor Wintergreen.

Edward steps into the empty shop and locks the door behind him. He sets his books and leather case on the workbench and studies the interior.

A fine layer of dust covers all surfaces. Anastasia stopped cleaning in here weeks back. He stands before the workbench and picks up each tool in turn; an awl, marking wheel, small hammer, sole knife. All belonged to his father and the wooden handles are worn smooth by the old man's grip.

He drops the knife on the bench and turns towards the connecting door. Which is when he sees them.

He doesn't know how he missed them when he first entered.

Perhaps it was not yet light enough.

Perhaps the shadows fell in such a way as to keep them hidden.

Regardless, there they sit on the floor in the middle of the room.

Given the night he has had, Edward is not entirely certain they are real. He walks over and crouches before them.

Reaches out and touches them.

Sure enough, they exist.

At first, the shoes appear to be made of silk. However, on closer inspection, Edward sees they are made of leather. Although the eye is most carefully deceived into believing otherwise.

Edward has never before seen such exquisite leather, so pale and smooth to the touch. And embroidered all about in fine stitches are one hundred tiny birds of every color. The shoes have a distinct heel and subtle arch. And they are exceedingly dainty, as though they have been designed for a child's foot.

They are almost too beautiful to touch with mortal hands. They are certainly too beautiful to wear on Houndstooth's muddy roads.

"Edward."

Edward starts at his name and hides the shoes behind

his back, staring up at Anastasia who stands in the connecting door.

There are dark circles under her eyes. Her hair is unkempt, pulled free of its usual braid. She is still in her nightclothes; they are creased and he can smell her sweat on the fabric.

"Where were you?" she asks.

"I took ill," he says, standing, but still feeling a strong desire to hide the shoes from her.

"Ill?" she says, coming forward. She moves to place her palm on his forehead but he steps away from her touch and she drops her hands to her sides.

"Quite ill," he says. "I was put to rest at the Wolf & Foxtail."

"You should have sent for me," she states, "I would have come."

"No need," he says, wishing she would leave so he could examine the shoes once more. "I was well cared for."

"Oh," she says. And then after a long moment of silence, "I am glad."

"Doctor Wintergreen will be stopping by later to check on me, if you would be good enough to put on the kettle when he arrives."

"Of course," she says. He smiles at her, wishing she would leave him alone with the shoes.

"Well," she says, taking a step back towards the connecting door, "I'll wash up."

He smiles at her, relaxes his shoulders and one of the shoes slips from his fingers.

He grabs for it, but too late, it strikes the ground and rolls away from him and towards her.

"What is this?" Anastasia asks, reaching down. He grabs for the precious shoe but his wife claims it first. He wants to scream at her to drop it. That it doesn't belong to her, it belongs to him.

"Why t'is beautiful," she says with a smile, "Did you make them for me?"

He wants to gag. The idea of her wearing these shoes sickens him. Not only are they far too tiny for her enormous feet. But if she were to wear them, it would only sully, contaminate and defile their beauty.

"Nay," he says, shrugging off the look of disappointment that spreads across her face, "I found them."

"Where?"

Edward curses. Wishing he had the time to think of a convincing lie. But the truth is out and so he gestures to where he is standing.

"How strange," Anastasia says and as she crosses to the door, he wants to snatch the shoe from her hand in case she should try to flee with it. But she does not leave, she simply inspects the lock.

"It does not appear to be molested. I wonder who left them here. And how they got in?"

Edward stays quiet, his fingers itching to reclaim the shoe in her hand.

"T'is a mystery," she says at last. "We could take them to the Sheriff. He may be able to find their owner."

The fingers of Edward's left hand curl into a fist. Give these beautiful creations to that pompous, patronizing plebeian? Not ever.

"Or we could place them in the window," Edward says, in a voice he almost doesn't recognize because he sounds much calmer than he feels. "Perhaps the owner will stop by to claim them." He studies the one in his hands, "they may have been brought to me for mending in some fashion."

Anastasia looks doubtful. But then she holds out the shoe to him and it requires all his will power not to snatch it from her fingers.

"T'is possible," she says, as he reclaims the shoe, feeling less panicked now that they are both in his possession. As Anastasia walks towards the door, he watches her wipe the hand that held the shoe against her nightclothes as though she were somehow dirtied by the experience of holding it.

Edward waits until she closes the door behind her before clutching both shoes to his chest. They are magnificent works of art, fit only for the most rarified of beauties. Certainly, such shoes would be far too expensive for any of the common folk in Houndstooth. Why, even his father never had the talent it would require to create shoes such as these.

He is drawn to see the shoes in full daylight and so he places them carefully in the shop window. Then, Edward sits down on his father's workbench so he can study their magnificence. The skill of their stitching and craftsmanship is unparalleled and the manner in which the sunlight sharpens the color of the birds makes them appear almost as though they are moving. They are truly marvelous creations and a secret part of his heart hopes they are never claimed so that he might have the privilege of possessing them for days to come.

A shadow falls over the shoes and Edward glances up in annoyance. How dare anyone block the sunlight from them?

But someone does.

A woman stands before the shop window, staring at the shoes. She is short and wide, built like a square with a lumpy face and skin the consistency of grey porridge. Her grey hair towers above her head like a honey-hive. On her chin is a large brown mole with three course hairs sprouting out of it like weeds. She is then joined by another; an extremely thin man, almost emaciated, who would be tall if he stood upright. However, he slumps forward, his arms loose and when he moves he reminds Edward of the way spiders scurry for dark corners when they are exposed to the light. The pair engage in a few lines of conversation and the woman points to the shoes.

Edward's heart seizes.

He has only just found these delightful creations; surely they cannot already be reclaimed? It takes everything in his will power not to snatch the shoes from the window and hide them. But then his heart calms. And even though he has not yet seen this woman's feet, he knows the shoes cannot belong to her. He cannot say why he knows this, he just does.

He watches the couple hover outside the window for several more agonizing moments and then the woman strides towards the shop door.

In an instant, she is standing before Edward.

The thin man, however, does not follow.

"Good morning," Edward says, yanking out his handkerchief to wipe the sweat from his brow.

"Is it?" she responds, her eyes glancing over him before adding, "Where are your shoes?"

Edward stares at her. His shoes? He looks around the shop. His father always made shoes to order so there was never any stock —

"Your shoes," she says, pointing at his feet and Edward realizes that since returning home, he is still barefoot, "I beg your pardon Madame —"

"I was already loath to patronize a shop as common as this one, especially now that I see the proprietor cares very little for social graces. But the shoes. I must have them. Wrap them at once."

Edward stares at the woman. While she is certainly the most ugly woman he has ever seen, her hair is clean and shiny and smells of lavender. And her dress. The fabric is red silk, and though her body has little shape aside from a square, the gown is tailored to perfection, adding the illusion of curves. Even her boots (and indeed her feet are as large and flat as he suspects), are made of only the finest black leather.

"Are you a dullard?" she asks, when he fails to move.

Edward flushes, "of course not."

"Then do as I command. I have not got all day."

"The shoes?" Edward asks, "they are yours?"

The woman focuses her sharp green eyes on him, "What my mistress wants, my mistress gets. I presume, given the shoes are displayed for view in your window, that they are for purchase?"

"Yes, my Lady," Edward finds himself saying.

"Then wrap them at once."

Edward scrambles to retrieve the shoes from the window. He is once again incredibly astonished at how smooth the leather is in his hands. He places them on the workbench and opens one of the drawers to retrieve a sheet of wrapping paper.

"Tck'a"

Edward stops to look over at the porridge-faced

woman. She holds out a red silk scarf.

"Wrap them in this."

He nods and retrieves the piece of silk, feeling a great emptiness in his heart when the shoes disappear within the red fabric. Only then does he realize they have not yet set a price. Moreover, he doesn't even know how much to charge for such magnificence.

"I trust this will cover their cost," the porridge-faced woman says, as though reading his mind. And she drops five gold coins onto the workbench. Never before in his life has Edward seen one gold coin, let alone five. If he works in the shop everyday for five years and is not required to pay any taxes, he may come close to earning the equivalent of one gold coin by the end of that time. But five? Without a doubt, he is suddenly the wealthiest man in Houndstooth.

"Yes, of course," Edward says, as he shoves the silk wrapped shoes into the woman's thick fingers.

"Good day," she says, looking at his bare feet, "I trust we meet no more."

And then she is gone.

Out of the shop.

But Edward is hardly aware of her departure. The gold is cold and heavy in his palm. He holds one up to the sunlight and it shines bright, almost glows. He bites down on the square piece and it tastes of metal. He laughs.

The connecting door opens to the shop and Edward shoves the gold pieces into his pocket.

"Who was that woman?" Anastasia asks, wiping her flour covered hands on her apron.

"What woman?" he asks.

"The woman leaving the shop."

"She came for the shoes," Edward says, for Anastasia will notice their absence.

"Did she say how they happened to come here?" she inquires.

"I forgot to ask," Edward lies, fingering the hidden gold pieces, "but she was glad to have them back."

"She reminds me of someone from Ferrybone," Anastasia says. "Someone from a long time ago."

Edward brushes past Anastasia on his way to the stairs, "I think I'll wash, change for lunch."

Anastasia nods. "There's the last of the beet soup you like so much."

"Excellent," Edward says, and then he's taking the stairs two at a time. Once in the bedroom, he shuts and bolts the door behind him. He crosses to the window, flips the curtain aside. Then he retrieves the gold coins from his pocket and holds them in the palm of his hand.

Whereas mere moments before, he found them cold and heavy, now they seem as warm and light as the sunshine itself. He is the luckiest man in Houndstooth, if not the world. He folds his fingers around them and holds his fist to his heart.

It is only then that he realizes the grey pouch with his bridal gold is missing from about his neck.

CHAPTER
SIX

Wherein a weasel
escapes a trap.

Anastasia lies in bed and stares at the crack in the ceiling. Ever since the roof fell in over the shop this past winter, the crack has been there. It looks like a wide gaping mouth, ready to swallow her whole. She feels listless this morning, unable to move. She wonders if she has caught whatever brain fever afflicted Edward and the others. But last night when Doctor Wintergreen stopped by to examine Edward (and pronounce him fully recovered), he assured Anastasia it was not contagious.

Indeed, it was somewhat incredulous to think Edward had ever been sick. Last night, he was full of energy, unable to sit still. He fidgeted all through the supper hour. And even though Anastasia made her rosehip biscuits, one of Edward's favorite, he hardly ate a morsel.

Instead, he had been obsessed with something he

carried in his pocket. He was constantly touching the fabric with a gesture of reassurance, as though he was concerned that whatever was there, might disappear on him. She was far too tired from her sleepless night and a long day of cleaning, to inquire into the matter. And so she said nothing when he begged off the meal and left the house for a brisk walk. She expected him to be gone all night again, but he had surprised her by returning within the hour with a bottle of something hidden in his coat. He then disappeared up the stairs and into his room where he spent the remainder of the evening.

Anastasia expected to fall asleep as soon as she climbed into bed. But she was certain there was an intruder in the house or the shop. She wasn't sure what led her to believe this; perhaps it was a noise, a scrape, a bump in the night. Perhaps it was a shift in the energy of the place, or the events of last night. Regardless of what it was, each time she climbed out of bed, lit a candle, wrapped herself in her night-coat and went downstairs to check, the doors and windows were always locked and nothing had been disturbed.

Regardless, she searched every nook, cranny, closet and crevice. She left no hiding place unsearched. She even went so far as to check Edward's room. She was surprised when he answered her knock, expecting him to be asleep. But he was not. A candle was lit and he held his fingers in a fist at his side, as though whatever had been in his pockets had now been transferred to his hand. He had not heard anything at all, but she was welcome to search his room if it would make her feel more at ease.

Anastasia peered in the room, but nothing seemed

amiss so she declined, wished him goodly dreams and returned to her own bed. That had been three hours past.

She is not usually a superstitious woman, but the air seems ominous tonight. She shudders and closes her eyes, but sleep does not come.

Edward lies in bed, the gold nestled safely in his right hand. He checks the bottle of champagne on the bedside table, but it is empty. He has been awake for hours, his brain creating multiple possibilities for a future he had nigh given up on. He decides he will run away from Houndstooth and his heart feels giddy, lightened by this decision. With the gold, the world is his. He could go to Ferrybone, set himself up as a Genteel-man. Won't Anastasia's father be surprised! Nay, he is still thinking so small. He can travel north, beyond Utterly Peak to the Kettle Islands. From there, he can hire a boat to deliver him to the continental countries.

There, the great wealth of Anastasia's father and other men can be his. He can announce himself unmarried. No one would need to know about his wife. Indeed, no one would even know him. He would simply be a wealthy young merchant from abroad.

He can search for a new bride. One with more beauty, greater wealth. He has the capital now. He can have anything his heart desires. He smiles, giggling in delight over his plan.

He jumps from bed and strides over to the wardrobe and dresses. He slips into the velvet smoking jacket

Anastasia's brother gifted him, dropping the gold pieces into the pocket. On the continent, he will have ten such coats. Maybe even twelve, one for each daylight hour. He quickly inspects the remainder of the garments in the wardrobe. Worn, thin, threadbare the lot of them. He doesn't need to take them. In fact, aside from the smoking jacket and the coins, he will leave all his possessions behind. They are no longer worthy of his greatness.

He smiles to himself in the mirror, pleased to see the yellow tinge from yesterday has disappeared. His eyes sparkle with vigor, though he has had no sleep. He splashes water on his face and decides a brisk walk through the Shade will help to bring his escape plan into focus. He dries his face and hands and dives down the stairs to the shop. He is moving so quickly he almost misses them. But whether it be a trick of the light or something else, a sudden flash draws his eye to the centre of the room.

The shoes. They have returned.

Nay.

Not the same shoes.

A different pair altogether.

But definitely made by the same hand. Edward would recognize that skill anywhere.

This time the shoes are decorated with the exotic beasts of the Asiantine. Striped cats and black and white bears. Orange foxes and ring-tailed primates.

There is a knock at the shop door.

Edward ignores it, his fingers shaking as he reaches for the shoes. Oh, exquisite leather, as soft and supple as yesterday's pair. Oh, divine stitches, once again so delicate and fine.

The hand at the door hardens and the knocking increases in volume.

But Edward wants one more minute with the shoes. He doesn't care where they came from, only that they are here. He holds each up to his nose and smells deep. It seems impossible, but they smell of roses. He rubs his cheek against the curve of the sole, astonished by its smoothness.

The knocking becomes more persistent and with a curse, Edward rises, and strides across the room. He places the shoes on his workbench and throws open the door.

There on the stoop stands the porridge-faced woman and her spider-like chaperone from yesterday.

Her eyes are cold, her lips pursed.

"Yes?" Edward demands.

The woman points to the cardboard notice in the window of the shop.

"Your sign reads, open at eight." She holds up a gold pocket watch and consults the hands, "it is now eight o' three."

"We're closed," Edward says, his hands itching to return to the shoes.

"I think not," the old woman responds, tucking the watch away into some hidden pocket and once again pointing to the notice, "t'is Tuesday. You are most definitely open." And then she brushes past him and walks into the shop. Her eyes immediately set upon the shoes.

"Ah, I see you have made another pair," she says, grabbing them.

Edward clenches his fingers into fists, for the desire to strike the shoes from the porridge-faced woman's hands is almost overwhelming.

"They're of a different design," Edward says.

"I can see that," the woman snaps, "and you should know, since my Mistress seems to delight in your wares, that she never wears the same item twice."

The old woman sets the shoes down once again on the workbench, draws out the familiar piece of red silk from yet another pocket and tosses it to Edward.

"Wrap them."

Edward does as she requests, his heart aggrieved that such beautiful creations were in his possession for so short a time.

Like the previous day, the old woman reaches into the velvet bag she carries on her arm and drops five gold pieces on the workbench. She then holds out her hands for the shoes. But Edward does not move.

"Seven," he says.

"Seven?" the porridge-faced woman echoes raising an eyebrow which causes the hairs on her mole to vibrate, "t'was only five yesterday."

"Yes," Edward says, clearing his throat, "well times are difficult are they not? With the rise in taxation and all.T'is seven."

The old woman studies him with very cold eyes and Edward has the sense that he has just earned himself an enemy. But still he does not relent. Finally, she says, "Very well," and tosses two more gold coins onto the bench.

Edward then hands her the package, his fingers eager to claim his coins.

The woman crosses towards the door, but stops before exiting.

"Mr. Cordwainer?"

Edward tears his eyes away from the gold in his palm.

"I would suggest the price remain steady. It would irritate my Mistress to pay more than seven gold coins for a pair of shoes and she does so hate to be irritated."

And with that she steps through the door, allowing it to slam shut behind her. Seven gold coins. Seven! For one pair of shoes.

Sweet Christos.

Edward's knees weaken and he drops to the workbench, drawing out the gold from yesterday. He mixes the two payments together. As of yesterday he was rich. Now he is undeniably wealthy. And should he stay in Houndstooth, he has no doubt there is more gold to come.

Something moves in the shadows off to his left. Edward shoves the gold coins in his pocket and twists his head but the room is empty. Strange, he thinks, he could have sworn

—

He reaches out, grabbing at the shadows. And much to his surprise, his fingers take hold of a piece of cloth and he hauls what he has caught into the light.

It is a tiny person.

Nay, not a person at all, although it resembles one in form.

The thing's arms and legs are short and stubby and it stands no higher than Edward's knees. Its face is long with a pointed chin covered in white whiskers. Its eyebrows are also white, thick and bushy. Its nose long and bumpy.Its eyes large and the most brilliant shade of emerald green. It wears a suit that appears to be made of burlap and holds a little leather satchel in its hands.

Edward has caught hold of its arm and it squeals trying to pull itself free of his grip.

He lifts the creature so that its feet no longer touch the floor.

"What are you?" Edward demands.

The creature squeals again and tries to bite Edward's hand. So Edward gives it a shake, causing the leather satchel to drop from the thing's fingers. As it strikes the floor, a variety of tools spills from within. Shoemaking tools.

"I am an Elf, Sir," the creature cries.

A cold chill settles over Edward.

"You made the shoes," he says.

The creature continues to wiggle and so Edward lifts it higher, until they are eye to eye.

"Answer, damn you," he says.

The creature finally stills.

"Yes, Sir."

"Why?" Edward demands.

"Because you wished it," the Elf responds.

"I did no such thing," Edward states.

"But you did, Sir. You wished to be the most famous man in all the Kingdom. I am here to grant you this desire."

Edward releases his hold and the creature yelps as it lands on the floor with a thud.

A wave of remembering washes over Edward. The night at the Wolf & Foxtail with Sophia—nay, not Sophia. But a woman with golden hair, large blue eyes, pink cheeks. Her skin was soft, her tongue was—

A terrifying cramp seizes Edward's guts. The color drains from his face.

"Magic is extinct."

"Not quite," the creature amends.

"But t'was punishable by death."

"If one was caught practicing, yes. But not all of us

were. Caught, that is."

Edward feels lightheaded so he sinks to the floor, his head between his knees.

"I assure you, Sir," the creature continues, "I am most discrete. No one ever need know magic is involved. But if you prefer I cease, I completely understand. I can leave now—"

The creature begins to gather his fallen tools and replace them in the leather satchel.

"Stop!" Edward orders and the creature halts. "No one ever need know?"

"Not at all, Sir. My Mistress and I guarantee discretion."

"Your Mistress?" Edward asks.

"Yes, Sir. I believe you met her at the Wolf & Foxtail? A little too ugly for one such as I, but I have heard humans think her quite pleasant to look upon."

"Rosemary is your Mistress?" Edward asks, and his skin warms and his blood rushes at the remembrance of her touch.

"Indeed, Sir. You should consider yourself privileged to have been selected by her."

Edward glances around the shop as though Rosemary herself might be standing in the shadows.

"Oh no, Sir, she is long gone."

"So you work for me now?" Edward asks.

"Not quite, Sir, I work for the wish," the creature states.

"T'is the same thing," Edward says. He fiddles with the gold coins that have taken up residence in his pocket.

"I suppose you'll be expecting compensation?"

"Oh no, Sir." The creature gasps as though offended, "My Mistress is very clear about that point. I work for free."

"Well then, I'll leave you to it, shall I?"

"Very good, Sir."

Edward watches the little creature snatch up its leather satchel and tools and dart back into the shadows.

And just like that it is gone from view.

Edward, however, doesn't move from his spot on the floor.

He needs to figure out how to dispose of Anastasia. He may be able to fool the dim-witted residents of Houndstooth into believing he is responsible for creating the beautiful shoes being sold from his shop, but fooling Anastasia is another matter all together. She has seen him make a pair of shoes (he made her first pair of sandals and boots), and she is quite aware of his skill level.

But more damning is that she knows about the first pair. Curses. He wishes she had never seen them. He has been careless, and must rectify that now.

A knock sounds at the door.

Christos.

If the porridge-faced woman has returned to demand he refund the two extra gold coins, he will slap her ugly face. He throws open the door. But t'is not the old woman at all.

Anastasia throws off the quilt and pads over to the bedroom door. Edward has been knocking for the past minute. At first she ignores him, pretending to sleep. But he persists and so she rises, swinging open the door.

He fidgets with a piece of paper in his hands.

"I'm sorry to awaken you, my love. But a Messenger

arrived with this for you."

He holds out a telegram and Anastasia takes it from his fingers. She flips it over. There are very few words.

The ink blurs before her eyes and Edward throws a supporting arm around her waist.

"Here, sit," he says, and leads her back to the bed.

Anastasia's hands shake and her throat thickens with tears.

"I must leave immediately," she says.

Edward pats her shoulder in comfort.

"I'll pack for you," he says, with almost a tinge of eagerness in his voice and opens the wardrobe to pull out her small travel case.

Anastasia glances down once again at the telegram. There are only five words. But they change her world.

Papa dying. Come at once.

Edward stands in the doorway of the shop and watches the carriage rattle its merry way down the cobblestone street. He wished for Anastasia to go and now she is gone.

From the shop behind him, he can hear the click and clack of the Elf's tiny tools.

A smiles creases his mouth.

Magic.

CHAPTER SEVEN

Wherein a fly lands
in a royal cup of tea.

Edward awakens with a pounding headache and a throat that feels like dry ashes. He opens his eyes and takes in the empty bottles of Continental wine scattered across the floor. On the beside table, is a box of the sweet tobacco cigars favored by Anastasia's Father.

Anastasia.

He closes his eyes.

After she departed yesterday, Edward visited the local money lender. He had taken one of the gold pieces to be broken into more manageable shillings. The man's eyes bugled in his head upon the sight of the gold, no doubt wondering where Edward had gotten such a large sum. But Edward felt no desire to explain. He cleaned out the money lender's entire stock of shillings with five hundred still owing and to be retrieved in two weeks.

Afterward, Edward visited the husbands of Carlotta and Betsy and purchased enough supplies (the very best cheeses, meats and breads), to last the week. In the afternoon, he visited Jenny's husband and had measurements taken for a new suit to be made from the most expensive twill available. He was uncertain where to order new shoes, after all, that might raise a few eyebrows. However, upon returning home a brand new pair of black leather continental shoes were waiting for him on the floor of the shop.

The figure next to him on the bed moans and snuggles closer. Bile rises in his throat at the sight of Sophia in his bed.

She had come by the house last night after midnight. However, Edward was still awake, searching for a secure spot to hide his gold. He is uncertain why he answered the door. Probably worried the neighbors might hear. She'd heard of Anastasia's departure and wanted to know why he didn't come by.

Edward said he was tired both from his illness and a long day's work and needed sleep.

But she pushed her way past him into the shop.

"I miss you, Edward," she whined, pressing herself against him like some glutinous mass of dough.

He pushed her away, disgusted by her drooping flesh and enflamed cheeks. She was drunk and her breath smelled of stale spirits.

"Go home, Sophia," he said.

But she was not to be denied.

"Edward," she persisted, encircling him once again with her arms.

He wrenched himself away from her then with such a

force, she stumbled and fell, cracking her head against the floor. There was a moment of terrible silence and for a moment he thought he might have killed her. But then she started to cry. Great big heaving gulps like a bloated bullfrog in mating season.

It was accompanied by a high-pitched keening wail and he began to worry someone on the street might hear and call the Sheriff.

"Darling," he pleaded, "I'm so very sorry." She shook him off continuing to cry, but he persisted, pawing at her hair, patting her shoulders, squeezing her swollen breasts.

"You hurt me," she hiccuped, her fingers exploring the swelling bump on her right temple.

"T'was an accident," he said, "I've been a right mess with everything that's happened today."

Her blubbering started to ebb and she wiped her snotty nose on the sleeve of her gown.

"You're so mean to me, Edward," she sniffed as he kissed her meaty neck.

"I know, Darling," he found himself saying, "I am so very sorry. Now come have a drink. You'll feel better."

He helped her to her feet and led her into the kitchen. He was reaching for a homemade raspberry wine given to Anastasia by Carlotta when he saw her eyes light upon the case of Continental. His fingers tightened at the idea of wasting a single translucent drop on the likes of her, but the bump on her head was developing into quite the bruise.

So he pulled one of the bottles and said, "Let us celebrate."

She giggled like an affected schoolgirl and fetched two of Anastasia's crystal glasses from the cupboard.

"What are we celebrating?" she asked, as he filled hers to the top.

"Why, us," he said and she giggled again as he poured himself only a half a glass. He toasted her beauty and downed his in one gulp, intending to send her on her way after the one drink. But their glasses never seemed to empty and suddenly they had consumed two bottles and she no longer looked like Sophia, but more like Rosemary.

So he dragged her upstairs, pushing her onto the bed. She helped him tear aside her dress and she screamed and screeched through the night as he battered himself against her.

Now t'was nearly six in the morning.

He must find a way to get rid of her. A cold chill runs along his back and he wonders if magic is really as easy as it seems.

He closes his eyes and wishes Sophia would disappear.

Three hours later Sophia finally departs out the back door, through the garden and to the cobblestone road. He stands at the window watching her leave and she stops three times to turn and blow kisses in his direction. It had been a near impossible task to get her out of the house.

Once he awakened her, she did not rise as he desired. Instead she rolled on top of him, pinning him to the bed, urging him to copulate with her. He deflected her advances, was even slow to respond but that did not dissuade her. She persisted until he was aroused and then once they were joined, she remained on top, riding him, her pendulous breasts swinging before his eyes, her face red and sweaty, grunting like some kind of farm animal.

Edward closed his eyes to shut out the sight of her, but the smell of her rank breath made it near impossible to imagine it was Rosemary who mounted him in Sophia's place.

After she finished, she declared she was going to sleep yet again. But Edward dragged her from the damp sheets and forced her to dress.

Even still, by the time she washed, curled her hair, made her way downstairs, insisted she be allowed to cook him breakfast, and tidied up the kitchen, it was coming upon the ninth hour. She had wanted to talk about a dream she had last night where she was certain someone had been in the bedroom touching her skin. But whenever she awoke she could see no one. She chided Edward, accusing him (in a very flirtatious manner), of molesting her while she slept. Edward protested but ultimately agreed (yes, t'was him), in order to get her out of the house.

When she finally departs, he utters a huge sigh, returning to the bedroom which still stinks of Sophia's sweat. He rips the sheets from the bed to have them laundered. Nay, he thinks, no need for that. He will simply buy new sheets. Ones that are of better quality, more suited to his newly acquired station in life.

He dresses in his smoking jacket, washes his hands so they will be clean and steps downstairs to the shop.

He holds his breath while opening the connecting door.

His faith is rewarded.

The shoes are there. In the same spot. Made from the same smooth leather. This time the left foot is emblazoned with the many phases of the moon, while the right foot has a map of the stars. All embroidered in the palest of silver thread.

He glances at his pocket watch (a quarter past ten), and flips the sign on the door from closed to open. T'is a good thing porridge-face was not early today, he thinks, for he is not in the mood for another of her lectures.

At nigh on four in the afternoon, Edward still sits at the workbench. He has not moved all day. Not to fetch food from the pantry, though his stomach complains about the absence of nourishment. Not to visit the water closet, though his bowels protest against the amount of wine he drank last night.

The street has stayed empty.

And if the Elf is present, Edward has yet to spy his shadow.

He consults his pocket watch yet again. What on earth could be keeping her? She as good as informed him she would be back again today.

He is tempted to close the shop and make his way to the Wolf & Foxtail. It would serve old porridge-face right if he were not here when she came to purchase her precious shoes. It would serve her right to be kept waiting, when she has done the same to him.

He knows they don't have an appointment.

And he also knows that her Mistress wants his shoes. He can smell it on the old woman. The fact that she didn't quibble when he raised the price underscores the fact that, in terms of the shoes, she must do as she is instructed.

He glances at his pocket watch again. Five minutes have passed.

He has no doubt she will come eventually. After all, the Elf said the wish must be fulfilled.

He will give her five more minutes and then he'll close up and go to the Pub for some dinner.

Ten at the most.

It is nearly midnight and Edward still sits at the workbench waiting. He has not stepped away from the room. Every time he tries, he feels as though he is caught in a web, unable to move, struck by fear that he may miss the old woman's arrival.

Somewhere behind him are the faint sounds of scraping and scurrying. It sounds like vermin, but Edward suspects it is the Elf at work.

He looks down at the eleven gold pieces in his hand. Perhaps the creature lied. Perhaps this is all he is meant to have. Perhaps there is no such thing as wishes or magic at all.

He returns the gold to his pocket and crosses to the front door, turning the lock.

Which is when he hears it. The clomp and clatter of hooves and wooden wheels against Houndstooth cobblestone. For a moment he thinks it must be the mail coach. But then he remembers it only travels at dawn.

Edward peers out the window to the street beyond and watches as the coach stops outside the shop. It is easy to see the horses are pedigreed. These are no mere work beasts making the daily post journey from Houndstooth to Ferrybone and back again.

The livery on the driver is of excellent quality, and even though it is dark, Edward can see the man's gold buttons gleam in the dark.

Moreover, the crest on the carriage door is that of the Royal House.

Sweat breaks out on Edward's forehead.

It must be the old woman. Come at last.

A figure emerges from the carriage and Edward recognizes the thin, spindly man. He is followed by a dark lump which can only be the porridge-faced woman. And then a third figure steps down.

Tiny, thin. Her head covered in a black mourning veil.

Christos. His client. It can only be the Princess.

Edward licks his palms, runs his hands over his hair and smooths the creases from his smoking jacket.

"Shoe man!" From outside, the voice of the porridge-faced woman is loud and demanding. Edward rushes to the door, unbolts it and swings it wide.

The old woman pushes her way past him, hauling with her the thin creature in the black veil.

"I hope we haven't kept you waiting," she says.

"Not at all" Edward says, bowing low, "I have been exceptionally busy today and only just finished my work."

"Hmph," she says, and then gestures with a hand towards the girl in black. "My charge," she says, "was exceedingly naughty today and so her punishment lasted well into the evening."

"Enough," says, a voice that sounds as though it were a mix of steel and song. "My Nanny's tongue is sometimes known to get the better of her."

Edward looks for who is speaking and realizes it is the girl. Her face is completely obscured by the veil. However, he can see that she wears the Elf's shoes. Their vibrant colors are in strict counterpoint to the black taffeta gown, the veil, and the cape of her mourning weeds.

"Do you know who I am?" the voice demands.

"Yes, your Highness," Edward states, bowing low yet again.

"That t'was my mother's name," the girl states, "and I am nothing like her, am I Nanny?"

"Not at all, my pet," the porridge-faced woman says.

"You may call me Princess Ambrosia."

"Yes, your Highness. Princess Ambrosia," Edward states.

"Now, where are the shoes?" the creature demands.

"Right here, your— Princess Ambrosia," Edward says, crossing to his desk. He pulls open the bottom drawer where he placed the shoes for safekeeping and lifts them out. The Princess's hands shoot out like two sharp claws and she grabs them from Edward.

"Light," she demands and with shaking hands Edward lights two candles and holds them near so she may inspect the shoes.

"Oh, Nanny," she breathes clutching them to her chest, "they are truly beautiful. I must have them."

"Seven?" Nanny says, pulling out her velvet drawstring bag.

"Ten," says Edward.

Nanny hesitates, her fingers rigid and white against the drawstring.

"I believe we agreed upon seven," she states.

"You are mistaken," Edward says, his eyes on the Princess as she cradles the shoes in her arms, "we agreed on ten."

"This place makes me very cross," the Princess Ambrosia says, as she glances about the interior of the shop, "it is dirty and poor. Pay the man, Nanny, so we might leave."

"Very well," Nanny states and Edward sees the old woman's eyes are impossibly cold. She pulls out ten gold coins and holds them out to Edward.

But before he can claim them she releases her hand and the coins drop to the floor.

"My apologies," Nanny says, but Edward knows the act was deliberate.

"Not at all," Edward says, biting his tongue, "it is late and you are tired."

Even though he can hear the gold calling to him, he leaves the coins on the floor for he refuses to kneel and collect them while the old woman is present.

"We expect a new pair each morning the Princess is in residence at the Summer Palace," Nanny states.

"Of course," Edward says.

"And every afternoon at three o' clock, you will deliver the shoes to the castle and I will make payment."

"Ten pieces," Edward states looking at the Princess.

"Ten pieces," Nanny says, through a clenched jaw.

"Are we done here?" the Princess asks.

And when Nanny nods, she sweeps out of the shop, the thin man opening the door for her to exit. As soon as they depart, Edward drops to his knees to sweep up the gold coins.

Which is when the door to the shop swings open and Nanny reenters. She wears a sly smile on her face, no doubt pleased to catch him in such a subservient position.

"You should know," Nanny states, "that Ambrosia does not like to share. If you make shoes for anyone other than her, she will punish you. Do you understand?"

"Yes," says Edward.

"Good," Nanny responds, and eyes the gold pieces he has yet to recover, "carry on."

Then out she strides, slamming the door behind her. Edward grabs the last gold coin, then crosses to the door and slides the bolt closed.

He mixes the pieces together with their previously acquired brethren. A shadow passes by the shop window and he turns to the side, covering the gold with his hand.

Is someone watching?

No, t'is the carriage pulling away in the street.

He needs to find a safe hiding spot for his treasure. Somewhere he alone will have access to. He grabs his worn leather satchel, the one that used to hold his father's shoemaking tools. No one, would have any reason to steal such a worthless item.

He can create a false bottom in the bag. It is the perfect hiding spot.

That night as he lies naked in bed, he takes hold of himself and imagines it is the Princess's hands on his skin.

Beneath the veil he wonders if she resembles Rosemary…

Chapter 8

Wherein a wolf wanders
through the Shade on his way
to a very different story.

Anastasia sits in the garden of her eldest sister, Saffron's, house. There is a small patch of grass between the butterbells and daffydils that is perfect for hiding. She sits, sipping a glass of sour plum juice, grateful for the time alone. Upon arrival in Ferrybone, the coach deposited Anastasia in the center of town. What had once been a thriving market place three months earlier, was no more. Now Ferrybone is desolate; most of the shops along High Street are closed, and those few that remain are in disarray. There was no one to meet her and so with bag in hand Anastasia walked the short distance to her parents' home. She was met with more desolation. The paint, which her father took pains to refresh every two months due to the hot Ferrybone sun, was faded and peeling. The windows were boarded and a flyer posted to the front door announced the property was for sale. Inquiries could be made at the bank. Regardless, she knocked until her knuckles were red but still no one answered the door.

Eventually one of the neighbors (someone new that Anastasia did not recognize), threw open her bedroom window, irritated by the continuous pounding, and shouted that the occupants had moved. Anastasia was perplexed by this turn of events. She tried to ask when this occurred, but the woman slammed closed the window, disappearing back into her home.

Anastasia then walked the half mile to Saffron's home. The once clean streets of Ferrybone were now littered with debris and dirt. It made walking difficult and so the trip took somewhat longer than she anticipated. By the time she arrived, she was parched. For it was well past noon and the sun was at its ripest.

It was at her sister's that Anastasia was met by the welcoming arms of her family who had all gathered under the one roof. Her mother was there, ensuring her bag was exchanged for a glass of cold apple cider. Anastasia could tell that her mother had aged greatly in three months. Her white hair no longer gleamed and there were dark circles under eyes.It was only after she was fed a meal of cold pheasant and crisp crackers with asparagus, that Anastasia received the whole story.

Papa had departed for an overseas trip to the Antioch Islands for trade. The heavy taxation imposed by the Princess forced him to find new avenues of income in order to replenish their household's fading coffers. Those who failed to pay had their family homes and lands stripped from their hands, faced imprisonment or worse.

Papa had been gone three weeks before Anastasia's mother began to worry. Yes, the Antioch Islands were, what seemed to her an immeasurable distance from Ferrybone, but the post was always reliable. But no word came from Papa to say he had arrived safely. A month passed. Then two. Bills demanded payment, the money ran low.

Her mother attempted to find him by contacting his business associates overseas. But no one had seen him. It was only when Anastasia's brother set out to retrace Papa's steps that they discovered he was lying ill in hospital. He had been stricken by red fever and lost to delirium. In order to raise the funds to cover his medical expenses, they were forced to sell the family home.

Saffron reorganized the basement of her house into a sick room for Papa. Primarily because there was no room elsewhere. Middle-sister, Helena and her two girls, were now occupying the spare room. But additionally, the fever that claimed Papa burned so hot he needed to be housed in the coolest possible location.

He had been fighting that fever for months now.

And no matter how many times the Doctor drained blood, applied leeches, mixed his tincture of dried mouse and batwing, the fever continued to savage Papa's mind and body.

Saffron wanted to keep Anastasia informed from the beginning, but Caroline refused, not wanting to worry her daughter. For she was convinced her husband would soon rise from his sick bed.

But now it was apparent there were few days left.

And so Saffron sent for Anastasia.

Anastasia enters Papa's sick room expecting the worst for she has seen prints of those stricken by the disease. So the hair loss, seeping sores, and foul stench of decay are unpleasant but not unexpected. But what drives the very breath from her body is how frail he looks. He has lost more than half his body weight. His bones stick out sharply under his skin so that he resembles a flesh covered skeleton. His lungs wheeze and rattle as he fights for every breath. And his eyes are pale, watery, unfocused and he starts like a small child at the sound of her footsteps.

"Papa?" she whispers, crossing the room to stand next to his bed.

She longs to take his hand, but Saffron warns against such action, lest the disease transfer to her.

"Caroline?" he breathes, seeking her out with his eyes.

"T'is Anastasia," she says, dipping a cloth into the bowl of water on the bedside table and wiping his brow.

"I know of no such person," he growls. "Caroline!"

"Papa, t'is I," she repeats, setting aside the cloth, "your daughter."

"I have but two daughters," he spits, "and neither carry that name. Get out!" He struggles, trying to rise but his legs twist in the sheets. "Get out!" He screams, striking out with his arms.

Anastasia takes a step back as her mother comes running into the room with Saffron.

"Hush, my dear," Caroline whispers taking his hand in her own.

"Get her out of here," he snarls, pointing a skeletal finger at Anastasia.

As Anastasia watches her mother stroke Papa's brow, Saffron takes her arm and pulls her back upstairs to the kitchen.

"He fades in and out of time," Saffron says, sitting Anastasia down at the table and pouring her a cup of raspberry tea. "One hour he is coherent, the next he demands to know what trickery is afoot because I am no longer a child."

"How much longer?" Anastasia asks.

Saffron reaches over and squeezes her hand, "the Doctor thinks no more than a week."

Anastasia blinks back her tears.

It seems impossible that one so strong could fade so completely in such a short amount of time. All her life, she pictured her father as invincible, and now here he is, his life chopped short by something she can't even see. She wants her Papa.

How is she to go on without his strength?

If he dies, she will never feel safe again.

Her heart pounds, her breathing becomes labored.

"Anastasia," Saffron says, squeezing her fingers, "T'will be all right."

"Nay, it will not," Anastasia says, "Not ever again."

And she pulls her hand away and runs from the room.

The next day he is better.

Though Anastasia is still terrified to enter the basement lest he not know her again. But her fear does not come to pass. Today, he recognizes her on sight and greets her with a smile. Welcomes her home, and asks after her travels. Then he apologizes that he has not yet bathed today for he is unable to rise from his bed.

Anastasia discards Saffron's advice not to touch him and folds him in her arms, resting her head on his shoulder, thankful once again for his touch. Though now he no longer feels like a safe place to land but rather a mere collection of sticks held together by skin. T'is impossible not to cry, though she wishes the tears would not fall.

"I am so sorry, Papa," she says.

"Come now," he says, wiping her eyes, "I have seen more than enough tears these past days." He pats the bed beside him and she curls up next to him.

"Are you in pain?" she asks.

"T'is nothing but a wee cold," he rasps and is taken hostage by a coughing fit. Anastasia holds his hand until the tremors subside, then helps him to a cooling drink of water.

"You should be outside playing dolls with your sisters," he smiles.

"I will, Papa. Later."

"Good girl," he says, closing his eyes.

And then he sleeps.

Anastasia watches over him. And prays.

The days pass in a blur.

Some days Papa recognizes Anastasia. Some days he does not. On the better days, she will sit on the bed and read aloud from his favorite tales. On the bad days, the only one allowed downstairs is Caroline. For only she can calm his fevered brow. On those days, Saffron and

Anastasia (and sometimes Helena if she is around), sit on the top step of the basement stairs and hold one another's hand for comfort. T'is on these days, when he is at his worst, that Caroline refuses to listen to anyone who tells her, her husband is dying.

Anastasia swallows the last of her juice and makes her way through the garden and into the house. She finds Saffron and Philip in the kitchen. From the looks on their faces, she can tell she has caught them mid-argument.

"Helena has disappeared again," Saffron says, giving her husband a meaningful look as he turns away and leaves the room. A mere three weeks after Papa returned, Helena was abandoned by her husband when he ran off with his seamstress. Days later, she along with Anastasia's two nieces, moved into the house as well. "I'm sure she's down at the wharfs and I can't bear for this family to have any more heartache. But Philip won't go look for her anymore."

Anastasia squeezes her sister's hand, "I'll go."

"You will?" Saffron asks, wiping her red eyes, "but t'is dark."

"I am not scared," says Anastasia.

"No," agrees Saffron with a look of wonder, "you really aren't, are you?"

"And besides," Anastasia continues, "I could do with a walk."

Anastasia walks along the deserted High Street. It is downhill to the wharf and it feels good to stretch her legs. She has remained stagnant for too many days. She misses the long walks she used to take in the Shade. In fact, she realizes she misses Houndstooth. The cluster of brightly colored cottages, the towering heights of Utterly Peak, the patch of violaheads in the back garden. She misses her room and the peace she finds there. She misses her friends. She wonders if Betsy still manages to foil the taxmen with her special scales. If Jenny has drank the last of her june-pip juice. Whether Margarite has added any more lace to her dresses.

A raucous laugh erupts from a dark alley and draws her attention back to the present. Every night since Anastasia returned to Ferrybone, (and a great many nights prior to her arrival, so Saffron informs her), Helena slips away at dusk to one of the myriad of cheap drink houses that cluster around the Ferrybone docks. If neither Saffron, nor Philip find her and force her to return, she stumbles home well past dawn smelling of stale smoke, cheap booze and other more base pursuits.

These drink houses are not at all like the companionable atmosphere of the Wolf & Foxtail. They are unkempt places with unwashed floors, overturned crates for stools and very few candles so that dark deeds may pass unnoticed in even darker corners. Anastasia feels no sense of trepidation as she surveys one ale house after another. She finds by covering the untouched left side of her face, she gains the freedom to pass unmolested through clusters of inebriated dockhands.

After searching four establishments, she finds her sister at The Alabaster Mermaid. Tucked into a tight corner, Helena sits between two sailors; her head on the dark haired man's shoulder, her hand on the blonde haired man's knee.

Anastasia pushes her way through the cramped room and stands before the wooden barrel that serves as a table.

"Helena," she says. But her sister does not seem to take note of her arrival. Instead she grabs the dark haired sailor's head and brings his mouth down to hers for a very wet kiss.

"Helena!" Anastasia raises her voice so she can be heard above the din.

Her sister releases the man much to his displeasure. But instead of turning towards Anastasia she grabs the blonde haired man and fixes a similarly sloppy kiss on him.

Anastasia reaches over the table, grabs her sister's arm and gives it a sharp twist.

"Christos," her sister spits, as she pulls away from the sailor to see Anastasia standing before her.

"Go on!" the dark haired man says, clenching his fingers into a fist and raising it toward Anastasia, "or I'll pummel yer."

"Leave it," Helena says, patting his knee, "t'is my sister is all." She looks Anastasia in the eye, "go home." And she locks herself around the blonde haired man and resumes her prior sport.

The dark haired man wraps his sinewy arm around Helena's shoulders.

"Go on, strumpet. Ya heard her."

Anastasia turns her face towards the light so the man has the pleasure of viewing her scars.

"I think not," she says.

"Christos," he breathes withdrawing his arm and sliding out from beside Helena. He punches his friend's leg, is rewarded with a growl.

"Get off her," he says, repeating the blow, "she's bloody Constantine's daughter." Even in the dim lighting Anastasia sees that the blonde haired man pales with his friend's words. He pushes Helena back and jumps to his feet, claiming his cap from the barrel and nodding to Helena, "Apologies, Miss. I'd appreciate it if you didn't tell your father about this little mix-up."

The dark haired man cuffs him across the back of his head and the two of them disappear into the crowd.

"You little troll," Helena spits, eyeing Anastasia. "They were mine for the night. Now I have to start over." She rises to follow the men but Anastasia blocks her way.

"T'is time to return home."

"Did Saffron send you?" Helena asks, resuming her seat and inspecting her tankard for any dregs of ale.

"She is worried."

"Worried? With her perfect husband. Perfect home. Don't be foolish. She's not capable of worry."

"Don't be cruel," Anastasia says, "you'll regret it on the morrow."

"Why do you defend her so?" Helena asks, tipping back the last drop of ale. "She was horrid to you as a child."

"She only wants what t'is best," Anastasia argues, "even if her manners are lacking."

"Well, you've certainly changed," Helena says, waving her tankard above her head, trying to catch the bar keep's eye.

"I have had to," says Anastasia, "Now get up, we are going home."

"Fortune? Fate? Forecast?" An old woman with a hump on her back the size of a sauce pan stumbles against Anastasia, bumping into their table. Her kerchief is pulled so low over her coarse grey hair that her eyes are all but hidden by the cloth. Her pointed chin is spotted with whiskers and her fingers are bony, the nails long and pointed. There is an ancient tattoo on her wrist, difficult to decipher, as the ink has bled through the skin with age. Perhaps a raven, a swan or some other bird.

"I'll take fortune," says Helena, pulling a haypenny from her glove and the old woman cackles.

"Helena, let us depart," Anastasia says, trying to ignore the fortune teller.

"You deprived me of my entertainment for the evening," Helena states, "t'is the least you can do before I return to Saffron's for my lecture."

Helena pats the empty crate next to her and motions for the old woman to sit.

"Papa would not want you consorting with magic," Anastasia hisses.

"T'isn't real," Helena says, "T'is fun. You do remember fun?"

Anastasia crosses her arms and sits on the empty crate to the other side of Helena.

She watches as the old woman takes Helena's right hand in her own.

"I call upon Mother Wind and Father Earth, Sister Sky and Brother Star, Shadow Moon and Darkling Sun to fix my eyes with the gift of sight, unravel the darkness and show me the light, fill my ears with what is good and right, reveal to me now the second sight."

The fortune teller blows across the surface of Helena's palm and her breath mists like a swirling fog.

Helena gasps and catches Anastasia's eye, "she's marvelous isn't she?"

"Shush," the old woman says, "you must be silent or the fates will not speak."

Helena presses her lips together and leans in. The fortune teller holds Helena's hand to her ear as though she is listening to it speak. She nods several times, then releases Helena.

"Well?" Helena demands.

"You have great passion, but you are grieving because the heart line is broken."

"Yes," Helena says, her eyes fixed on the old woman.

"To love again you must find what has been lost or you shall never be found."

"And what have I lost?" Helena asks.

"T'is not for me to answer," the old woman says, pressing her palm against Helena's heart, "the truth is here."

"T'is nonsense," Anastasia says, "may we please leave now?"

"She is a non-believer, your sister," the fortune teller says, peering up at Anastasia. Then she gestures, "give me your hand."

"No. The penalty for magic —"

"T'is pretend, Anastasia," Helena sighs.

"Then how did she know we were sisters?"

"Please, the whole town knows Papa. Now give her your hand and then we'll leave."

"Do you promise?" Anastasia asks.

"Promise," Helena says, touching her heart.

Anastasia turns toward the old woman who hunches before her and holds out her hand.

The old woman again repeats her chant. When she blows across her palm, Anastasia's skin feels suddenly cold and she shivers. The desire to pull her hand away is very strong. But then the old woman holds it to her ear as though to listen and the din of the bar seems to fade away until Anastasia can hear only the fortune teller's voice.

"There is great sadness in your world," the old woman says, "for you wish for a different life."

Anastasia is silent. A different life? One in which her husband loved her. One in which she could have children. A comfortable home. Yes, perhaps she does want something different. But her choice is made and the time for wishes is the territory of childhood and she has long since passed over those borders.

The old woman tips her head so Anastasia can at last see her eyes. They are a brilliant blue, and the color is calm and peaceful. The old woman places her hand on Anastasia's heart and warmth seems to spread from her fingers.

"Do you not?" the old woman asks, pressing her fingers against Anastasia's breastbone.

"Yes," Anastasia breathes, "I wish my life were different."

The clarity in the fortune teller's eyes shifts and they cloud over as though with cataracts. The old woman drops her tattooed hand from Anastasia's chest and her voice drops an octave.

"I see death. Awful, painful, terrifying death," she states, the words dropping from her mouth like winter sleet.

"Yes," Helena agrees, with great sadness, "t'is our Papa. He is sick with fever."

"Nay, nay," the woman says, shaking her head and pointing to Anastasia, "the death I see? T'is hers."

Anastasia strides up the steep hill to the top of High Street. She can hear Helena huffing and puffing behind her.

"I am sorry," Helena calls out, "Anastasia. Please, slow your steps."

Anastasia halts at the old newspapiary shop and waits for her sister to arrive.

"I am truly sorry," Helena repeats, gasping from the exertion of climbing the hill.

"You need to stop," Anastasia says, as she watches her sister, two stone overweight, struggle to regain her breathe.

"Stop what?" Helena asks. "T'was meant to be fun."

"I am not speaking of the fortune teller," says Anastasia, gesturing to Helena's body, to the direction of the wharves, "I am speaking of this."

Helena looks up at Anastasia, "T'wasn't my fault. Peter broke my heart."

"T'is true," Anastasia says, touching her sister's shoulder, "but t'is you who are breaking everything else."

Helena's face suddenly crumples and she sinks to the street, sobbing. Anastasia crouches before her sister, holding her until the last cry vacates her throat. Then she wipes the tears and snot from Helena's face, kisses her brow.

"Time to come home, Helena" Anastasia says. And then she helps her sister to rise.

T'is near dawn when Anastasia and Saffron finally get Helena to bed, accept every last one of her apologies, assure her of their love, confirm she will never be without them. And when Anastasia finally strips away her dress and climbs into bed she realizes her grey silk pouch with her bridal gold is missing from around her neck.

CHAPTER NINE

Wherein something
rather lovely is broken.

Ever since Anastasia left town, Edward's hours have been remarkably alike. He sleeps late, usually awakening with a dry thirst. He claims the Princess's shoes from the shop floor and places them in the display window. Today, the left shoe has a carriage much like the Princess's own and the right, has seven prancing black horses. Although he agreed not to make shoes for anyone other than the Princess, he does not see the harm in displaying his craftsmanship for the townspeople to admire. After, he has a late lunch (some cheese, salted pork, dry bread), a cold bath and then changes into one of his new suits. He claims the Princess's shoes from the shop and wraps them for delivery. Then he walks the five miles to the Summer Palace.

He is met at the front gates by the tall thin man (Mr.

Tittletattle is his name, Edward has discovered), who escorts him through a maze of rooms and into the East Gallery, in the interior of the castle. The hallway is lined with the portraits of a great many severe looking men, and even severer looking women. There he meets Nanny, hands her the shoes and, in return, receives his payment. His father's leather satchel is now so weighted with gold it has become far too heavy to carry back and forth to the palace. So instead, he carefully conceals it under the floorboards in his bedroom.

Afterwards, he returns home where he paces the shop, unsure of how to occupy his time. But knowing he must stay at the shop to maintain the appearance that he is shoe-making. When the dinner hour finally arrives, he sets out once again, this time to the Wolf & Foxtail for a kidney pie, chips and a couple of pints.

He rarely sees the Elf. And if he does, it is only out of the corner of his eye. He is more apt to hear him scurrying about the shadowy corners of the shop as he sets about his work.

Today, however, is different. Yesterday, Nanny instructed him to bring his kit so that he might measure the Princess's feet. And so today, he immerses himself in a hot bath which he scents with some of Anastasia's lavender oil. He washes his hair, and trims some of the longer edges with a tiny pair of scalloped scissors from Anastasia's sewing basket. He takes his father's straight razor to the stubble on his cheeks and chin. Plucks a few stray hairs from his eyebrows and dresses in a black suit. He slicks back his hair with some more of Anastasia's lavender oil and examines his appearance in the cracked bedroom mirror.

Presentable enough for a Princess, he thinks. He

takes the stairs to the shop and extracts the shoes from the display window. He is pleased to see the cluster of townspeople that have gathered to view them.

He tucks the shoes into a silk drawstring bag fashioned by Jenny's husband, ensures he has his measure, a notebook and pencil in his pocket and steps outside the shop, locking the door.

A shadow passes behind him and he stops.

"Edward?"

He turns to see it is Sophia's father, Frederick. His face is drawn as though he has had little sleep. His eyes are bleary, his hair not combed and his chin, grizzled with grey stubble.

"Is Sophia here?" the man asks.

Edward shakes his head. "No, of course not."

"Have you seen her of late?" he asks, following Edward as he makes his way up the street.

"Nay," Edward states, wishing the old man would leave. "Not for many days." But Frederick doesn't leave. Instead he, grabs Edward's arm, slowing his pace.

"What have you done with my daughter?"

"Done?" Edward asks, annoyed, "I have done nothing with her."

"She's missing." Frederick says. "Hasn't been home in days."

"Well, t'is nothing to do with me," Edward says, "now excuse me, I cannot be late." And he shakes his arm free and steps around Frederick, hurrying up the road.

Sophia.

Funny, he hadn't seen her in quite some time. He stayed clear of her since their last encounter. And the few times she came knocking after midnight, he ignored her demand for entry, the subsequent cries, and at last her angry shouts. Nay, instead of Sophia's bed, he prefers his own company. Returning home to sit by the fire and fall asleep drinking a bottle of Continental wine.

But come to think of it, he hasn't seen her at the Wolf & Foxtail either.

He glances back to see Frederick still standing in the street, staring after him. He is much relieved when he enters the outer reaches of the Shade and the man disappears from view.

As Edward steps into the Princess's chamber, Mr. Tittletattle closes the door behind him. Inside, the vaulted ceilings are at least twenty feet high. Tapestries cover every inch of wall. The windows are bedecked in yards of velvet drapery. A thick fur rug lies in front of a fireplace so large one could stand in it. And the inferno burning within, throws off a wave of heat that makes the air heavy and suffocating. A large bed with silken covers, curtains and a phalanx of pillows stands in the center of the room.

There is a vanity that holds a collection of bottles and powders. And a full length mirror affixed to the wall beside it.

The Princess Ambrosia steps out of a small antechamber to the right.

She is completely nude.

Edward stares at her body which is so thin, it is almost skeletal. There is no meat on her bones, even her breasts are small and flat.

Nanny enters the room behind the Princess and Edward's eyes shift to the side to fix on one of the tapestries. On it, a knight is gored by a unicorn's horn, while his own sword is impaled in the beast's side. It is unclear which of the two figures has landed the death blow.

"Princess," Nanny says, holding out yesterday's shoes. Edward thought them by far the finest of the lot, fanciful creations that depicted red coated Genteel-men on horseback on one shoe, with a calamity of hounds chasing a matching red fox on the other.

The Princess Ambrosia takes the shoes from Nanny, then crosses to the fireplace and tosses them in to the inferno.

"Do you mind?" she asks spinning about to face Edward. Her voice. He had forgotten its sound, but now it rings in his ears like sunshine sparkling on water.

"Mind?" Edward says, trying to focus on her face and not her naked flesh. This is the first time he has seen the Princess. He heard rumors of her great beauty, but he didn't expect her to look like this. She has pale blue hair piled high and braided with silken red ribbons. She has full pink lips. Her eyes appear grey and then purple and then blue, depending on the fiery flames. Her skin is like porcelain and she is hairless everywhere. Even her eyebrows are drawn on with a piece of charcoal. Her fingers and limbs fragile, but commanding. She is small, but most definitely a woman.

"Shoe man, I asked you a question," the Princess says, and her voice sharpens to remind him of winter.

He refocuses on her voice, cannot fathom what she is asking and is forced to ask, "Do I mind what, your High-,

Princess Ambrosia?"

"That I destroy your shoes."

He turns his eyes to the fire. Yesterday's shoes are completely engulfed in flame.

"Did they displease you, Princess?" he asks and sweat breaks out along his forehead, collar, and upper lip.

"Not at all," she says, leaning up against the flames as though to warm her skin, "they were by far my favorite pair."

"Then why burn them?" he asks.

"T'is so very easy to tire of beautiful objects. And when one does, what was once beautiful to the eye becomes ordinary, common, cheap." She walks over to Edward to stand before him. "The only way to keep beauty alive is to not only reinvent it, but destroy that which already exists. Thus, it can never be diluted by existing in more places than one. Now," she says, focusing on the silk bag like a hawkling discovering prey, "give me my shoes."

Edward wrenches open the drawstring bag and withdraws the new pair.

The Princess Ambrosia grabs them from him, her nails raking across his fingers in her eagerness to claim them.

"Oh," she says, studying them closely, "they are truly magnificent. Nanny, look."

Nanny has taken a seat next to the fireplace with her knitting. Her needles click rhythmically as she works the red wool and she provides only a cursory glance at the shoes.

"Very nice, dear."

Ambrosia swings about, walks over to the bed and sits.

"You will put them on my feet now," she says, and holds the shoes out for Edward.

He follows her over to the bed, takes the shoes from her hands and kneels before her. He takes her right heel in his hand, marveling at how small and delicate it is. He places the shoe onto her foot, ensures the fit is snug.

When he releases her foot she places it on his left shoulder. He glances up, but that places him eye level with the smooth folds of skin between her legs.

He shifts his eyes and takes hold of her left foot, fitting the second shoe. When he finishes, she places that foot on his other shoulder.

Edward remains kneeling, his eyes fixed to the floor.

"Do I disgust you, shoe man?" the Princess Ambrosia asks.

"Of course not," Edward states, still staring at the floor.

"Then look at me."

Edward does so, stretching his neck so that he can see her face.

"Very good," she says, holding his gaze. And then— "What do you think?"

Edward's tongue appears to have dried in his mouth and it takes him a moment to wet his lips so that he might answer.

"Begging your pardon, Highness? Princess Ambrosia," he says, and his voice is rough even to his ears.

The Princess Ambrosia pushes against him with her feet, spreading her legs wider.

"How do I look?"

"Wonderful," Edward answers, glancing over at Nanny who still sits knitting before the fire. Ambrosia kicks at him with both feet, knocking him back onto the floor.

"You are making the shoe man uncomfortable, Nanny," Ambrosia pouts.

"Tck'a," says the old woman.

"That means she cares not," says Ambrosia, as Edward climbs to his feet. She drops back onto the bed and pulls her knees up to examine each shoe with more care. Her fingers trace the fox's whiskers, the coachman's trousers, the horses' manes. "However do you do it?" she asks, and then runs her fingers along each sole, "And the leather. So soft."

"That t'would be a secret," Edward says with a forced laugh.

The Princess props herself up on her elbows and a shadow falls across her face as though his answer is not acceptable. For a long moment, Edward holds his breath expecting her to lash out. But then she smiles, exposing sharp white teeth.

"I suppose we must all have our little secrets," she states. Then she waves her foot before him. "Start measuring," she orders.

Edward hovers above her like an anxious bird, as he draws his ebony and ivory measure stick from his pocket along with his notebook and pencil

"I'll have to remove the shoe," he says.

"Do it."

His fingers take hold of the shoe once more and with great care he removes it from her right foot and sets it on the mattress. As he reaches for his measure, she wiggles her foot from his grasp and places it on his thigh. She rubs it against him, inching higher until her heel rests against his groin.

"Your Highness."

She digs her heel deeper.

"Princess Ambrosia."

His fingers grab her ankle, holding her foot in place. Edward glances over at Nanny who is engrossed in her knitting.

"Are you going to measure?" the Princess asks.

"Of course," says Edward.

"Then get on with it before I have you executed."

The blood drains from Edward's face and sweat breaks out across his forehead. He drops his measure tool and his fingers fumble to reclaim it.

"Oh, Nanny, I have scared the shoe man."

"Tck'a" says Nanny.

Ambrosia gives a carefree laugh, as Edward's shaking hands place her foot inside the measure. He adjusts the lever, then releases his hold and records her foot's length and width in his notebook. As he does so, she raises her hips from the bed, and then drops back to the mattress, "I'm waiting," she says.

Edward feels his pulse in his penis. It throbs, wanting to conquer the creature on the bed. He glances over at Nanny, so focused on her knitting. Then back at the Princess. He bites hard on his tongue, hoping the pain and blood will draw him back to his senses. Ambrosia flips the other shoe off her foot and it flies past him to strike the wall. He claims her left foot in his hand and takes his measuring stick in the other. Her feet are so small and delicate, cool to the touch. Her hips twitch again and she spreads her legs again, widening the gap at her thighs.

"Hurry," she whines, pushing her bottom lip out like the spout on a cream jug.

Edward takes the measurement and quickly releases her foot, grabbing his notebook and stepping away from the bed. The Princess Ambrosia rises and comes to stand before him.

"Did you know Nanny doesn't like you?" she asks.

Edward shakes his head as he glances at the old woman and her needles.

"Doesn't matter," Ambrosia says, "I like you."

Edward's heart pumps fast as she stands on her tiptoes and sniffs his neck.

"Do you like me, Edward?" she asks.

"Of course your Highness. Princess Ambrosia," he says, not caring his voice is hoarse as he steps back yet again and bumps into the wall behind him.

She fills the space in front of him, trapping him there, as she studies his face. Then her small fingers grab for his penis through the cloth of his pants. Edward groans and presses his head back against the wall.

"Are you married, shoe man?" she asks.

Married? With her fingers squeezing him Edward can hardly recall his own name. But the memory of Anastasia is like a ghostly presence and she rises up between them.

"Yes," he gasps as she apply more pressure.

"You remember," Nanny says, from her chair across the room, "that girl, I told you about."

"Oh yes," Ambrosia hisses, "Anastasia. Well, I shall have to invite her to dinner at the palace."

"I don't think that t'is a good idea," Edward says.

Her slap stings his cheek, catches him off guard.

Even Nanny looks up from her knitting at the sound.

"What did you say, shoe man?" Ambrosia asks, and there is steel in her voice, her eyes and the grip of her hand. Edward is on the verge of release and his brain struggles to regain control. Her fingers tighten again, causing him to cry out.

"Of course, dinner," he gasps.

"Lovely," Ambrosia says, "don't you agree, Nanny?"

"Lovely," the old woman echoes.

Her fingers squeeze so hard, she's hurting him. He can bear it no longer so he grabs her hand to stop her, but somehow she has roped his fingers through hers and they work him together. Finally when he can stand to be touched no longer, she gives a sharp twist of her wrist and Edward comes in his pants with a yelp.

"Get out" she says, dropping her hand, "I'm very tired."

"Yes, your Highness. Princess."

Edward scurries to the door where Mr. Tittletattle opens it before he can touch the handle. He flees into the Eastern Gallery and doesn't stop for a breath until he is well beyond the palace's front gate.

Ambrosia walks the length of the room in her new shoes, pausing in front of Nanny who is still attending to the red wool.

"What do you think of the shoe man, Nanny?"

The old woman tosses her a disapproving look. "He's much too common for the likes of you, my pet. Your father would not approve."

"Tck'a," Ambrosia says, wiggling her hips, "best you punish me then."

"Very well," Nanny says, setting her knitting aside and rising from her chair to collect the poker from its stand at the fireplace.

Edward keeps running until he reaches the outer border of the Shade, beyond which lies the rooftops of Houndstooth. With the Princess as a client, his fortune is made. And he calculates how many gold coins will be housed in his pockets by year end. Why, it will be more wealth than any one man (or woman), has in all the Kingdom (aside from the Princess Ambrosia herself). He slows to a stop and catches his breath.

The Princess finds him desirable.

He laughs out loud. The Princess! How he wishes he could share this new development with his mother.

He will need to rise to Ambrosia's status. Which naturally means the shop and house need improvement. Only a mansion (like the ones Anastasia pointed out to him in Ferrybone), will do. But that will take time to plan and build. And he feels a sudden urgency to elevate himself at once. Thus, the most prudent course of action will be to undertake a renovation of the house and shop. He'll have new glass in the windows, fresh paint on the walls (inside and out), new modern furnishings, carpets, draperies (not the ones inherited from his father's grandmother, the ones with which his mother 'made do').

Edward wonders with whom he can speak about such things. If Anastasia were here, she might know. But he has no desire to contact her and inform her of his plan. She may grow suspicious and return home. The potter's wife. What was her name again? Stella?

She was known to have an eye for delicate things. After all, she was the talk of Houndstooth five summers afore, when she was hired by the Queen to redecorate the dining hall after Utterly Peak gave way and large chunks of ice and rock destroyed the east wing. The majority of the crops were lost that summer as the village men were forced from their lands, to help rebuild the Palace. And Stella, known for her bewitching glazes and hand thrown pots, had caught the eye of the Queen and been invited to attend to the interior details once the structure was restored.

While the King had paid minimal wages to his laborers, the Queen had been most generous to Stella and the town watched as her and her husband's wealth had grown. Some say the cost of this unnatural gain was her husband's life, for he had died the very next winter of exposure, having gotten lost in the woods after an overzealous night of drinking at the Wolf & Foxtail. Stella's husband always struck Edward as a bit fool and a lot of a drunk, and therefore such talk was simply because the townspeople were jealous of her success.

Regardless, after Stella was widowed, Edward was surprised she chose to remain in Houndstooth. But stay she did. Yes, Stella is the one to talk to. But first, a drink, to quench his thirst after the walk from the Palace.

It is not yet the dinner hour when Edward arrives at the Wolf & Foxtail. And, therefore, he is surprised to see the area in front of the fireplace filled with villagers. They gather around Frederick who stands at the center talking with the Sheriff.

Edward pushes his way through to the bar, where Margarite's husband is standing in for Sophia. He pours Edward a pint of cold bitter ale.

"Why the gathering?" Edward asks, placing a haypenny for his drink on the hard maple bar.

"They searched the woods today," Margarite's husband

says, picking up the coin and dropping it into the till. "No sign of Sophia."

"Maybe she left for Ferrybone," Edward suggests.

Margarite's husband looks surprised, "Now why would she do a fool thing like that? Nay," he shakes his head, "Sophia loved Houndstooth. She would never leave."

Edward shrugs his shoulders, takes a long swallow of the bitter brew.

"Two women in the past week." Margarite's husband says, pouring another pint, "Makes the blood run cold."

"Two?" Edward asks, setting down his tankard, "Who else?"

"You haven't heard?" the man questions, and it is Edward's turn to shake his head.

"Jenny. The tailor's wife. Went out for her evening constitutional last Wednesday and never came home. At first, they thought the scrywolves got her but now with Sophia gone?" The man shrugs, "t'is strange."

He walks the newly poured pint down to the other end of the bar, leaving Edward alone with his thoughts.

Jenny. Edward has a vague remembrance of a woman dressed in multi-colored skirts and shawls, stumbling around town, stinking of june-pip juice. He thinks she is one of Anastasia's friends, but as to what she actually looks like, he cannot recall. Edward glances over once more at the cluster of villagers and sees the Sheriff watching him.

He finishes his drink with haste, as he has no desire to speak with the Sheriff. T'is a pity Sophia is missing, he thinks, as he slips down the hallway to the back door of the Pub. For after his encounter with the Princess, he wouldn't mind some evening company. Perhaps he'll return to the Wolf & Foxtail later, when spirits and propriety are much loosened by the liberal hand of liquor. Yes, at that time he may find one the less rigid daughters of Houndstooth up for a wee bit of fun.

But first, he thinks as he steps out into the courtyard, business.

When Edward leaves Stella's, he is drunk on excitement. His meeting with her was a resounding success. She was able to provide him with numerous samples, books to peruse (oh the books, with their illustrations full of sumptuous furnishings which can all be his for the right price), and a plethora of her own ideas for both the house and shop. They discussed silk draperies, Cherry-wood furnishings, Germanic porcelains, Sapperton pottery, Romanic stone, Elegiac marble and more. Stella, with her agile fingers, drew quick sketches on how she could translate each of his rooms (no matter the size), into a place to rival any palace. There was even a plan to enlarge the workroom by building an attached storage room at the back of the house for the Elf—although Stella certainly wasn't aware of its purpose.

Stella didn't question Edward's sudden influx of wealth; in fact, she said she heard rumors of the unique shoes he was creating for the Princess and congratulated him on his good fortune and finely honed skills.

She sent him home with a handful of drawings and an accounting of the various expenditures for him to peruse. Although this undertaking would be costly, it would hardly affect his collection of gold. Edward considers stopping by the Wolf & Foxtail once more, but seeing as how the crowd still gathers (and wanting to avoid the Sheriff), he turns his feet towards home.

The shop is completely dark. For some reason, the curtains are closed over the display window (something Edward never does), and this accounts for the absolute darkness in the room. But as his hands are full of Stella's books and charts, he forgoes lighting a candle and steps his way from memory, across the shop towards the connecting door.

He has nearly arrived, when he trips over an object on the floor. He cries out, dropping the drawings, hoping to prevent a fall. But fails, twisting his ankle and landing with a hard thump.

"Bloody Cross," he curses, fumbling in his pocket for a matchbox and wondering what it was that has tripped him. He finds the box, yanks free a match and strikes. The smell of sulphur fills his nostrils as he holds the flame aloft.

A discarded heap of clothes lies on the floor.

He peers closer.

Nay, not clothes.

The match burns down and the flame sears his fingers.

He curses again, dropping the match to the floor where it extinguishes.

He lights another and this time he jumps to his feet (careful to avoid the object on the floor), and locates a candle on the workbench. He lights the wick, then turns back to the heap on the floor.

T'is Sophia.

She lies face down, her shirt bright red against her pale

skin. Her skirts tangled in her legs. She is completely and utterly still.

"Sophia?" Edward asks.

But he gets no answer in return. He crouches down to poke her in the shoulder. Which is when he realizes she is not wearing a shirt. The skin has simply been peeled from her back.

A blackness pricks at the edges of Edward's mind and he sinks to his knees, one hand against the wall for support.

What dread horror has occurred here?

A scurrying sound startles Edward and he stumbles away from the body.

It is the Elf.

With strips of white skin draped over one of his arms.

"Bloody Hell," Edward breathes.

The Elf blinks at him, frozen. Like a shivermouse that has been sighted by a hawk.

"I apologize, Sir. I will dispose of this mess immediately."

"What have you done?" Edward mutters.

The Elf's jaw works back and forth as though searching for words, "Sir, I am simply making shoes."

"What about her?" Edward demands. "Sophia. What did you do to her?" He shuffles back until he is resting against the wall for support.

The Elf glances at the body on the floor, then back at Edward.

"Begging your pardon, Sir, that is a Sophia?" it asks.

"Yes," Edward snaps.

"Then, Sir, I am using Sophia's leather to make shoes. I had my eye on her for quite some time. I could see from the night she spent here (you do remember that night don't you?), that her skin was quite supple and well tended. Remarkable for a village girl."

"You don't make shoes from human skin," Edward says.

The Elf blinks as though it doesn't understand.

"Goat, cow, dog for Christos's sake," Edward's says, and his voice is so shrill he hardly recognizes it as his own.

"Oh no," the Elf says, shaking his head and placing the skins onto the workbench, "I've tried those, Sir, but the quality is not the same. The finest cuts are always from humans."

The Elf approaches Sophia, grabs her arm and gives it a sharp tug. Sophia, or rather, her body, rolls over onto its back, the head lolling towards Edward. Her eyes are open in an expression of horror. Her mouth is wide as though she were caught in a scream. There is a deep, dark cut across her throat, but no blood. She has been drained dry.

An explosion sounds nearby, and Edward jumps, looking at the Elf in alarm. The sound repeats. This time it is more familiar. Not an explosion. Knocking on the door.

"Edward?"

The Sheriff.

"Christos," Edward mutters, jumping to his feet and grabbing hold of Sophia's arm, "we've got to get rid of her."

"Be at peace," the Elf says, "he has no knowledge of these events. Now hand me your cloak."

Edward does as instructed, watching as the Elf throws the garment over Sophia's corpse, rendering her near invisible in the gloom.

"The door," the Elf suggests and Edward nods. He

crosses the room and opens the door, stepping outside and closing it behind him just as the Sheriff is turning to walk away.

"Good day, Sheriff."

"More like evening," the man corrects, his keen eyes examining Edward.

"Yes, of course," Edward states, keeping his hand clenched on the knob lest the Sheriff attempt to force an entry.

"How fares your wife's father?" the Sheriff asks.

"Much improved," Edward says, "he should be restored to health any day now." Not that Edward knows, for he has not heard a single word from Anastasia since she departed. But he does not want the Sheriff to know this. He forces his mouth into a smile, "If you'll excuse me, I am extremely busy."

"You were not at the search today," the Sheriff says.

"Nay," says Edward, and coughs in an exaggerated fashion. "Bit of a cold coming on." Edward doesn't know why he lies. It would be easy enough to say he knew nothing of the search. But the words are out now. To reclaim them, would be to raise suspicion. For a long moment the Sheriff says nothing, simply watches him. Until at last he bows his head.

"Have a good night, Mr. Cordwainer. Stay safe."

"Good night," Edward responds, watching the Sheriff walk up the street towards the Pub. Stay safe. What did that bloody well mean? Edward shakes with anger and damns the Sheriff for thinking he can threaten him. Wait until he discovers Edward has become a favorite of the Princess Ambrosia's.

The Princess.

The thought of her clears Edward's head.

He turns and steps back into the shop.

The shock of almost being discovered has somewhat lessened the horror of Sophia's body. And when the Elf strips her of Edward's cloak, he finds he is compelled to to watch as the creature draws a measuring tool from his pocket and sets it against Sophia's naked, but still skinned chest.

"You have done this before?" Edward asks.

"Many times," the Elf smiles, drawing out a sharp cutting tool.

"Jenny?" Edward asks, wiping the sweat from his brow.

"I am not familiar with their names, Sir."

"Ugly girl. Lots of skirts. Frizzy hair."

"Ah, yes. Jenny. The skin was well preserved although it did take some time to treat the alcohol smell."

The Elf places his knife against Sophia's skin and slices into the flesh.

Edward tries to look away, but his eyes are snared by the sight of the blade in Sophia's skin. So instead he says, "you have to stop this."

The Elf lowers his tool to look at Edward.

"I cannot, Sir. If I stop now, it will impact what is to come and that will make my Mistress exceedingly angry. And she is very disagreeable when she is angered. I fear what she might do to the both of us."

"Me?" Edward says, wiping his sweaty hands on the velvet of his coat, "Oh no. I have no part in this."

"But you do," the Elf corrects, "you wished to be the most famous man in all the Kingdom. This requires I use the best tools, the best threads, the best leather."

There is a long moment of silence as Edward stares into Sophia's unblinking eyes.

"I will summon my Mistress although I fear there will be consequences for both of us." The Elf sets down his knife and brings his hands together as though to clap.

"Wait!" Edward orders, and the Elf stills, "What kind of consequences?"

"Well if I am lucky my Mistress may simply tear out my guts with her teeth or use my bones for her evening fire. As for you, I am not quite certain, for I have never had a human choose not to complete a wish before. But since you are decided —" The Elf attempts to clap again, but this time Edward grabs the creature's wrists.

"Wait," he says, staring down at the Elf. "Wait."

"Very well, Sir," the Elf says as Edward releases him. He hops onto the workbench and watches Edward pace the room. Edward circles around Sophia's body three times before he finally stops in front of the Elf.

"What do you do with the bodies?" he asks the creature.

"Oh, Sir, please be assured they will never be found. I am an expert at my job. In fact, of all my Mistress's workers I am considered the best."

"So Sophia, Jenny? They will never be traced here?"

"No, Sir. I am most careful to cover my tracks. My Mistress expects nothing less."

"Good, good," Edward says, wiping his palms on the knees of his trousers. He turns again to look at Sophia.

"Please, Sir. Do not cause yourself unnecessary worry. She will be gone come morning."

"Good," Edward says, turning his back on the Elf to gather the fallen charts, books and drawings that Stella gave him. Then he walks over to the connecting door.

"Carry on."

Edward doesn't recall closing the door to the shop behind him, nor climbing the stairs to his bedroom, or discarding his clothes. But here he is, naked, curled up on the mattress. He is extremely cold, as though he has spent the better part of the day at the high extremes of Utterly Peak. But he lacks the energy to wrap himself in a blanket. For his bones feel as though they have turned to stone.

He closes his eyes. But Sophia's face, her expression of horror, her gaping throat stare back at him. He blinks away her visage, grateful he managed to light a candle.

I didn't know, he tells himself. *I didn't know.*

Edward rubs his fists against his eyes. He is not responsible for the Elf, has no control over him. So if the Elf chooses to fulfill the contract in such a manner as … well, in such a manner as Edward witnessed downstairs, then it has nothing to do with him. Absolutely nothing.

I didn't know, he says.

He will practice the phrase all through the night, until not only can he convince another that it is the truth *(I didn't know)*, but himself as well.

I didn't know.

It is not until nearly dawn that he realizes he forgot to claim his ten gold pieces for the day's shoes from Nanny.

CHAPTER
TEN

Wherein a tooth gives
cause for complaint.

Anastasia asks the carriage driver to let her out two
miles from Houndstooth. Her feet feel restless, her
stomach in knots. She is distracted, nervous, ill
tempered. She has been away almost nigh on two months.
Helena and Saffron tried to convince her to stay, but the
house was becoming claustrophobic and she could no
longer sit and listen to her mother's heart wrenching cries.

Papa died the day after the new moon.

Anastasia was awoken at dawn to see Saffron standing
above her.

"T'is time," her sister said, as Anastasia blinked the
sleep from her eyes.

Papa gradually worsened over the night until at last his
lungs were full of fluid and he was all but drowning.

They were each given a few moments alone to

say their goodbyes and Anastasia was last to go down to the basement. She stepped over to the bed where Papa lay. He no longer had the strength to smile, but she saw from the way his eyes brightened when she approached, that he recognized her.

She grabbed his hand, uncaring how firm her grip. Thinking if she held tight enough, he would not be able to slip away.

"Anastasia," he whispered.

"I am here, Papa," she said, kissing the sweat from his forehead.

"I have done you a terrible wrong."

"Nay, Papa" she said, "never."

"I should not have made you stay with Edward," he coughed, "No good will come of him. Unbind it with him," he urged. "At first opportunity." He gripped her hand as though desperate for an answer, "promise me."

"I promise, Papa."

"Good girl," he sighed.

The candle flickered, sputtered, and died, dousing the room in darkness. But Anastasia did not want to release his hand to search for the matches.

"Anastasia?" His voice had been weak, and he sounded so very tired.

"Yes, Papa?"

"Have you ever seen such a magnificent sunrise as this?"

She heard a soft sigh and then his hand relaxed in hers.

"Papa? Papa?"

She must have screamed the last, because Saffron and Helena ran down from upstairs, bringing much needed light.

Papa's mouth was slack, his eyes empty. Gone. Never to be reclaimed.

From behind her sisters, their mother arrived, erupting into a great piercing wail.

It took Saffron several hours to convince Anastasia to release Papa's hand. And several more before she would permit herself to be removed from the room.

Anastasia stops to listen to the birds, the sound of the wind in the trees, the purity of the silence. Her fingers reach up to the touch the grey silk pouch around her neck. But, then she remembers that it is gone. The day after she and Helena encountered the fortune teller, she returned to the Alabaster Mermaid to inquire after the old woman. But neither the barkeep, nor any of the patrons remembered her presence.

She continues walking and soon her feet leave the dirt packed road and meet the familiar cobblestone streets of Houndstooth. The Wolf & Foxtail looks quiet. There are a collection of weathered posters on the wooden doors and Anastasia stops to read.

Missing.

Sophia. Jenny.

Missing? What has happened here? She quickens her pace and sees a crowd gathers outside the bakery. Betsy. Anastasia's walk turns into a run but as she draws near, she sees the crowd is not gathered outside the bakery at all. They are in front of her home. Although she almost doesn't recognize it. The outside of the building has been given a brilliant yellow coat of paint, with bright red shutters and a leaf green door. White geraniums, purple violets, and pink chrysanthemums spill from newly fastened planters beneath each window.

A red and yellow striped awning is perched over the door to keep one dry during the rain and sleet. The windows sparkle as though they have all been recently washed or (upon closer examination), replaced.

The gaggle of children and villagers peer into the shop's display window. Anastasia approaches, standing on tiptoes so she can see. But the crowd is too thick and her view is blocked. So Anastasia makes her way to the front door and slips her key in the lock. She half expects it not to work, but it does. And so she opens the door and steps into the shop, locking it behind her and setting her satchel on the floor. Like the outside, the interior has undergone a substantial transformation. The floor boards have all been polished, stained, and waxed and shine a bright cherry red. The walls are painted egg blue. There is a yellow satin couch with red cushions. A low table before it, houses a somewhat dusty silver tea service. Three massive silver candelabras with twenty candles each are placed prominently in the room, though not one of the thick beeswax candles has yet been lit. There is a large wool mat with an intricate design in gold thread (is it of shoes?), placed in front of the door that connects to their home. The workbench has been replaced and relocated to the rear of the shop. All the tools that now rest there are new, although they still look unused.

And there, in the back wall, is a new door. Anastasia tests the knob, but it is locked. She presses her ear against the door, but t'is quiet on the other side.

She walks over to the window where the crowd gathers outside. In the display case, sit an otherworldly pair of shoes. At first she thinks they are the same shoes that

Edward found in the shop the day she left. They have the same buttery leather, the same intricate needlework. But although they are of the same hand, these shoes are remarkably different, decorated with an armada of ships. Their white sails plumped by the wind. Their hulls cutting through turquoise waters. Cannons popping through port holes in preparation for battle.

Ignoring the cries of protest from outside, Anastasia reaches in and removes the shoes from the window. She doesn't like holding them; they feel damp to the touch, almost as though they are sweating.

She crosses to the connecting door and enters their home. The steps leading up to the second floor have now been carpeted.

"Edward?" Anastasia calls upstairs, but hears no response.

Still holding the shoes, she steps into the kitchen. A new copper stove with two ovens has replaced the old iron one. The table and chairs are new as well. Made of a hard wood, they are sturdy, reliable. She opens the pantry to see the larder filled with enough food for ten winters. A peek outside shows that aside from a well worn path to the water closet, the garden is completely overgrown and choked with weeds.

Anastasia closes the back door, feeling like a trespasser in her own home. Where is Edward? She retraces her steps back to the stairs. The second floor hallway has also been carpeted and her footsteps make no sound as she walks the short distance to Edward's room.

Thick velvet curtains cover the windows blocking out light. A new cherry wood bureau, wardrobe and matching bed (twice the size of the old one), fill the room. There are more candle holders here, these ones lit, dripping onto the carpet, creating miniature mountains of wax. Finely tailored clothes made of expensive velvet, cotton, and silk are tossed onto the bed, the bureau, the floor. There are a cluster of empty wine bottles in the corner. And more on the bed. Where Edward lies, fully clothed, his father's worn leather shoemaking satchel in his arms.

Anastasia grabs hold of his ankle and gives him a shake. "Edward."

He awakes with a shout, scrambling away from her touch, yanking a kitchen knife out from its hiding place beneath the blankets.

"Stay back!" he orders, pointing the knife in her direction, "stay back."

"Edward," Anastasia says, "t'is your wife. Anastasia."

Edward blinks several times as though he does not recognize her. Then the hand that holds the knife wavers, and drops to his side. There are dark circles under his eyes. He has not shaved. His breath stinks from stale liquor.

"I thought you were —, never mind," he says.

She waits a moment longer, but he does not continue.

"Edward," she asks, indicating the room, "what has happened here?"

Edward drops the knife on a pillow and runs a hand over his eyes, looking about the messy bedroom.

"You should have written you were coming, I would have had someone in to clean."

"I do not mean the room, I mean the house, the shop." She lifts her hand that still holds the shoes, "these."

"Give me those," Edward growls, snatching them from her, clutching them to his chest.

"Where did you get them?" Anastasia asks.

"I made them," he says.

"Do not be silly," Anastasia says, and regrets it at once when she sees the look of hurt upon her husband's face. She waits a moment before continuing. "Edward, where did these things come from?"

"I bought them."

"We have no money."

He looks at the shoes cradled in his arms and draws a finger along each as though caressing them.

"I've hired someone."

"Who?"

Edward rises, reaching for a silk bag in which he places the shoes. Then he steps around Anastasia to the bureau. Examines his reflection in the mirror.

"T'is a secret," Edward says, pouring lavender oil into his hands, and splashing it on his hair and cheeks. Then he wipes his hands against his trousers.

"Edward," Anastasia says, "please speak to me."

"I'm off to the Palace," he says, shoving his hand into a jar of dried mint leaves and stuffing several into his mouth to chew.

"The Palace?" Anastasia asks.

"Who do you think buys all the shoes?" he asks, grabbing the silken bundle and his father's leather satchel as he steps around her to the hall. Anastasia does not move until she hears the outer shop door close. Then she makes her way to her bedroom.

It has not changed one bit. The single bed with the thin blankets, the dresser with one shaky leg, the pitted mirror, the broken window.

All still the same.

She places her hand on her heart, until it calms, much relieved that some things have not changed.

Edward stops on the path to the Palace and sets down the leather satchel. He started carrying it again. Even though it has grown exceedingly heavy as the gold coins multiplied. But he can't imagine leaving it behind in the shop. He isn't sure he can entirely trust the Elf not to steal his treasure. Aren't there old wives tales about elves and their love of gold? (Or perhaps it is dwarves, Edward isn't quite sure.) Whichever it is, Edward can't imagine being parted from his treasure for any length of time. And now that Anastasia is returned, he will have to be even more cautious.

Goddess Blood.

Edward had forgotten about Anastasia. He recalled missing her for the first few days. But soon the space she once occupied, no longer seemed so empty. And so he had simply forgotten her.

Although he was alarmed by her sudden return, she had awoken him from the dream, and for that he was grateful.

Every night for the past month, when he closed his eyes to sleep, Sophia would come to him. The dream (if it was one), always started the same. She would scratch her broken nails on his bedroom door, whispering his name. And although he would try to awaken, he would find himself frozen in place on the bed. Then somehow she would creep inside the room and over to the bed.

Already naked, with her long black hair trailing down her spine like a horse's mane. Her voluptuous breasts would swing wildly as she mounted him and her decaying thighs were quick to grip his hips, pinning him in place. As soon as she straddled him, the skin on her throat would split open as though severed by an invisible blade. And blood would spill from the gash, coating her breasts, running down her flesh to stain the area where they were joined together. But this was no ordinary blood. Wherever it touched him, it burned his skin as though it were hot candle wax or acid. He would try to push her aside but her hands were like iron fists, holding him in place while a terrible laugh echoed in her throat. He would always awaken with a shout.

And although she was gone when he opened his eyes, her presence stayed with him the remainder of the day.

As the nightmare grew, so too did his fame as a shoemaker (not only in Houndstooth but in a few of the surrounding villages as well). Every morning, when he rose and went down to the workshop, he found a crowd outside waiting for him to place the Princess's newest shoes in the window. It was a heady feeling to watch the villagers jostle each other as they tried to get close to his creations. And he really did consider the shoes as belonging to him. For aside from that last encounter with the Elf, their paths never crossed. Sometimes Edward wondered if the Elf actually existed. Perhaps it was he, Edward, who was working in the shop each day, cutting and sewing the leather and stitching the intricate designs. It was just that he couldn't recall doing so.

Edward had been making his daily excursions to the palace. At which time, he would meet with Nanny, and exchange the shoes for coin. And although his blood would anticipate the Princess every time he reached the Palace, he has not seen her since that first visit to her rooms.

He hears the bells on the church strike three, grabs the satchel and hurries up the path to the Palace gate. As usual, Mr. Tittletattle awaits to guide him to the eastern wing. Only this time, Nanny is not waiting for him and he is led directly into the Princess's rooms.

He finds Nanny seated in her chair before the massive fireplace, knitting. The Princess Ambrosia is sprawled naked on the fur rug, her hair a vibrant orange, bound in bows and towering a good foot above her head.

She turns to look at him, a scowl upon her perfect lips.

"You are late, shoe man."

"I am very sorry, my lady," Edward says, his sweaty hands clutching the black satchel.

"And I am very cross and have a good mind to punish you."

Edward freezes, his breath caught in his throat.

"Begging you pardon, my lady. I will not be late again. My wife is returned from Ferrybone and it caught me by surprise—"

"Fie and fiddlesticks your wife," the Princess says, waving her hand about, "you, shoe man, are bankrupting my Kingdom."

She climbs to her feet and snaps her fingers at Edward.

"Bankrupting?" Edward asks, holding out the silken bundle that contains her shoes.

"Who do you think pays for these?" the Princess

asks, grabbing the shoes and pulling them free of their wrapping.

Edward doesn't answer because it hasn't actually occurred to him how the Princess gets her money. He just assumes she has it.

"I will have to raise taxes again if you insist on raising the price," (they were now fifteen gold coins a pair). Edward yanks a silk handkerchief from his pocket and wipes his sweaty brow.

"Although, I can see you're putting my coin to good use," the Princess says, stepping forward to brush a piece of lint from his velvet covered shoulder. The briefest contact from her hand is enough to make Edward's blood rush. He attempts to hide his erection, but the Princess bats his hands aside and laughs.

"Do you like the shoe man's new suit, Nanny?"

There is no response, only the click of needles.

"She still doesn't like you," Ambrosia says her free hand traveling down his shirt to his waist band. "Poor, boy," she whispers, her fingers seeking him out through the cloth of his trousers.

Edward stifles the groan that wants to escape.

"But I do think you should give me my next shoes as a present," she says rubbing him, "after all, I've made you an extremely wealthy man."

With her fingers working him, Edward has trouble thinking. He is desperate for the gold, but at the same time, it seems only reasonable to give her one pair of shoes. After all, she is quite correct. She has made him the richest man in the Kingdom. Where is the harm in gifting her one pair?

"Shoe man?" she cajoles.

"Agreed," he gasps as her strokes become more firm.

"Excellent," she says, releasing him. "Now get out." And she wanders over to the fireplace and throws herself on the fur rug once more. Edward reels from the loss of her touch. He wants her hand back on him applying pressure, but Mr. Tittletattle is now standing there, holding the door open, an expectant look upon his face. Edward grabs his leather satchel and crosses towards the door.

"Shoe man," the Princess says, and he glances back to watch her roll towards him on the rug, "your wife?"

"Yes?" Edward asks.

"Bring her to dinner. Tonight."

Edward wants to decline, to deny, disassemble. But the set of her shoulders warns him he should not even try.

"Yes, your Highness. Ambrosia," he says and gives a little bow. Then he looks at Nanny. Her eyes are on him and she smiles. But it is all teeth.

Edward watches as Ambrosia drapes Nanny's knitting over her bare shoulder and it is then that Edward realizes Nanny knits the hair the Princess wears upon her head.

He shudders, turns away and follows Mr. Tittletattle out the door.

The Palace dining room is impressive in its size. The ceiling rises almost to the heavens and silver and gold candelabras hold what appear to be a thousand illuminated candles. The floor is covered in thick Prussian carpets and the walls are hung with paintings of cherubs at war with scrywolves and other strange creatures. An abundance of hacked limbs, spilled guts and swollen tongues belie the fact that this is a room meant for dining.

Even though Anastasia was born into a merchant family, she has never before seen such extravagant riches. Not even when she was a child and spent time at the King's Castle in Ferrybone, were there such luxuries. The table at which Anastasia and Edward sit is enormous. There are three place settings and each and every piece of porcelain, stem of cutlery and crystal glass is unique. The thick smell of incense issues forth from holders over the fireplace, threatening to choke the occupants.

Anastasia takes a long swallow of water from her glass.

She wears the green dress her mother gifted her with upon her first visit home and she has bound and braided her hair in the latest ridiculous fashion of the continent. It has been so long since she attired her hair in such a fashion, that her fingers were clumsy from lack of practice. She and Edward have been waiting in silence for a half an hour, neither one speaking. Edward is hunched in his chair as though he wishes he were elsewhere.

Anastasia sets her empty glass on the table which is when the door swings opens and Ambrosia enters.

Anastasia and Edward both rise from their seats. It has been many years since Anastasia last met the Princess and, although that moment is cemented in Anastasia's memory, she doubts Ambrosia even remembers. Tonight, the Princess is dressed in a floor-length skirt made of a thousand slender twigs. Her bodice is made of butterfly wings. Spider legs adorn her lashes, making them seem even longer. And the white wig that sits high on her head is decorated with stuffed birds, green leaves, and gold ribbons. A stole made up of fifty foxtails is draped about her bare shoulders. And upon her arm is a fabric band that holds a brooch shaped like a peacock. Jade and turquoise stones for tail feathers and ruby chips for eyes.

And, of course, she wears the shoes.

The Princess Ambrosia walks towards Anastasia, both hands outstretched in greeting, a wide smile upon her face.

"Anastasia, how good to see you."

Anastasia takes the Princess's hands. Her fingers are cold and hard, like dull knives. And when her lips brush both of Anastasia's cheeks, she is overwhelmed by the sickeningly sweet smell of lilies.

The Princess steps back, still holding onto Anastasia's hands, studying her face. Unafraid to examine her scars.

"How long has it been?"

"A great many years, Princess," Anastasia responds with a bow.

"Tck'a," the Princess says, "we are old friends. Call me Ambrosia." Then the Princess turns to face Edward. "Did you know Anastasia and I were childhood playmates?"

Edward stares first at Anastasia, then at Ambrosia, shaking his head.

Ambrosia gives Anastasia's hand a playful tug before releasing her. "Bad girl, keeping secrets from your husband. Now sit," she says, gesturing to them both and makes her way to the head of the table to ring a little golden bell.

Immediately a footman enters and crosses to a sideboard that is populated by a phalanx of decanters, each filled with a different wine, port, cordial, or brandy. He selects a bottle and fills each of their glasses before departing.

Ambrosia raises her glass towards Anastasia.

"To old friends."

Anastasia responds in kind, then takes a sip of the sweet wine.

"And new," says Ambrosia, turning towards Edward.

But Edward doesn't respond to the toast, he simply downs his drink in a single gulp.

Anastasia listens to the Princess recount the story of their last meeting. It was many years past, the night of the King's fortieth birthday. The Queen arranged an extravagant birthday party at Castle Ferrybone, inviting regents, princes and emperors from royal families the known world over. The entire Kingdom was invited and villagers arrived in hordes from the length and breadth of the land.

There was entertainment for seven days without end. Fiddle-faddles and juggle-players, fire-breathers and bird-talkers. There were story-stealers and rabble-rousers, wanderers and truth-tellers. An army of tents swallowed up the castle grounds and one could taste delicacies from every corner of the realm; there were sweetmeats and garlic breads from the southern provinces; licorice chews and apple taffy from the east. Raspberry teas and chocolate coffee from the west and dried dolphfish and watercrust from the cold northern waters.

It was Anastasia's first outing after the fire and when her parents were invited by the King and Queen to join a midnight feast, she was left in the company of Ambrosia and her silly friends. Anastasia had once considered them her playmates, but now they simply ignored her or when they thought she wasn't paying attention, whispered and pointed at her newly blemished face.

Ambrosia herself had, at first, seemed friendly.

Gathering the the girls together, taking Anastasia by the hand, leading them to a room deep within the castle walls.

"You musn't tell anyone I've brought you here," Ambrosia said, as she opened the many locks, "but this room, t'is haunted."

She flung open the door to reveal an ordinary enough room, although one that was poorly furnished.

"In this room, a mad knight once carved his mistress into tiny bits for betraying him with another," Ambrosia said, pointing to the single bed with four mattresses piled one on top of the other. "And her horrible shrieking can still be heard as his ghost returns each night to slay her again and again."

The girls clustered together in the centre of the room, Anastasia standing next to the empty fireplace.

Ambrosia kept a finger to her lips, hushing any of her playmates who tried to speak.

"Listen," she whispered.

And then it started. A terrible screeching that echoed in the walls and sent the girls screaming from the room. Anastasia had been the last of the pack and when she reached the door Ambrosia slammed it in her face.

And too late, Anastasia heard the click of the lock.

Regardless, Anastasia grabbed for the doorknob but it was most definitely bolted. She pounded on the door, demanding her release. But it did not open.

Anastasia could hear the girls giggling on the other side but no matter how much she pleaded or cried out they did not respond.

The knight's ghost attacked her then. A great flapping shadow that flew at her with a terrible cry. She felt her bladder give way and screamed herself into a faint.

When Anastasia finally revived, she opened her eyes to find herself on the floor beside the door. And there, perched on the mattress, was the ghost. Only it was no supernatural thing. Instead, a brown scream-owl with yellow unblinking eyes and a matching beak tipped its head to watch her.

Anastasia rose to her feet expecting the owl to attack, but it did not. It simply watched. She took a step towards it, and then another. Holding out a hand in supplication. When she came close enough to touch the bird, it stretched out its neck and nibbled her fingertips. Then it took a few hops on the bed and rolled its head, waiting for Anastasia to climb onto the mattress.

As soon as she had done so, the owl spread its wings, circled the room twice and flew into the fireplace and up the chimney. Anastasia sat for a moment, and then exhausted from having been so afraid, she curled up in the middle of the bed. But the mattress was exceptionally uncomfortable. And she found no matter which way she lay, something hard buried within, dug into her flesh, bruising her skin.

In the morning when she awoke, Anastasia rose and pushed aside the mattresses, searching for the cause of her discomfort. It took some searching and all she could find was a small iridescent pearl no larger than a seed.

It was shortly thereafter that she was discovered by a maid and released into the arms of her mother and Papa. Her mother had chastised her for hiding, but Papa simply squeezed her shoulder and gave thanks to the King and Queen for their hospitality. As they departed, Anastasia handed the Queen the pearl she found beneath the mattresses, in case it had been mislaid.

The Queen turned very pale at this and insisted on being permitted to look at Anastasia's legs. Whereupon she had seen the girl's bruises and launched into a fit of hysterics. The royal physician had been sent for and Anastasia's family slipped away for home. This had been the last time Anastasia had been to the palace, let alone enjoyed the company of the King and Queen.

Ambrosia seemed to have forgotten her cruelty of that day. Instead, she was regaling Edward about the escapades of silly girls and professed Anastasia to be most brave for volunteering to sleep the night in the haunted room.

Anastasia swallows a fork-full of sweetbread and when she looks up from her plate, she sees both Edward and Ambrosia have their eyes upon her.

"The Princess Ambrosia was asking about your father," Edward says. "If he's quite recovered?"

Anastasia wipes her mouth with the serviette and takes a sip of wine to steady her hands.

"He is dead," Anastasia says, and can feel the prick of sadness in her eyes.

"Oh, fa," the Princess says, covering her mouth with her hand, "I am so very sorry."

"Dead?" Edward says, staring at her, "You did not say."

She had not, no. But in truth, they had not spoken since she awoke him from his bed. Aside from Edward ordering her to dress and accompany him to the Palace that evening.

"Well, we must raise a glass to your Papa," Ambrosia says, holding up her crystal goblet, "and bind ourselves as sisters for we have both had beloved fathers taken from us too soon."

"Thank you, Princess," Anastasia says, raising her glass and sipping her wine.

"Now," Ambrosia states, as she deposits her empty glass on the table, pushes back her chair and rises, "Edward and I have some business to discuss."

Edward blinks, his hand frozen mid-way to his mouth with a forkful of liverwurst.

"We do?" he asks, glancing over at Anastasia, his cheeks reddening.

"Do we not have an appointment," Ambrosia asks, "for you to address the pinching in the right toe area of my shoes?"

"Of course, of course," Edward states, dropping his fork to his plate as he stumbles to his feet.

Anastasia rises as well and holds out her hand to the Princess, "thank you for the lovely meal."

Ambrosia takes her fingers in farewell, saying, "please, sit. Edward won't be long. I'll have some port and cakes brought in for you."

Anastasia curtsies and then Ambrosia rises on her tiptoes and kisses Anastasia's left cheek, her wet tongue brushing over the skin. Anastasia jerks aside, covering her cheek with her hand.

Ambrosia smiles as though nothing untoward has happened.

"It was marvelous to see you," she says, "we must do this again."

And then she releases Anastasia's hand and strides from the dining hall. Edward gives his wife a parting glance, and follows after the Princess. A pair of footmen enter, one carrying a three tiered plate stacked with tarts, sweets and mince pies. He sets it before Anastasia. The other approaches the sideboard and selects a rich burgundy port which he pours into her empty glass.

When they finish their duties, they exit leaving Anastasia alone in the room.

Anastasia shakes her head, refusing yet another glass of port offered by the footman. She has had too many drinks as it is (was it three or four or perhaps even five?), and her stomach can accept no more of the sweet drink. It has been nigh on two hours since Edward and Anastasia departed from the dining hall.

She now knows their disappearance has very little to do with shoes. Anastasia is not surprised Ambrosia is attracted to Edward, for he is an extremely handsome man. As for Edward? Well, Anastasia doubts he would have the strength to refute Ambrosia's advances even if he wanted to. Ever since childhood, the Princess always had a strange tenacity to get what she wanted.

"Would you fetch my wrap?" she asks the footman, as he returns the decanter to the sideboard.

"Ma'am," he says nodding, and disappears from the room. Anastasia rises from the table and exits into the hallway after him.

The room is a long gallery of many portraits. She finds one of Ambrosia's father, the King. It seems a very strange thing to see his face when he is no longer alive. In the painting, his eyes are alight with laughter, his mouth open in a wide grin. He holds an atlas in one hand and a bright blue feathered quill in the other. Anastasia recognizes the objects. She herself turned the pages of that leather-bound atlas. And that very same blue feather she held against her cheek, astonished by its softness. Both were gifts her father brought home from his travels for his friend, the King.

"Ma'am." The footman returns with her wool cloak and settles it over her shoulders.

"Thank you," she says. "When you see my husband, would you tell him I have returned to town?"

The man clicks his heels together, "very good, Ma'am."

"Goodnight," she says, and makes her way down the long corridor of portraits, through a multitude of morning rooms, conservatories, and parlors to the front entrance. A hunched man in a black chimney pot hat opens the palace door for her to depart. As she passes, he smiles at her and she sees that each of his teeth has been filed to a sharp point.

She shudders and steps out into the blackness of the night. The door closes with a thud behind her.

There are no lanterns out here to light the dark. Nor does Anastasia have a candle (or matches), to help her find her way through the Shade to town. For a moment, she considers knocking on the castle door and requesting a lantern from the man in the chimney pot hat. But then the heavy cloud cover parts and a full moon lights the grounds.

She hurries, cutting across the wide strip of lawn to the edge of the Shade and in moments the path that leads to Houndstooth is at her feet.

Within twenty minutes she'll be home.

Home.

She desires its safety.

And so she enters the woods.

CHAPTER
ELEVEN

Wherein an elf discovers
a craving for salted pork.

dward stands naked in the Princess's room. He has been standing as such for two hours. For as soon as they reached her room, Ambrosia ordered him to disrobe.

This was it, he thought, forgetting at once about his wife still seated in the dining room. His fingers made quick work of stripping away his shoes, socks, cravat, shirt, trousers and under layer. Which is when Nanny stormed into the room, ordering him to dress and depart at once.

Edward reached for his trousers to cover himself, however Ambrosia, intervened, demanding Edward remain as he was. The Princess then commanded the old woman to depart, but Nanny refused. The Princess issued every threat in her arsenal: torture, execution, disemboweling, excommunication. But Nanny would not budge; insisting she was responsible for Ambrosia's well being and would continue to be so despite her mistress's inclination to consort with trash.

Edward supposed he was the trash Nanny was referring to, and determined that when he and the Princess were at last alone, he would urge her to be rid of the old woman. The yelling continued for the greater part of an hour, until finally Ambrosia ordered Edward to once again remain where he was, and the two women departed.

And so here he stands with his arms crossed, rocking back and forth on his feet, annoyed that he has been kept waiting for such an extended length of time. He is not the Princess's plaything, to be ordered about with impunity. He decides to give her two more minutes. Then he will dress and depart. Regardless of the consequences.

There are thirteen seconds remaining on the clock, when the door opens and the Princess returns alone. She is naked (except for her shoes), and she closes the door behind her and turns the lock. Her eyes are red from crying, her cheeks stained from tears. And there are red welts across her thighs and buttocks as though she has been struck.

Anastasia stands in the thick of the Shade. The moon which provided initial light upon entering the forest, has now retreated behind thick clouds, stranding Anastasia in the dark. T'was foolish to attempt the walk without light. But now that she has strayed from the path and is lost, she must choose to remain where she is or keep going.

The church bells strike ten, reminding her she should have been home by now.

And by the sound of the bells, Houndstooth is off towards her right. But the brush and trees and undergrowth is so thick, she is uncertain as to how to make her way through. If she takes the incorrect path again, it will be another hour before the church bells signal their location.

Perhaps it would simply be best to wait out the night in the woods. For when dawn arrives, it will be far easier to find the path to town.

She searches the dark for a place to rest and finds a fallen tree trunk.

However, no sooner does she settle upon it, then the clouds open, and it begins to rain.

Ambrosia wipes her nose on the back of her hand, as she steps over to the full length mirror and examines the welts that mar her smooth skin. Then, still ignoring Edward, she turns to her vanity, selects a feather puff, dabs it in fine white talc and powders her face, covering the red blotches made by her tears. When finished, she tosses the puff aside and adjusts her white curls so they frame her breasts.

Finally she turns to face Edward.

"I'm tired, shoe man," she says, "get out."

A roaring sound fills Edward's ears and it is almost as though he is possessed by a demon. For he finds himself crossing the room, grabbing her by the arms and pinning her against the glass mirror. He presses his skin against hers and shudders.

Flesh to flesh. She is cold, hard, like marble.

His mouth suctions onto her neck and he bites her skin.
She wrenches her right hand free and slaps his cheek.

"I did not give you leave to touch me."

But anger at being made to wait, not just tonight, but
for the past six weeks, rages inside Edward. And he raises
his own hand, striking her cheek in retaliation. Her head
slams to the side, cracking the mirror, shifting her wig so
that it sits askew on her head.

Ambrosia lets loose with a high keening cry of rage and
launches herself at him, raining blows upon his head and
chest, her claws ripping and tearing at his skin. Edward
is certain striking the Princess is an executable offense if
ever there is one. But there is no going back.

He blocks her assault, tossing her into the vanity,
sending her pots of powder, perfumes and potions
crashing to smithereens. Then she falls to the floor. And
this time her wig completely dislodges, revealing a shorn
head.

She spits at him, hisses, but he ignores her, grabbing
hold of both her ankles and dragging her over to the bed.

Anastasia stumbles over a patch of grumbleberries and
the inch long thorns rip through the light fabric of her
dress, scratching her legs and drawing blood. At first,
the thick canopy of trees provide some protection from
the heavy drops, but eventually the sheer volume of rain
finds its way through. She shivers for her dress, hair, and
shoes are now thoroughly soaked by rain. She yanks
her skirts free of the bramble and steps in the opposite
direction. Half an hour ago, she was certain she was

nearing Houndstooth, but that hope has near evaporated.

She is completely lost. Her hands shake from cold. Her feet feel heavy and ungainly. Each raindrop on her head, like the prick from an embroider needle.

She explores the leaves before her with her hands, trying to find a way out of the bramble. A branch snaps and she immediately stills. That wasn't her, was it? She stands motionless, trying without luck, to decipher shapes in the dark.

She has been trying not to think of the scrywolves. Or of her missing friends. And what may have happened to them on a similar dark night.

Perhaps the sound was simply a branch dislodged by the rain. Her heart calms and she gathers her skirts to try another path.

Snap.

Anastasia twists her head to the side.

T'is not the sound of rain on a branch.

Snap.

T'is the sound of a foot breaking a twig.

Snap.

Someone is in the woods with her.

Snap.

And they are following her. Because each snap is louder than the last.

Her heart flutters in her chest like a caged bird and she covers her mouth with both hands, so as not to make a sound. Too scared to even breathe.

Whoever is in the woods with her has now stopped moving as well. It cannot be a scrywolf because surely it would have attacked by now. What if it is her husband? Perhaps, without lantern or candle, he is lost as well. At which, she would feel very silly hiding here in the bushes. But if it is Edward, why does he not call out for her? Perhaps he is equally scared, unsure of who walks ahead of him in the dark.

"Edward?" she calls, and her voice is as shaky as her fingers.

There is no response and Anastasia's heart beats faster.

"Edward, is that you?"

But again, nothing.

Nay, not nothing. Breathing. Hot breath. On her neck.

She forgets about hiding and bolts like a fox driven from its den by the dogs during a hunt. Tearing through the woods, uncaring of bramble, branch or bush.

Uncaring of how much noise she makes.

Anastasia simply runs.

"You bastard," the Princess Ambrosia hisses, as she tries to twist free of Edward's grasp. But the moment he drops her ankles, he seizes her around the waist, twisting her so that she faces away from him. She turns her head to bite him but he stays out of her reach. Hoisting her into his arms and dropping her face down on the bed. She scrambles forward, her hands grasping for hold on the down comforter. But Edward grabs her by the waist, pulling her towards him, shoving himself between her legs.

The sweet smell of her sweat stings his nostrils and he drops on top of her, crushing her breasts and bones into the mattress.

She screams out for Nanny, bucking beneath him, trying

to dislodge him from her back. He seals his hand across her mouth silencing her. She manages to free a hand and strikes back at him and something sharp slices his arm. She has something in her grasp.

He releases her mouth, grabbing hold of her wrist and squeezes until her hand opens. His mother's peacock pin drops to the bed. Edward grabs hold of it and hurls it across the room. It strikes the mantelpiece of the great fireplace and falls in amongst the flames.

Edward uses his knees to separate her bony thighs. He presses one hand down on the back of her neck to keep her head pinned in place. She screams loud and long, but no one comes running. With his other hand, Edward grabs hold of his penis and positions himself at the entrance of the smooth folds of flesh he has been craving these past six weeks.

The Princess suddenly goes very quiet and stills, as though to prepare herself for what is to come. And in that moment Edward plunges deep into her, a shout of triumph and glory on his lips.

Anastasia runs past a curving hedge and straight into a wall, slamming into it with such force that she is knocked off her feet. She lies on the ground, stunned by the impact.

A hand touches her arm and she screams, scrambling away, trying to reorient herself.

A match flares, illuminating the dark, revealing the Sheriff.

He looks at her with surprise, "Anastasia?"

She bursts into tears and immediately feels foolish. She can see now she is at the border of Houndstooth, with the illuminated windows of her neighbors a few hundred feet up the road.

"I am sorry," she says, wiping her cheeks with the handkerchief he pulls from his pocket and hands to her.

"I thought you were in Ferrybone," he says, "What are you doing here?"

"I returned this morning and was at the palace with Edward," she says, blowing her nose.

The Sheriff looks over her shoulder and into the darkness as though looking for her husband.

"I came back alone," she says "but I got lost. And frightened because I think someone is following me."

The Sheriff stiffens.

"Are you hurt?" he asks, and when she shakes her head, he helps her to her feet. His hands are warm on her skin, her sleeves having been torn away in her flight.

A branch snaps in the dark and Anastasia presses close to him, her fingers finding his arm for comfort.

He digs into his pocket and pulls out a key which he presses into her fingers. "Go to the jail and wait for me."

"Where are you going?" she asks.

He gestures with his head towards the wood. "I am going to find whoever is following you. Now go." He gives her a little shove in the direction of town. "I'll come see you when I'm done."

"Be careful," she says.

He smiles, saying, "go on." But she stays to watch him approach the woods in the spot from which she emerged. Seconds later, the darkness swallows him up.

Anastasia is once more left alone.

She turns her back on the forest and hurries towards Houndstooth and the sanctuary of the jail.

Edward's body is slick with sweat, his skin and blood on fire. The Princess has stopped resisting and so he releases his grip on her neck and instead takes hold of her hips, noticing his grasp has left bruises on her skin.

As he slows his movement, she twists her head and their eyes meet.

"Harder," she spits, "make it hurt."

Although there is no joy in it, Edward smiles.

And does as she demands.

The jail is a small building on the outskirts of Houndstooth. It seldom has guests, save for the odd drunkard from the Wolf & Foxtail. Inside, the room is divided into two sections. On the left is a small cell with a cot and on the right is the Sheriff's chair and desk (covered with notes and scraps of paper), two lanterns (one of which Anastasia lit with a taper from the fire), a shelf with books on law and a tin of tea, a cabinet with coats, and a small pot-bellied stove that keeps the room toasty warm. There is a chart on the wall with a map of Houndstooth.

Anastasia finds a kettle in the cabinet, and boils water for tea. She moves the Sheriff's chair in front of the fire, so that her hair and dress will dry. She has been waiting for nearly an hour now and the bitter cold that sunk into her bones, has now all but fled.

Through the window, Anastasia sees a halo of light

approach the jail. She pours a second cup of tea, adds two spoonfuls of sugar and stirs.

The door scrapes open and the Sheriff enters, dousing his lantern and setting it on the floor.

His shoulders and hair are wet from the rain.

Anastasia rises and holds out the mug of tea which he takes from her hands.

"Please," she says, indicating the chair before the fire.

The Sheriff takes long swallows of the hot tea, emptying his mug almost immediately.

"Nay please keep warm," he says indicating the chair.

"Thank you," she says, but before she resumes sitting, she takes his mug and refills it.

He strips off his coat and hangs it on a peg next to the stove. Then he removes his boots and crosses to the cupboard. Fetches a glass bottle and clean cloth and returns to her side.

"Your legs," he says, gesturing to her.

Anastasia looks down at her ruined dress. Her skirts hang in tatters about her knees. The skin of her calves is torn and bloody from the brambles. Anastasia sets her tea aside and reaches for the cloth, but the Sheriff says, "allow me."

"Thank you," Anastasia says. The Sheriff kneels before her and unstops the glass jar, pouring a good measure of the clear alcohol into the cloth.

"Did you find anyone?" she asks.

The Sheriff shakes his head, "not a sign."

"T'was not my imagination," she says, "I am certain of it."

"I believe you," he says, gripping the back of her leg in his hand. Despite the fact he has been out in the cold, his fingers are warm and her skin immediately feels hot. Anastasia grips both handles of the chair as the Sheriff dabs the soft cloth against the scratches, wiping away the blood, disinfecting the cuts.

The room grows very quiet or perhaps it is her breathing that grows loud. Regardless, it is all that Anastasia can hear as she looks down on the Sheriff's head, his shoulders, his hands on the bare skin of first one leg, then the other.

Anastasia places a hand against her right cheek for her scar feels as though it is very hot, almost on fire once again. She knows the alcohol must sting but she has gone numb to any sensation but the warmth of his fingers. She does not want him to just touch her legs. There are other places on her body, places that have not been injured or bruised, that now demand his touch. But all too soon he is releasing her legs and sitting back from her on the floor.

"How is that?" he asks, looking up at her.

Anastasia feels incapable of speech, so she can only nod.

"Good," he says, standing. "Are you well enough to return home?"

Anastasia nods again, watching him cross the room to return the cloth and glass jar to the cabinet. He is obviously unaffected by their encounter and she feels tired and ridiculous for imagining that what she desires may in any way be reciprocated. She knows she is far from desirable. She covers her scars with her hand once more, wishing she could rip away the side of her face and replace it with something else.

The Sheriff grabs a dry coat from the cupboard and holds it out to Anastasia, "I'll walk you home." Then he's reaching for his damp boots.

She slips his coat over her cloak. It is twice her size and she wraps her arms around herself for comfort. She cannot bear to look at him. She feels too vulnerable. When he is ready, she follows him out into the cold. Water drips from the eaves and from the trees. It is the only sound as they walk together.

Anastasia's feet hurry towards the shop. She simply wants to climb into bed. She takes the key from her cloak but her fingers shake and she cannot find the lock.

The Sheriff takes the key from her and unlocks the door, opening it wide.

"Thank you," she says, stepping inside.

"Anastasia," he says, and she turns towards him, although she still cannot meet his eyes.

He places his hand on her chin and, forces her to look at him.

"No more walking alone. Not at night."

She nods.

"And lock the door behind you."

She nods again, waiting for him to release her.

But he does not and his fingers tighten.

"You're hurting me," she breathes.

"I am sorry," he says, and releases his grip.

Anastasia surges forward, her hands grasping his strong shoulders, pressing her mouth against his. His lips are soft, the stubble on his chin prickly. Her heart near explodes in her chest from the contact, but then his hands are grasping her wrists, setting her back, separating their mouths.

"No," he says.

A rash of color floods Anastasia's face.

I am sorry, she thinks, wanting the words to be heard, but unable to speak.

"No," he repeats, and turns and walks off into the dark.

Anastasia closes the door and locks it behind her, dropping onto the velvet settee. Hot tears fill her eyes but she refuses to let them fall.

At least for a few minutes.

Edward lies exhausted on the damp sheets of the Princess's bed. Ambrosia's arms and legs are wrapped around him like some kind of parasite.

If he so much as moves an inch from her side, she digs her sharp nails into his skin or bites at him with her teeth.

She is not afraid to draw blood.

The Sheriff lays on the cot inside the cell. There is a draft from a crack in the stone wall and the lantern throws strange and terrible shadows across the ceiling. He can still feel Anastasia's small frame against his own. Her lips, her breath, her sweat. She was nervous; her pulse running scared under his fingers.

It had been Margarite who first alerted him to her presence. She was letting Griswold the Angry Cat out for its evening shivermouse and could hear stumbling and crashing about in the area of the Shade that bordered their cottage. Margarite sent her husband to fetch him and he had come at once. He hadn't expected to find anything other than an emaciated scrywolf at best.

But there she was.·

Anastasia.

Appearing out of the darkness like a ghost. Indeed, he wasn't even sure that she was real until he touched her. For she had disappeared from Houndstooth as suddenly as Sophia and Jenny. Indeed, he had wondered for many long days if she was the first to go missing. Perhaps Margarite's fears had come true and Edward had disposed of her after all.

But Edward had been most adamant when queried, that Anastasia was simply at her parents. And a querying telegram to the Sheriff's counterpart in Ferrybone confirmed her presence in that city. He had not known she was returned, not until she ran him over in her flight.

The first time he saw Anastasia in Houndstooth he was astonished. It truly seemed divinely blessed that both of them should find their way to this town. But when she didn't recognize him, words failed in his mouth. And each time thereafter he found himself too paralyzed to speak the truth. Now he, who has never been afraid in his life, is terrified. For if she discovers who he is, she is certain to despise him for his indecision, his cowardice, his lies. He would expect nothing less.

It is also clear Anastasia could have been his tonight. And it took all of his will power to turn her aside. For there is nothing he wants more, than to be at her side. And yet ... he curses the pledge he made to the Goddess to do no more harm. Anastasia can not be his, not while bound to another.

The Sheriff wonders if it is time to leave. He thought this place would be his salvation, a place of quiet where the nightmares of the war would fade. But now this triumvirate of three incidents make him suspect some greater hand at work. The night at the Wolf & Foxtail (which Doctor Wintergreen still advocated was faulty ale even though the tests proved otherwise). Jenny and Sophia missing. The fact that both he and Anastasia are here.

Alone, these incidents were of no particular note. Together, they suggested a more complex being was moving people about as though they were mere players on a chess board. No one would believe him, of course. For magic (if indeed something magical was afoot), was a very tricky thing, near impossible to prove, and thought to be long extinct.

He closes his eyes and not for the first time, wishes he had never come to Houndstooth.

Anastasia awakens with a start.

For a moment, she is frightened, uncertain of her surroundings. She is not in her room at Saffron's, nor in her room in Houndstooth. Then she remembers; the dinner at the Palace, getting lost in the forest, the Sheriff escorting her home. She touches her lips, then sits, groaning as her body aches from her flight through the forest.

She runs her hands along her scratched arms. Her throat is parched, demanding her thirst be quenched. There is a scuttling sound in the corner. She pulls her feet up onto the settee, certain it is a shivermouse. But when she glances into the shadows, she sees it is not vermin at all.

Instead it is a little creature, that would only reach her knees if she were to stand next to it. It is thin, almost emaciated. It wears a ragged cloth around its waist. It appears a child except the wispy beard on its bony chin says otherwise. In its spindly hands, the creature holds a pair of shoes. Edward had not mentioned it was a dwarf he hired to make the shoes. She'd heard of them before, but they were usually found in the southern mountain ranges and worked with metal and woodcraft.

Some villagers thought dwarves to be practitioners of foul deeds. Anastasia, of course, attributed this prejudice to their small stature and the fact they were rumored to be secretive, sly creatures that kept to themselves and did not like to be troubled by the ills of the outer world. No wonder Edward had kept his assistant's identity secret.

Anastasia holds her breath as she watches the creature place the shoes in the middle of the shop floor, then scurry towards the back wall.

A small hole opens where no door was before, and the creature disappears through it.

Anastasia waits a few moments, then releases her breath and rises. She crosses to the workbench and lights one of the many beeswax candles. Then she crouches down to inspect the shoes. These ones show an elephantine hunt. On one shoe are the hunters, men in red uniforms with firesticks and spears and mongrel dogs with a taste for blood.

On the other shoe are the dead elephantines, their tusks pointed to the heavens. A hunter (who looks impossibly like the late-King), stands next to one of the dead, his hand on the creature's head, a look of pride on his face.

Anastasia sets the shoes once more on the floor and walks across to where she saw the creature disappear. She crouches down and runs her hand along the wall. The candle flame flickers and so she holds the light closer.

Set into the larger door, which is still locked, is a smaller door cut so carefully into the wood it is almost invisible. It comes to about her knee and there is no handle, so she guesses it must only open from the inside.

She thinks for a moment then rises and makes her way to the kitchen. She places the candle in a holder then selects one of the new copper pans. She stirs the embers in the fire and adds two new dry logs.

From the icebox outside, she grabs a bottle of fresh goat milk and pours it into the copper pan. While the milk warms she enters the pantry and pulls out a selection of sharp cheddar cheeses, cinnamon sweetbreads, and spicy meats. She cuts each into chunks suitable for a child's hand and places them on a plate.

When the milk has warmed, she pours it into the mug she uses for measuring flour. Then she places the plate and mug on a tray, and grabbing the candle, carries the dishes back to the shop. She sets the tray in front of the little door and knocks.

She waits a minute before knocking again. When there is still no answer, she leaves the tray where it is, makes her way out of the shop and upstairs where she falls into bed and a very dreamless sleep.

Edward leans his forehead against the shop door. It is almost dawn and he is exhausted. The Princess kept him from sleep the whole of the night. Whenever he tried to leave or even felt himself sinking into slumber, she would be on him again, sucking at him like some kind of leech, demanding attention.

He pushes up his sleeves, baring his arms. Like his back, they are covered in her scratches, almost deliberately placed, as though she wanted to mark him for her own.

Edward turns and sees the shoes waiting for him. He shuffles over and claims them from the floor, not even stopping to look at the design. All he wants now is sleep. He places the shoes in the shop window and heads towards the connecting door. But something on the floor at the back of the shop catches his attention. He heads over and finds an empty cup and plate on the floor.

Edward can't think why they would be here. Perhaps the creature is stealing food. He returns them to the kitchen.

From there, he heads upstairs, grabs his father's leather satchel from its hiding spot, and climbs into bed.

For the first night in weeks, Sophia does not interrupt his sleep.

As Anastasia passes Edward's room the next morning, she can hear him snoring. She pushes open his bedroom door to see him still fully clothed, lying on top of the blankets. The smell of stale alcohol and lily assaults her nose. She closes the door once more and continues downstairs to the shop. When she opens the door, she sees the plate and mug are no longer where she placed them. A cool breeze stirs the air, freshening her lungs but she doesn't remember the window being open last night.

She crosses to the front of the store. Broken glass fills the display.

The shoes.

They are not in the window. Not on the floor. She does a quick search of the shop.

They are gone.

Anastasia scrambles upstairs to Edward's room and throws open the door. She crosses to his bed and gives him a shake.

"Edward, you must rise."

"Go way," he mumbles, "sick."

"Edward, the shoes are gone."

He sits bolt upright, stares at her with red eyes.

"What?"

"The shop has been burgled. The shoes are gone. I saw them last night but —"

Edward is gone, flying out of bed, pushing past her and running downstairs.

Anastasia follows and finds him at the window.

"No, no, no, no, no," he says, sifting through the broken glass as though the shoes could possibly be hiding beneath the shattered shards.

"Edward," Anastasia says, grabbing his hands, "use care, you will cut yourself."

He shakes her hands away, stumbling against the wall as though in need of support.

"I am a dead man."

"Edward, I'm sure the Princess will understand if —"

"She'll understand nothing," he spits. "If she knows someone else has her shoes, t'is all over. That was our agreement."

"Then perhaps you should not have placed them in the window," she says, watching him tear at his hair.

He glares at her, forming his fingers into fists and for a moment, she thinks he might strike out. But then he crosses to the door at the back of the room and kicks it.

"Elf. Get out here." He kicks the door again and again, "Elf."

The tiny door opens and the creature Anastasia saw last night pops out its head. Edward grabs the Elf by the arm and hauls him into the workroom.

"I need another pair of shoes. Today."

The Elf squeals and tries to pull free of Edward's grasp.

"I cannot, Sir, I am most tired from my prior efforts."

Edward shakes the creature and it cries out.

"You will do as I say, or you will die. Do you understand?"

"Edward," Anastasia says, crossing to his side, "t'is just a child." She grabs hold of Edward's hand, trying to pry his fingers from the creature's arm. But Edward blocks her, knocking his elbow into her face.

A sharp explosion of pain radiates from her nose and Anastasia drops to the floor, the metallic taste of blood in her mouth.

Edward shakes the creature once more, "you will make me another pair before the appointed hour."

"You're hurting him," Anastasia says through bloody lips, as she climbs to her knees and tries once more to free the creature.

Edward places his foot against her chest and shoves. A thousand stars burst into Anastasia's vision from the force of the kick.

"Am I not your master?" Edward demands.

"Yes," the creature cries.

"Good," Edward says, dropping the Elf to the floor. Then Edward turns towards Anastasia. She cares not for what she sees in his eyes and crawls towards the front door. But Edward follows, standing over her, placing his foot on the small of her back, pinning her to the floor.

"That is no child," Edward says, crouching down, "that is an Elf. And it belongs to me."

Anastasia lies very still, hoping he will depart without causing further injury.

"I have a good mind to punish you," he says, crouching low and running a hard finger down her spine.

A sharp chill takes hold of her and Anastasia kicks out at him scrambling forward.

But Edward grabs her with both hands, his forearm across the back of her neck, pressing her right cheek to the floor. The rest of his body weight sinks onto her back and she cannot move.

He runs his tongue over her unblemished cheek, at the same time his free hand squirrels under her body to grasp her left breast in his bruising fingers.

Anastasia tries to scream but cannot find the breath.

"T'is a good thing you are so ugly," he whispers in her ear. Then he spits on her cheek, releases her and walks over the door. It slams behind him as he exits the shop.

Anastasia curls into a ball, wiping her sleeve along her cheek removing the spittle. A noise sounds behind her and she turns to see the little creature watching her.

Then it steps through the door, and closes it behind him. Leaving Anastasia alone in the room.

Nay, not alone. She can hear someone crying.

It takes her a few moments to realize it is she.

Anastasia sits on her bed, a cold cloth pressed to her nose.

As soon as she had breath, she roused herself from the floor and fled to her room.

She has been sitting here all morning and afternoon, listening to the sound of hammering as the old window is removed and a new one installed. Now it is quiet.

The Elf must have delivered a second pair of shoes for she heard Edward leave five minutes ago for the Palace. Her small satchel sits next to her on the floor. She will not stay here a moment longer. She will find another way to unbind this marriage. For she wants nothing more to do with Edward. But she cannot leave that creature to her husband's madness.

She rises from the bed and examines her face in the mirror. There is a large bruise forming around her left eye and nose. Her lip is split. And her eyes look empty. She touches the swollen flesh, is rewarded with pain. It makes her feel alive, gives her the energy to move.

Anastasia steps down the hallway to the stairs. She knows she has at least another hour before Edward returns, so the sooner they depart, the closer to Ferrybone she and the Elf will be.

She crouches down and knocks softly on the little door.

"T'is I," she whispers, "Anastasia."

There is no answer. She presses her ear to the wood and can hear the sound of metal.

She knocks again.

But there is still no response.

Anastasia stands and tries the knob. And much to her surprise, the door opens.

She steps into a little room. One that previously did not exist. There is a candle lit in the corner and she can see that the interior resembles a workroom. There is a little workbench, shoe leather hanging in strips on racks, a miniature knife, measure, and other tools.

The Elf sits at the workbench embroidering. He looks up as Anastasia approaches.

She holds out her hand, "come, little one, we are leaving."

But the creature shakes his head and lifts his right leg. There is a metal ring around his ankle, attached to a chain which is affixed to the wall.

Anastasia grabs the chain in both hands and pulls but the metal is strong.

"Edward did this?"

The creature nods.

"I will find a tool and free you," Anastasia says, rising.

"Nay, concern yourself not, my Lady," the Elf says, "I am contracted to your husband. My obligation remains here and here I will remain."

"Still," Anastasia says, sinking to her knees and setting down the chain, "t'isn't right you be treated in such an ill manner."

"Such treatment and I are old friends, my lady."

Anastasia grabs the bottom of her petticoat and tears a strip from the cotton.

"Here," she says, approaching the Elf. She wraps the fabric around his thin leg where the metal is affixed and chafes his skin.

"Thank you, my lady."

The Elf then resumes his work, hunching over the shoe, the little needle flying in and out of the leather, bringing a peacock to life. She glances at the workbench and sees that the other shoe has yet to be constructed.

Then she looks over at the door. If she means to leave

Houndstooth, she must do so now. Edward will return before long.

She looks back to see the Elf watching.

"You should go, my Lady. I will be well."

Anastasia touches the bruise on her face, then sits on the floor next to the Elf.

"Here, let me help," she says, reaching for his implements. "I was quite good at the needle when I was younger."

The Elf watches her stitch for a moment, and then as if pleased by her work, turns to address the still unfinished pieces of leather on the workbench.

"Do you have a name?" Anastasia asks.

"None," says the Elf, "beyond creature, thing, or pestilence."

"Well then we must find you one," Anastasia says.

PART THREE

CHAPTER ONE

Wherein an angry cat
smells a rat.

Edward pops a raspberry chocolate into his mouth and chews. He has already delivered the Princess's shoes and now the day, as it did the day before and the one before that, has opened into great big nothingness. His life is stagnant. He eats, sleeps, delivers shoes, slakes the Princess's lust (if she so desires), and nothing more. The townspeople regard him as as a brilliant shoemaker. But if they only knew the truth. That he is nothing more than a glorified errand boy.

He pats his expanded waistline (it has grown of late due to his insistence on only the finest foods and wines), grateful for the daily walk to and from the palace which keeps his weight somewhat in check. He watches Anastasia, seated across the table, sip her nettle tea. She has participated very little in their new found wealth, choosing to wear her same plain Houndstooth dresses and eat what she grows in her garden or obtains from neighbors. The only thing she has asked of him, was an allowance to purchase books. And she sits now with her nose in yet another tome, this one titled: *Womyn's Wisdom; Potions, Brews & Balms.*

She strayed from home very little over the past month as the bruises on her face healed. And even now she has little scraps of fabric wound around the tips of three of her fingers. But he knows they cover needle pricks. One dark night, two weeks past, he heard her rise in the night. He followed her in secret, down the stairs and watched her enter the Elf's cell. At first, he suspected she was going to release the creature and he knew in that moment he would kill her. So he fetched a butcher knife from the kitchen and waited for her in a shadowy corner of the shop. But she did not emerge for five minutes, ten minutes, almost an hour. And when she did exit, she was alone and so he cowered in the dark and watched her cross into the kitchen. In a few minutes, she returned, carrying a mug of warm milk and a sandwich of raw onions and vinegary pickles. She then disappeared back into the Elf's cell.

Edward crept forward and peered into the room, careful that he wouldn't be seen. The little Elf was eating the sandwich prepared by Anastasia while she embroidered one of the Princess's shoes. Every now and then, the little Elf would marvel at her work or point out an exceptionally clever stitch. It was a companionable sort of silence and Edward felt a twinge of jealousy. He wondered how long the two of them had been meeting to share the work. He had first noticed Anastasia seemed more tired than usual three weeks prior. And then she had started staying up later than he, and sleeping in. Edward thought Anastasia was simply trying to avoid him. But no, she had been a second pair of hands for the little Elf. No wonder the little creature had been able to increase his production on the number of shoes Edward was now demanding on a daily basis. The creature had an assistant. At first, Edward thought the Elf would refuse to make more than one pair a night, until he realized the Elf had to do as he was instructed. And should Edward, demand one hundred pairs, the Elf would be obligated to provide.

Ever since the shoes were stolen from the shop window (and were rumored to have been worn by a lesser royal on the Continent), Edward held several meetings with prominent merchants from cities at the other ends of the Kingdom. They came to Houndstooth under cover of darkness. They held hushed conversations deep in the Shade. And when the illicit shoes were delivered, even more gold found its way into Edward's coffers.

Edward felt no guilt about making shoes for other feet. For the Princess hadn't paid him for the last two dozen pairs he'd delivered. Therefore, he had to find other means to grow his wealth. And if a merchant from the continent was willing to pay ten, twenty, thirty gold pieces to have his daughter wear a pair of shoes from the Princess's famed shoemaker, then so be it. Edward would provide. As long as the transaction was kept secret.

He no longer places the shoes in the store window, much to the villagers chagrin. Instead, they are kept in a shatterproof glass box within a cage that is built into the floor of the shop. If a villager wants to see the Princess's shoes, he or she can pay two shillings for the privilege of the viewing. Edward considers this a reasonable charge (though it equals one days pay for the average farmer). The newspapiary man is forced to pay much more (primarily because he draws reproductions of the shoes for the local daily).

Edward knows Anastasia must be working longer alongside the Elf to deal with the increase in demand. Yet, she has not once complained. Instead her cheeks seem rosier, her eyes brighter, her mood lighter.

Edward watches Anastasia sip the last of her tea. She has spoken to him very little since their encounter on the shop floor. And he doesn't remember when he started joining her in the kitchen for afternoon tea. Possibly ten days ago. She said nothing when he sat opposite her (still didn't), instead she seemed completely absorbed in whatever book she was reading. But she appeared to tolerate his presence or at least she never asked him to leave. And now, with her unbound hair falling forward to frame her face, he realizes she looks almost pretty. True, he only ever looks at the left side of her face. But somehow, the scars don't seem as prominent anymore. Her grey eyes are always warm when speaking to the Elf and her mouth has a kindly smile. Her body is curved and he imagines she is much softer to lie next to, than the angles and sharp edges of the Princess. She often smells of the garden, of their home, of Houndstooth and he wonders what it would be like to curl up next to her. Sleep would no doubt be peaceful.

Edward shifts in his chair and feels his blood stir, wonders if he can persuade Anastasia to accompany him upstairs to his bed. He clears his throat to speak and sees she is staring at him.

"Yes?" he says, realizing she has asked him a question, although he doesn't recall her words.

"I need to pick up some items in town. Is there anything you require?"

"No," Edward says, shaking his head.

She rises from her chair, placing her mug in the basin.

"Will you be back for supper?" he asks.

She sets her book on the shelf by the table and looks over at him.

"I suppose so," she says.

"I thought I might cook that partridge for us."

Anastasia watches him for a moment, "that would be nice."

He smiles at her and hands her the shopping basket.

"Thank you," she says, and steps out the back door. Through the window, he watches her cross the yard to the street and disappear from view. Yes, they'll have the partridge tonight. With some of that new wine he imported. T'is strong stuff. A couple drinks of that and his wife should be good and pliable. He can even slip a little sleeping draught into her drink, to secure her compliance. Yes, he thinks, nodding. That sounds like a perfect evening. And he slips his hand into his trousers and starts to rub.

Anastasia lays the child-size shirt she has sewn on the counter of the All-Goods-Shop and examines the buttons on display. While she may have a good hand at embroidery (and is becoming even more accomplished), sewing is not her strength. This is her fourth attempt at making a shirt for the Elf, and although it is still somewhat lopsided, she is rather proud of her efforts. It is bright yellow, like the butterglove that grows in her garden, and is made of soft flannel to keep him warm through the upcoming winter. Now all it needs is buttons and she selects four black ones shaped like birds.

A shadow falls across the material and she turns to see the Sheriff standing next to her.

"Hello, Anastasia."

Her cheeks color for she has not talked to him since the night of the kiss. And though it was weeks ago, it suddenly feels very recent.

"I see congratulations are in order," he says, indicating the shirt.

Anastasia blinks at him, her brow furrowed. Congratulations?

"Oh no. No," she says, "t'is not for me, but a friend."

"Ah," he says, and lapses into silence.

Anastasia notices the Sheriff looks more haggard than when she last saw him. There are dark circles under his eyes, his hair is uncombed, his clothes unwashed, rumpled, stained. He utters a yawn and smells of last night's coffee .

"Would you like some tea?" she asks, placing her hand on his arm.

He looks down at her and a bleary smile crosses his face.

"Thank you, I'd like that very much."

Anastasia and the Sheriff sit in the window of the bakery. There are two cups of hot jasmine tea before them and Anastasia orders a plate of pastries when the Sheriff says he is uncertain as to when he last ate.

"I've been meaning to stop by about the shoes," he says.

"The shoes?" Anastasia asks. Wondering why he would be interested in what the Princess wears on her feet.

"I heard of the theft. Thought Edward might report them stolen. But he never did. And I've been so busy with the missing women, I'm afraid I've neglected some of my other duties."

"T'is all right," Anastasia reassures, "Edward replaced them."

"Good," he says nodding and yawns again. "T'is the women," he says at last. "Eight gone."

"Eight?" Anastasia echoes. She had been to the village vigil two weeks prior when the number of missing women reached five, but wasn't aware of any further trouble.

"I've kept the last three quiet, hoping to find some leads. But nothing." He takes a long sip of tea, rubs at the bristles on his unshaved chin. "There's pressure from the Palace as folks are threatening to withhold taxes if the women aren't found. Can't say I blame them."

Anastasia reaches across the table and squeezes his hand. He looks up at her.

"You haven't been out after dark, have you?" he asks.

"Nay," she says. "I have kept that promise."

"Good," he says.

Betsy stops by to deliver the plate of pastries and refill the hot water in the tea pot. She tosses Anastasia a wink as she returns to the counter.

"Have you thought of setting a trap?" Anastasia asks, ignoring Betsy.

"I've discussed it with the Mayoral," he says, removing his fingers from hers to take up his cup, "but what God fearing woman would agree to be the bait?"

"You may be surprised," Anastasia states.

"I may," the Sheriff responds, then lowers his voice and leans towards her, "but I fear no mere man is taking these women."

"What do you mean?" Anastasia asks, as she freshens their drinks.

"You'll think me mad," he says.

"Nay," Anastasia says, picking up her tea cup, "never."

The Sheriff breaks off a corner of lavender biscuit and pops it into his mouth to chew. Once he's swallowed, he looks back at her.

"I think there's magic involved."

"How can that be?" Anastasia asks, setting down her cup, "t'is extinct."

The Sheriff simply looks at her and takes another bite of his biscuit.

"Isn't it?" she asks.

"Some say t'was how war was won in the Asiantine," the Sheriff says. "They say the King used magic."

"But those are rumors," Anastasia counters.

"Perhaps," the Sheriff says, finishing his last bite of biscuit and selecting another, "but for those of us that were there, it did indeed seem as though an unseen hand played a role in our success."

"In what way?" Anastasia asks, a knot forming in her stomach.

"For three days, the sun never set as we fought in trenches that ran waist deep with the blood of the enemy. And all that time our arms never tired. We divested ourselves of our armor because the temperature was so hot it would have cooked us, yet not once during those long hours of hell did we know thirst. And if we were struck a blow—well, see for yourself," he says yanking his collar back and dipping his head. A ragged scar runs across the back of his neck. "That blow should have severed head from spine. And instead t'was no more than a scratch."

"Are you saying these women used magic? And now suffer the consequences? Because I assure you they did not. "

"Not necessarily," he says. "They could be dead at the expense of another's success."

The knot in Anastasia's stomach grows tighter.

"See, t'was never the use of magic that was the danger," the Sheriff says, "It was the cost. If one prospers by unnatural means, another must perish by that same standard. It doesn't necessarily have to be the same person. T'is why it was first banned, then punishable by death, then destroyed or made extinct. Magic is a living force, too fickle to control, though some would certainly try."

The color drains from Anastasia's face.

"I must go," she says, grabbing her basket and standing, "I am sorry."

The Sheriff rises from the table.

"I'll walk you home," he says, draining the last of his tea.

"Nay, nay," she says, setting a few coins on the table to cover the cost of the tea and pastries, "I will be fine."

And then Anastasia turns and runs out of the shop.

Anastasia bursts through the back door and into the kitchen to find Edward standing at the counter plucking feathers from the partridge.

"Ah, my love, you are back early."

"The Elf. He has to stop making shoes," she breathes.

Edward stares at her, his fingers full of feathers.

"What are you talking about?"

"The Elf. I think he is here because of some magical force," she states. "And somehow that same magic is responsible for the women disappearing."

Edward blinks at her, then shakes his hands free of feathers and rinses them in the basin.

"How?" he asks.

"I know not how they are related," Anastasia says, dropping her basket on the table, "I wish that I did."

"What has brought this on?" Edward asks.

"I was speaking to the Sheriff," she says, and immediately bites her tongue. She knows that Edward detests the man.

"The Sheriff?" Edward asks, raising his brow.

"It matters not who said it," she says, annoyed her cheeks flush, "merely that it might be possible. In which case the Elf cannot continue his work."

Edward reaches for an empty glass on the counter, fills it with wine.

"Have a drink," he says, holding out the glass, "calm your nerves."

"I do not want calm," she states. "Edward this is important."

Edward is silent, thinking, swirling the wine in the glass. Finally he speaks. "Very well. Did you tell the Sheriff about the Elf?"

"Nay," Anastasia says, "I wanted to speak to you first."

Edward nods his head and holds out the glass yet again.

"Are you sure? T'is a very calming drop."

"Edward," Anastasia repeats.

"Alright," he relents, tossing the contents in the sink and depositing the glass on the counter. "We will talk to the Elf. But I am certain there is no magic involved."

Anastasia squeezes his arm, "thank you, Edward."

He nods again and smiles at her, "of course, my love."

Anastasia crosses the kitchen and enters the shop, with Edward close behind her. She swings open the door to the Elf's cell and enters. He is fast asleep on the little cot the two of them built together.

Anastasia turns expecting to see Edward. But he is not there. Instead the door closes behind her.

"Edward?"

She hears the sound of metal rubbing against metal.

"Edward?"

Anastasia grabs hold of the knob and tries to open the door. But it is locked.

"Edward!"

There is no response.

She glances over at the Elf.

He has awoken, is looking up at her with large eyes.

Edward listens to Anastasia pound on the door. She has been doing so for nearly two hours. At first he thought someone outside on the street might hear. But Stella made the room of a hard wood, and very little noise escapes. He doesn't know what to do with Anastasia. He just knows she cannot stop the magic. He needs more gold. Not for much longer. Just a few more days. He has a large delivery of shoes (thirty pairs in all), to be finalized on Sunday. After that, Anastasia can do as she would like.

He is uncertain when he began to formulate his plan to escape Houndstooth. Perhaps t'was when he realized how suffocating the Princess had become. As their time together increased, the more she would whine, pout and threaten every time he left her bed. Her jealousy had focused on Anastasia and while at one point, Edward would have been glad to have been delivered from his wife, he now found himself intervening on her behalf. Insisting Anastasia was a crucial part of the shoemaking process. That it was, in fact, her hands that stitched the embroidery the Princess loved so much.

He knows the Princess will never allow him to leave and thus he will have to disappear. And after the Sunday delivery (to a merchant from the Asiantine), he will have enough gold to last him a lifetime. He had thought this afternoon while she was in town, that he would invite Anastasia to accompany him when he left Houndstooth for the continent. But now he understands she will be a hinderance. He needs to go alone.

Edward consults his pocket watch. Anastasia has quieted within the cell and it is now growing dark. Edward checks the lock on the door to the Elf's cell. It is strong, cannot be broken. The blacksmith assured him the locking mechanism and bolts were of the sturdiest steel. Edward grabs his father's leather satchel and tests the weight. It has become most heavy, now that the false bottom is stuffed with gold pieces. But Edward finds, he simply cannot leave it behind. He ensures that his tools are inside and stands at the window waiting for night to fall over Houndstooth.

He cannot leave too early. Nor, too late. Recently the hunt has become more difficult. Because of the missing women, villagers are more cautious. They no longer take evening walks, they stay inside their homes. And Edward has had to become bolder. When he first chained the Elf to the wall and was forced to become the creature's hands and feet in the world, Edward recoiled at the prospect of being the one to collect the leather. But he had grown in skill, following the Elf's precise instructions on how to kill, drain the body, and then skin it. How the Elf disposed of the remainder of the body, Edward did not know. He presumed it was magic.

When Edward had taken Mary-Anne (the Pardoner's daughter), he had been too cautious with the kill (terrified he would hurt her), and more than half her skin was lost in the ensuing fight. Things had gone better with Buttercup (the Candlemaker's wife), and Hester (the stone mason's niece). But with fewer women out at night, Edward found he was now taking greater risks. When he harvested Cressida, he'd walked right up to her door and knocked, stating that Anastasia was stricken with the first pangs of motherhood and could she provide assistance. Cressida, of course, agreed at once, grabbing a selection of herbs and balms and accompanying him out into the dark as though she had nothing to fear.

They'd walked the main street back to the shop and Edward was petrified they would be seen together. But it was late, and the villagers had gone into hiding. Edward wasn't scared once Cressida entered the shop. He'd gotten quicker with his blade, with the Elf continuing to advise him on how to dispatch his prey with very little noise. He still wasn't used to the thrashing and squealing that accompanied a kill, to say nothing of the blood (there was always so very much of it). But the Elf had trained him how to pull the skin away from the muscle so it wouldn't tear. How best to fold it so it would not permanently crease.

Once Anastasia began working with the Elf, Edward started drugging her evening tea on the nights he hunted. It wouldn't do for her to learn where the leather came from. Tonight, he knows exactly on which door he will knock. It was always tricky to select the perfect specimen. He tried to choose women with larger builds so there was more skin to harvest and he would have to hunt less often. But he also couldn't pick elderly woman. He did that once (hoping that after his ordeal with Mary-Anne he could find one that didn't fight back). But Widow Goldspan turned out to be a useless kill as the leather was too fragile to be of any use. No, the younger the kill, the smoother the leather.

Edward checks his pocket watch to see that the hours have flown and the time for the hunt is nigh. He listens once more at the door to the Elf's cell, and all is quiet. He tests the lock again, then crosses the room and slips out of the shop.

The night air is dark. Cool. Silent.

Not even the vermin stir tonight. He steps with quiet feet (and he has most certainly learned that skill over these past two months), along the cobblestones of Houndstooth. Then he slips into the alleyway between the All-Goods-Shop and the Butcher. And waits.

Tonight he has plans for Betsy, the baker's wife. Betsy is a hefty woman, grown fat on tarts, treacle, pastries and pies. He is hoping her skin will be more than sufficient for the last batch of shoes. He has been saving her for the right occasion when he needs the Elf to produce a surplus. And now that time has come. Moreover, her husband left town yesterday, taking the horse and cart down south to collect yeast and other supplies not available in Houndstooth. And when her husband leaves town, Betsy always spends the night at Margarite's (according to Anastasia), for she is afraid to be on her own.

A patch of light appears on the street across the way from him and Edward realizes it is Betsy with her lantern. She steps out of the shop, locking the door behind her. She looks both ways up and down the street but Edward knows the dark is his friend and that he is hidden from view. When Betsy is certain no one lingers, she leaves the front step, turning right and waddles in the direction of Margarite's.

Edward's heart pounds in his chest, his hands grow sweaty. A red haze appears before his eyes as it always does when he prepares to harvest the leather. Given her girth, Edward does not anticipate a fight; Betsy is too ungainly to resist. He reaches into his father's shoemaking satchel and grabs hold of his knife.

His heart instantly calms.

He waits until Betsy rounds the corner and then he steps out of the alley and follows, as silent as her shadow.

Anastasia slumps against the locked door. Henry (the Elf chose this name as it reminded him of the old King), crouches before her a look of grave concern on his face.

"Tell me," she asks of the little creature, "has magic been involved in this enterprise?"

The Elf's head hangs low as he acknowledges Anastasia's question.

"So t'is my fault my friends were brought to ruin," Anastasia says, hiding her face with her hands.

"My lady," Henry says, twisting his bony fingers together, "t'was Sir Edward entirely."

"Nay," Anastasia says, dropping her hands, "I suspected something was amiss. But, I could not place it. Now eight women are missing because I silenced my tongue." She looks up at the creature with tired eyes, "You realize this has to stop, Henry? That Edward cannot be allowed to continue?"

"You mustn't interfere," Henry says, the wispy hairs on his chin quivering and glancing about the room as though afraid they may be overheard, "for if you do, my Mistress will cause you great harm."

"But t'is wrong," Anastasia says, "and balance must be restored."

"Please, my lady," Henry crouches before her on his knees, plucking at her skirts, "I cannot protect you, she is far too powerful."

Anastasia is quiet for several long minutes. After which she leans forward and kisses Henry on the forehead. "I understand, Henry, and thank you for your concern. But if I must give my life to make amends, it must be so."

Henry wraps his arms around Anastasia's neck and buries his face against her shoulder, weeping like a small child.

Anastasia rubs his curved back, murmurs comfort into his ear.

At last when he has no more tears to shed, he steps back to look at her, "You have given me more kindness than I have ever received, my lady, and as such I am in your debt."

"Nay," Anastasia says, wiping his eyes with her handkerchief, "t'is I who owe you. You have made this past month in Houndstooth most bearable. I am honored to call you friend."

"Then I shall help you as I can, my lady," Henry says, "you must go seek safety with your Sheriff."

"How?" Anastasia asks, rapping her knuckles against the door, "we are locked in this dreadful room."

Henry rises and paces the floor, "you must close your eyes and whatever you may hear or smell, you musn't open them until I am finished. Is that understood?"

"Yes," says Anastasia, covering her eyes with her hands, "but how?"

She feels Henry pat her knee, "My dear lady, whenever a wish nears completion, there is always a little magic left for extras."

Anastasia smiles and feels Henry place a kiss on her scarred cheek. "My apologies," he says with a whisper, "for alarming you that night in the woods. Now that we are friends, I would never cause you harm."

A cool gust of wind blows against Anastasia's face.

"Henry?" she asks.

There is no response.

"Henry?"

Still nothing. But the ground beneath her feels different. She removes her hands, keeping her eyes scrunched tight. Her fingers touch the ground beside her and she feels dirt.

She opens her eyes. Henry is no longer there and she

is no longer seated on the floor of the room. But rather in her garden out back of the house with the cold night air pricking at her skin.

Anastasia doesn't stop to wonder at the magic.

She climbs to her feet and runs.

Edward follows Betsy, vigilant not to make a sound. Margarite's house is on the outskirts of the village, on the rise of a hill overlooking the Shade. It is a lonely stretch of road, carved through the woods, with a thick row of trees on either side. It is the perfect spot to kill Betsy. No lanterns or torches light the dark and heavy cloud cover ensures not even tonight will the moon spoil his plans.

Betsy waddles along the dirt road, oblivious to his presence. In the dark, she looks less like a woman and more like a cow, unaware of the wolf in her shadow. She sings a stupid Houndstooth ditty about a wooden shoe sailing among the stars. It makes her easy to follow, and when he loses sight of her once, then twice amongst the shadowy tress, he still knows exactly where she is. He places his father's leather case next to a thick stump by the roadside. Though out in the open, the night is his friend, disguising the black leather as just another shadow. Edward will need two hands to hunt and they have finally arrived at the turn and there, on the rise, is Margarite's house.

Betsy arrives at the wooden gate and reaches for the clasp. But Edward is already running forward, the knife firmly in his right hand, raising it for the kill. He can see the soft skin of her neck, smell her sweat, feel the rasp of her wool shawl under his fingers —

"He's right here!" Betsy screams, spinning around, striking out with her basket. It slams into Edward's chest, knocking him off balance and he stumbles over a low bramble bush and lands flat on his back.

"Bloody woman, silence!" a male voice curses. And Edward immediately recognizes it as belonging to the Sheriff.

"Bastard!" Betsy shrieks, kicking at Edward with her feet. He drops the knife, covering his face with both hands so she cannot recognize him. He hears running footsteps, more male voices and dogs (Oh God, no, not dogs), and realizes the Sheriff is not alone.

Edward rolls over onto his side, grabbing up handfuls of mud, smearing it on his face to cover his skin. Then he rolls down the rise of the hill, keeping low to avoid being seen.

"He went that way!" Betsy shouts, and although he cannot see her, Edward knows Betsy is pointing in his direction.

The dark grows lighter and Edward sees the men now have torches and lanterns and lamps.

"Who was it?" one of them calls.

"Did anyone see?"

Edward stays low, crawling like a dog through the mud. But then, the traitorous moon asserts herself, illuminating the road with her bright glory.

"This way!" the Sheriff shouts and Edward turns to see the torches heading in his direction.

He scrambles to his feet and dives into the Shade, grateful for its dark shadows. He stumbles through the thick brush and brambles, tripping on a twisting tree root which sends him catapulting into the mire. He sinks beneath the tepid water like a stone, the mud pulling at his clothes, dragging him down to the place of nightmares. But just before he is lost forever, Edward reaches out and grabs a handful of reeds, hauling himself from the mire's grip, forcing his head above the surface, his lungs gasping for oxygen.

He shakes from the cold and his fingers and toes and arms and legs grow numb. But he forces himself to stay submerged, emerging for breath whenever his lungs begin to burn. When he surfaces, he smells the flaming torches, hears the men's voices, the dogs' growls. He waits in cold dread to be found.

In fact, he wants to be found. His muscles ache, and he is so very cold and tired. He feels as though he has felt this way for a lifetime. When was the last time he felt warmth? Felt peace? Felt joy? He cannot remember. His life before the Elf now seems a haze, a blur, a distant memory. Why don't these men pull him from this foul place where he is buried? He needs to be rescued. Why can't they see that? But they find him not. And after what seems to Edward hours, the lanterns disappear, the men's voices fade, the dogs quiet. And soon the Shade is dark once more.

Edward, however, still doesn't emerge. Not for a long time. And when he finally does haul his aching, half-froze carcass from the mire, he lies gasping on the forest floor, wondering how he will ever find his satchel.

A lone scrywolf scavenging in the Shade for prey, wanders past and gives him nothing more than a cursory sniff.

Anastasia paces the floor of the Sheriff's office. Her anxiety has increased ten-fold upon finding him absent. And each hour that passes since her arrival feels an eternity. Where can the Sheriff be? She grabs for her cloak, wrapping it about her shoulders, determined to seek him out. Regardless of her promise to avoid the night.

But before she can reach the door, it opens and the Sheriff stands before her. His breeches, shirt, boots are all stained with mud. There are scratches on his face, a broken twig in his hair. He holds a leather satchel in one hand and there is dirt under his fingernails.

"I have something to confess," she says, before he can speak.

He sets the leather bag down on the table and slips out of his coat, hanging it on the peg by the fire.

"Of course, but first this," he says, withdrawing a silver flask from his coat pocket and unscrewing the cap to take a long swallow. Then he holds it out to her, raises his eyebrow.

Anastasia takes it from his hand and holds it to her nose. The strong smell of brandywine overwhelms her senses and she gags. But she feels scattered, and so she takes a long swallow, coughing, allowing the alcohol to bring her back into focus.

The Sheriff sinks into his chair and removes his boots as Anastasia sets the flask on his desk.

"Better?" he asks.

She wipes her mouth and nods.

"Now what has brought you out at this hour?" he asks, glancing at the clock that stands on his desk.

Anastasia covers her mouth with both hands and paces the room. She has been wanting this moment for hours and now she feels paralyzed, unable to speak.

He rises from his chair and crosses the room to stand before her.

"Take your time," he says rubbing her arm.

She rocks back and forth on her feet for a moment, then drops her hands, "I've done a terrible thing," she says at last. She waits for him to speak, but he remains quiet, his face hidden in the shadows.

"T'is the shoes," she says at last, "Edward does not make them."

She watches his shoulders relax as though he was worried her admission was to be far worse.

"There's no law against selling something one doesn't make," he says and she can hear his smile.

"There is if magic's involved," Anastasia says, the words tumbling out. She presses her cold hands against her hot cheeks, trying to cool them, grateful the secret is no longer inside, polluting her. He steps forward and she turns her head away. She cannot bear to have him look upon her.

"Anastasia, look at me."

She shakes her head. What must he think of her now?

His fingers find her chin, twisting her head towards him and so she shuts her eyes. She feels his touch on her scars and she tries to push away his hand. But he grabs hold of her fingers.

"Look at me," he says.

And so she does.

His face looks no different than before. She sees no hate or loathing or rage there. His eyes are still kind, although the smile upon seeing her has drifted into something else.

"The leather satchel," he says, releasing her to point at

his desk, "do you recognize it?"

Anastasia thinks it an odd question given the admission she has just made. However, she looks over and studies its contours. It is familiar. She has seen it on many an occasion.

"T'is Edward's," she says, and then turns back to the Sheriff, "why do you have it?"

Edward stumbles into the shop and slams the door behind him, turning the key in the lock. He runs upstairs, stripping away his mud soaked clothes with numb fingers, winding them up into a ball, tossing them on the bed. He dunks his head into the basin of water that sits on the washstand and scrubs. When most of the mud is gone he stands, shaking the water from his head, soaping his hands. He sprinkles Anastasia's lavender oil over his skin then pats himself dry with a soiled shirt. He tosses the dirty water out the window, ensures no trace of grime remains.

He crosses to the wardrobe, grabbing for a clean shirt, his velvet smoking jacket, pressed trousers, new shoes. He dresses with great haste, then heads downstairs to the shop. The lock on the back room is still secure. He presses his ear against the door, but cannot hear anything from within. Anastasia must have fallen asleep. He steps outside the shop, locking the door behind him and pries loose a cobblestone from the road.

He picks it up and hurls it through the front window, smashing the glass.

He stops to think, his mind reeling, trying to recall if

there is anything else. His clothes. He curses, unlocks the door with hurried fingers and runs back to his bedroom, retrieving the soiled garments. He feels unhinged by the loss of his satchel. He had begun to make his way back to Margarite's, but as he slipped within five hundred yards, he could see the Sheriff had posted men and dogs to guard the cottage.

And then to his great horror. The Sheriff appeared with his (how dare he!), leather satchel in hand.

And so Edward was forced to creep away, leaving his gold in the hands of that beast. No matter, he will claim it on the morrow. It will be no great feat to tell the Sheriff the shop was burgled in the night and his bag was stolen. Poor Betsy must have come across the thief. The Sheriff will have no proof he was involved, for he will have an unbreakable witness.

He steps out of the shop and scurries up the alleyway to the Shade. His heart beats as though it were a runaway horse and he stops to calm his breathing. Everything will be well. He will deny any knowledge of these events. The Princess will provide him an alibi. He wipes the sweat from his brow, crouches down and jams his soiled clothes into a hollow log.

Anastasia.

Goddess Blood. What if she is found locked in the room? Damnation. He should have simply had the Elf use her for leather. That would have taken care of both his problems. He curses again, aggrieved by his own stupidity.

Anastasia rises from the Sheriff's chair as he enters the jail, a look of expectation upon her face.

The Sheriff shakes his head, "no sign of him. Though the front window has been broken once more."

"What about the room at the back of the shop?" Anastasia asks.

"Nay," he says yawning, "we broke down the door, but t'was empty. I've posted men there. They'll keep watch, arrest him when he returns."

Anastasia nods, but wonders about Henry. Hopes he kept some magic to free himself. She looks up to see the Sheriff watching her, "I should go. Find a place to stay."

"You are welcome here," he states, indicating the floor above. "I have a room upstairs."

"What about you?" she asks.

"I'll take the cot," he says, motioning to the empty jail cell.

"I do not want to dislodge you" Anastasia says.

"Not at all," he grabs the lantern she lit on the desk, says "follow me," and leads her up a narrow staircase to the second floor.

Through the doorway is a small room with a low ceiling. It contains a single bed, a clothes cupboard, a small table with a chair. There is a small fireplace. A stack of newspapers, another of books and a wash basin.

"I'll leave you to it," he says, placing the lantern on the table and nodding at her. Then he steps out of the room and closes the door behind him.

Anastasia sits down on the edge of the bed. His pajamas are folded on his pillow. She picks them up and holds them to her nose. They smell of him. She returns them to their pillow, then crosses the room to the washstand. Her face looks gaunt, pale in the mirror. Her hair is tangled, escaping its braid. She unties the binding and combs her fingers through the long tresses. Then she washes her hands and face, drying them with the small towel that hangs over the back of a chair.

Anastasia unhooks her skirt, unbuttons her blouse and removes both. Then her shoes, bloomers, stockings. She can sleep in her petticoat.

She folds her clothes and sets them on the the the chair. On the table in front, there is a small wooden bowl. It holds a key, a needle and thread, an acorn and a pink ribbon. With one singed end.

All color drains from Anastasia's face as she reaches out with trembling fingers for the ribbon.

For she has seen it before.

Edward paces the length of the hall as he consults his pocket watch. He has been kept waiting for half an hour. Every time a footman enters the corridor, he expects to see the Sheriff and his men. His stomach is in knots. He must speak to the Princess. And speak to her now. He restores the watch to his pocket and returns to the closed door, beyond which is Ambrosia's chamber.

He bangs his fist against the hard wood door once more. But still there is no answer.

Edward resumes his pacing. His story is solid. He has spent the night at the Palace. Surely, with all he has done for the Princess, she will grant him that small favor.

Edward is at the far end of the hall when the door to the Princess's room finally opens. He hurries forward only to see it is not his lover, but Nanny who steps out, closing the door behind her.

"Well?" he demands, "did you tell her I need to speak with her?"

Nanny holds out a pair of shoes.

"What are these?" she asks.

"What do they bloody look like?" he asks.

"Are they yours?"

"Of course they're mine," he snarls, "now let me pass."

"Then pray," Nanny says, in a voice colder than the glaciers on Utterly Peak, "tell me why they were purchased from a merchant in Gnomadic Cross."

Christos.

Edward's stomach hardens into a knot.

Christos, Christos, Christos.

"Listen," Edward says, "there has been a mistake."

"Show him out," Nanny says, and Edward turns to see Mr. Tittletattle has entered the room and stands silently behind him. "He is no longer welcome in this house."

"Please," Edward says, but Mr. Tittletattle places an iron grip around Edward's neck and drags him away from the Princess's door.

"T'is not my fault, I beg you!" Edward screams, trying to grab hold of a table so as to slow his departure.

"Wait," says a voice. And Edward recognizes it as belonging to Ambrosia. Mr. Tittletattle releases his hold on Edward and he drops to his knees on the thin carpet that stretches the entire length of the room.

The Princess steps towards him dressed in a gown made of animal bones and egg shells.

"Explain," she says.

"T'is Anastasia," Edward gasps. "she wanted more

gold. So she pressured me to make more shoes. I tried to tell her I worked only for you but she wouldn't listen."

"Nonsense," Nanny snaps.

"Silence," the Princess says, her eyes flashing and Nanny presses her lips together in a disapproving scowl. Ambrosia steps before him and lifts his chin in her hand.

"Nanny tells me you need my help, shoe man."

Edward nods.

"Why?"

"Anastasia told the Sheriff I'm responsible for killing those women. She wants to get rid of me and keep the gold so she's telling him lies."

"And did you kill them?"

"No!" Edward cries, "I don't know anything about it."

Ambrosia is silent for a long time, stroking his cheek with her thumb.

"You want me to mend these troubles?" she asks.

"Yes," he says, and when she drops her hold on his face, he prostrates himself on the floor before her, kissing her feet, kissing her shoes.

"You've been a very bad, bad shoe man," Ambrosia says, placing a foot on the back of his neck and pressing his head against the floor.

"Yes, yes," Edward agrees, feeling his penis throb, "very bad."

Anastasia removes her foot releasing him.

"Get up," she orders.

Edward scrambles to his feet stripping away his shirt, boots, socks, trousers. In seconds he's undressed, his penis hard and ready. And for the first time, he doesn't care that both Nanny and Mr. Tittletattle are in the room.

"Nanny," Ambrosia says, staring Edward directly in

the eyes. "Punish him."

Edward's mouth falls open.

"My pleasure, dear," Nanny says, unfastening her dress.

Edward wants to protest, to deny. But one look in Ambrosia's eyes tells him this is the path to forgiveness. And so he silences his tongue.

Both now and when Nanny takes hold of him.

Anastasia steps downstairs to the Sheriff's office. She stands in the doorway and watches him sit on the edge of the cot and drink from his flask. Then she enters the room and pads over to the cell.

He stands when he catches sight of her and she stops. Frozen in place.

"What is it?" he asks.

But she cannot speak.

"Anastasia?" he asks, exiting the cell and walking over to her, "are you ill?"

She can smell the brandywine on his breath as she holds up the ribbon.

His eyes catch sight of it and a very loud silence settles between them.

Finally, he raises his eyes to hers.

"T'is mine," she says.

"Yes."

"You are the boy from down the street. The one I would buy Papa's newspapers from."

"Yes," he repeats.

"You were there that night," she says, placing a hand on

her scarred cheek, "you put out the flames."

He drops his head and nods.

"Why did you never say anything?" she asks.

"I wanted to," he says, "but each time I saw you, words failed me. I am a coward."

"No," she breathes, scrunching the ribbon tight in her hand, "not a coward."

"A liar?" he asks, meeting her eyes.

"Nay," she says, shaking her head.

"Then what?" he asks.

"My savior," Anastasia says.

And then his mouth is pressed against hers. And his hands. Those large, strong, warm, glorious hands. Anastasia shivers and it is not because she is cold.

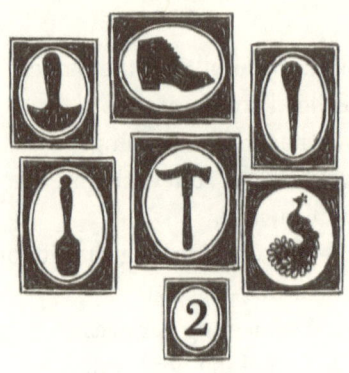

CHAPTER
TWO

Wherein fate and fortune
become strange bedfellows.

A nastasia does not remember arriving in the Sheriff's bedroom. One moment she was downstairs. Now she is not. From the time his mouth met hers, her former life ceased to exist and an entirely new one unfolded before her. Now they are here, collapsed in a tangle of limbs on his narrow bed. He lies beneath her, while she sprawls across his chest and thighs, her hair falling over his face, the strands damp from when they interfered with a kiss. She feels awkward. Her fingers, both stiff and clumsy against his shoulders, as though they were attached to someone else's hands. She tries to keep her face turned to the right. Not so that he does not have to witness her scars at so close a vantage. Rather, so that her vulnerability may not be read.

But he takes her chin in his hand and turns her face so

she looks upon him directly.

His eyes are dark and watchful. His cheeks flushed. His breath deep.

"Anastasia," he says, tucking longs strands of hair behind one of her ears, "you are very quiet."

"I have not done this before," she says, "and I do not wish to disappoint."

"Not with your husband?" he asks, although there is no look of surprise upon his face.

Anastasia shakes her head, covering her scarred cheek with her hand, "he did not want my imperfection."

"Then more the fool is he," says the Sheriff, "for I wish you to know you are seen."

"Then you must help me," Anastasia says, "for I know not what to do with my hands." Or legs. Or anything else for that matter.

"You may do whatever you wish," he says.

And so she touches him. First his face. Exploring the wrinkles at his eyes, rubbing her palms over the rough of his chin and cheeks. Combing her fingers through his hair. Finding a small dry leaf entreasured there. Next burrowing her hands under the fabric of his tunic and seeking out the scars on his back. Feeling each and every bump and ridge. Wondering who dealt them. Giving thanks they did not end his life. Her breath quickens as though she has been on the run. She feels constrained in her petticoat. And each touch of its fabric against her flesh sets her skin further afire.

She presses her mouth against the roughness of his neck and bites, sucking on his skin, tasting him. His hand clasps the nape of her neck, pinning her there and her fingers dig into his back, her knees grabbing hold of his thighs. It is as though she is drowning and he is the thing that will keep her afloat.

Anastasia wants him to take hold of her. So she shakes off his touch on her neck, taking his hands in hers and placing them on her calves. His fingers are rough and callused and his touch along her skin sends shivers along her spine. His hands move higher, pushing aside her petticoat to find her thighs, spreading her wide, so that she can press against the hardness of the flesh beneath his trousers. And then his fingers are touching her soft folds and she grabs hold of his arms so that she does not splinter into pieces.

As his fingers stroke her flesh, her hips move in counterpoint to his touch. But she wants more. She grabs hold of his shoulders, lifting herself to give him room to use both hands.

She feels the rush of approaching pleasure and cannot stop the moan that escapes her lips. She stares deep into his eyes, their breath in perfect time, as his fingers slip against her. She is wet and ready, wanting their flesh combined.

Wanting the ache tended to.

Wanting.

"Release me," he breathes.

And so she does.

Edward stumbles along the road towards Houndstooth, his body bruised and tender. But a huge burden has been lifted from his shoulders. If the damned Sheriff tries to pin these murders on him now, the Princess will have him executed. He walks quickly past Margarite's, checking for his black satchel even though he knows it is not there. The area is quiet, the mud outside the garden gate, disturbed and he can see the broken bramble branches from where he crawled away into the dark. He squares his shoulders as he approaches the main street. Before he meets with the Sheriff, he has one last item to attend to: Anastasia.

"Edward?"

He turns to see Stella standing in the door of her home, her shawl draped over her shoulders. Her long grey hair is gathered back in a knot and her bright green eyes watch him with concern.

"Are you well?" she asks.

"Of course," he states. "Why?"

"Your shop was broken into again. With the Sheriff and his men there all morning, I thought perhaps you had been harmed."

Damnation, Edward thinks. The Sheriff was already waiting for him. He had hoped to have enough time to get rid of Anastasia before the man arrived. That bloody Nanny. If she hadn't been so exquisitely thorough with her punishment, he would have been home much earlier. He has to assume the Sheriff has discovered Anastasia. No matter. He can convince the man that she is mad, what with her ravings of magic. And therefore, he had no choice but to confine her.

"I am quite alright," he says, "I was away last night on business."

"You look tired," she continues, "would you like to come in for a cup of tea?"

Tired. Yes, *I am very tired,* Edward thinks. He is unsure of the time, but he is certain he has been awake for more than a day. And the last thing he wants to deal with at the moment (considering the Princess has not yet had an opportunity to speak with the man), is the Sheriff's cross-examination.

"Yes," he says, smiling at Stella, "I would like that very much."

He follows her into the shop, then closes and locks the door behind them. Inside it smells of cedar, incense, exotic lands.

"I'll put the kettle on," she says, but Edward places his hand on her arm, stopping her. It has been awhile since he and Stella had last been in bed. He supposes the first time was those many months ago (or at least, it felt like months), when he first approached her about fixing the house and shop. Without her husband, she was lonely. And Edward was happy to oblige. Stella had a soft touch, an ample bosom, rosy cheeks. Being with her wasn't like making love to the Princess, who had so many corners it was like being in bed with a scarecrow. He appreciated the way Stella would undulate and roll under him. She moved slowly and … lovingly.

Moreover, she was more than willing to keep their dalliance a secret.

Edward slides his fingers down her arm and takes her hand in his own.

She smiles and leads him through thick velvet curtains and into the store room. In the corner is a pile of floor mats, imported from Turkistan. The room smells of pine and feels as warm and secure as a cave.

They strip away their clothes and he stills as he hears her gasp.

"Oh, Edward."

He looks down at himself, sees the welts that cover his chest and thighs.

"T'is nothing," he says.

"Nay," she says, running her fingertips over them, "someone has done you a great wrong." She presses her lips against a bruise but he pushes her away.

"Don't."

She stumbles against the wall, her eyes uncertain.

"I am sorry," he says, covering the bruises with his hands, "I could not stop them."

"Nay," she says, stepping forward once again and drawing him down to the mats, "do not feel ashamed."

She lies before him and he covers her flesh with his own, entering her, closing his eyes. He can hear her calling his name as he moves, but the mire claims him and he is sinking once more beneath the mud and cold water, drowning in foulness. The stench of rot fills his nose and mouth and he gags. Now he can hear bleating, and he thinks of Sophia. And now mooing, and he is enraged that Betsy wants to expose him to the Sheriff. He has done nothing to her but love her and she has betrayed him.

His head aches terribly and his bones are exhausted. He is almost too tired to move. If Betsy would just remain still beneath him, if she would only be quiet, everything would be fine. But she continues to bleat and so he covers her mouth with his hand. He wonders when he became this tired. It seems as if he has always been so. But surely there was a time (when he was a child for example), when his soul did not feel old and brittle. He has done nothing but good for these women, this village, the Kingdom and yet his deeds are never acknowledged.

He grunts loudly, jerking and finishes, collapsing onto Betsy (why on earth would he choose her to bed?), their flesh sticking together. He is utterly spent. For the longest time, he remains as still as she.

Finally he opens his eyes and rolls away from Stella. Feeling very confused. Wasn't he with Betsy? Regardless, he removes his hand from her mouth and mutters an apology. But Stella doesn't hear him.

Her eyes are wide open, staring into oblivion.

"Stella?" He pokes her but she still doesn't move.

"Stella?" He holds his hand above her mouth but no breath emerges.

Edward sits back against the wall and considers his predicament. No one knows he is here. And he still needs leather for the Elf.

He stands, searching the shelves of the stockroom until he finds a copper blade. The metal is sharp, draws blood when he tests it with his thumb.

Then he rolls Stella over onto her front and starts slicing.

Anastasia lies in the Sheriff's bed, curled in a nest of quilts. She has been awake most of the night. When the Sheriff would fall asleep, she would lie awake and study the hard planes of his face by the light of the candle. She has touched every inch of him now. The hard calluses on his fingers, the grey hairs that mixed with the brown on his brow, the scars on his back from his time in the trenches.

She heard him depart almost an hour ago. He whispered goodbye in her ear, kissed her brow, and bade her sleep. She was hoping that he was on his way to arrest Edward. She didn't know why her husband started attacking women. Perhaps being so close to magic had turned him mad.

Anastasia rises. There is fresh water in both the pitcher and basin. She washes her face and hands. Sniffs her shoulder. Can smell the Sheriff there.

She hangs the damp towel on the back of the chair and dresses. Her fingers fumble with each hook and stay, tie and ribbon. Her body feels tender, sore, happy. But it also feels changed. As though it has assumed another shape, one she is unused to occupying.

She ties her hair back with the pink ribbon and steps downstairs. There is hot coffee on the stove and a cranbuckle scone from Betsy's shop, on a plate.

She smiles and sits down to eat. But a knock on the door interrupts all but her first sip of hot coffee.

Anastasia rises and opens the door.

A rather short squat woman with hair like steel wool stands before her.

She squints up at Anastasia, as though studying her face.

"Hello," Anastasia says, "I am afraid the Sheriff is away at the moment."

"The Sheriff?" the woman asks, "Oh no, t'is you I've come to see."

"Me?" Anastasia asks.

"Yes. The Sheriff urgently requires your presence at the Palace."

"Is everything all right?" Anastasia asks, grabbing her cloak.

"T'is best you ask him," the woman states.

"Yes, of course," Anastasia says, closing the door and following the woman up the street.

Edward freezes, his hand poised over Stella's chest. He has heard a noise. At least he thinks he has. He is uncertain. And his mind, troubled by the proceedings of last night, seems an unreliable friend. After all, he remembers locking Stella's door himself, so there is no way an intruder could have entered. But still he waits, holding his breath. All is quiet. Unnaturally so. But such silence is a necessary requirement for unnatural acts. Edward counts the seconds. The minutes. And still he waits. He has already skinned the flesh from Stella's back and thighs. There is very little left to harvest.

After what must be ten minutes, Edward laughs and uses his forearm to wipe the sweat from his upper lip. His mind is playing tricks on him. And his nerves are in a heightened state of anxiety, causing his fingers to stiffen, resulting in jagged and uncontrolled cuts. And he is covered in Stella's blood.

This will be his last kill and then he will be free. Free of Anastasia, the Princess, the bloody Elf. Free of shoes, Houndstooth, the porridge-faced Nanny. The damnable Sheriff. Even if he cannot retrieve his gold, he will have enough from Sunday's exchange to last him a lifetime. The velvet curtain behind him twitches, but he laughs and ignores it. He will no longer trust his mind to guide him to the truth. At least, not until he has shaken this pitiable town from his feet.

He laughs again and feels a resurgence of energy and renews cutting with vigor. When he's finished, he delicately folds the skin and places each piece in one of Stella's baskets from the store. Then he sits back on his haunches and surveys Stella's remains.

T'is a pity, he thinks, *she was quite lovely.*

The curtain shifts again and this time he glances over his shoulder to reassure himself.

But there is someone there.

Three someones.

The Sheriff and two men.

Each has a pistol.

All are pointing at him.

Edward looks at Stella, at the knife, at his bloody hands.

"T'is not what you think," he says, but the Sheriff brings his pistol down on top of Edward's skull.

Pain explodes in his brain and he sinks into blissful blackness.

Anastasia follows Nanny through the maze of Palace rooms and into an inner chamber. There she finds Ambrosia standing naked on a chair before a roaring fire. A young woman, with a measuring tape draped around her neck, stands before Ambrosia her hands between the Princess's legs.

"Get out," Ambrosia orders, kicking the girl away upon seeing Anastasia and Nanny enter the room. The girl scrambles to fetch her pin cushion and scissors and runs from the room.

Ambrosia steps down from the chair, grabbing a length of tulle from the floor and winding it about her body. Then she delivers a wide smile to Anastasia, "Anastasia, how are you?"

"I am well," Anastasia says, her eyes glancing away from the sheerness of the Princess's wrap. "I am here to see the Sheriff."

"Come sit," Ambrosia says, taking Anastasia by the hand and leading her over to a small table with two spindly chairs. She claps her hands, "Nanny, some tea."

"That is not necessary," Anastasia intercedes, "the Sheriff."

"Can wait until we have tea," Ambrosia states, glancing at Nanny. The short squat woman nods her head and exits.

"Now be seated," Ambrosia says, pulling out a chair and motioning for Anastasia to sit. Anastasia does as requested. But Ambrosia does not immediately join her. Instead she lingers, her fingers sliding along Anastasia's smooth cheek, her throat, her collar bone, dropping to skim the skin just beneath her bodice.

"So pretty," Ambrosia murmurs.

Anastasia grips her fingers together, forcing herself not to pull away. They remain as such for another minute until finally Ambrosia removes her hand and joins Anastasia across the table.

"We must become better friends," the Princess says, "after all, this is a village of paupers and peasants." She leans across the table and squeezes Anastasia's hand, "Not you, of course."

Anastasia pulls her hand away, wishing the old woman would hurry and bring the tea. Ambrosia leans back in her chair, lifts a foot and studies her shoe.

"Your husband really is the most amazing craftsman." She points her foot at Anastasia, "Do you not agree?"

"Yes, Princess. Ambrosia."

The door then opens and the old woman enters carrying a silver tray, teapot, cream, sugar, and porcelain cups.

"Excellent, Nanny. Thank you," Ambrosia says,

clapping her hands, "I'll pour."

Nanny sets the tray before Ambrosia and the Princess pours out the steaming golden liquid.

"Milk?" Ambrosia asks Anastasia, pointing to the creamer.

"No thank you," Anastasia says.

"Sugar?"

"Nay."

Ambrosia sets a cup before Anastasia then lifts her own and takes a long swallow.

Anastasia ignores the tea, looking expectantly at the Princess.

"My dear, this tea is from my father's fields. You really must try it."

Anastasia lifts the delicate cup and takes a swallow. There are hints of mint, jasmine, pepper. The Princess is correct. It is quite delicious.

"Excellent," Ambrosia says, setting down her cup.

"The Sheriff," Anastasia says, and Ambrosia looks up at her.

"What about him?" The Princess asks.

"He sent for me," Anastasia states. When neither woman responds, she feels a cold chill run down her spine. "Did he not?" she asks. A sweat now breaks across her forehead and she feels dizzy. Her stomach hardens as though she has swallowed stones. Anastasia tries to rise, but her limbs feel quite useless. Unresponsive. A burning sensation settles in her blood.

Spittle forms at the corners of her mouth and she suddenly seems incapable of swallowing.

"Something amiss?" Ambrosia asks.

Anastasia tries to speak but the words catch in her

throat like hooks in a fish. She gasps, fighting for breath.

Ambrosia rises and walks around the table towards her.

Anastasia wants to flee but she cannot. Nor can she remain upright. She jerks back, sliding from the chair, tumbling to the floor, her muscles convulsing.

Help, she thinks. *Help!*

But Ambrosia does not seek help. Nor does Nanny.

Instead Ambrosia sinks to the floor beside her, drawing Anastasia's head into her lap.

"That will be the poison," Ambrosia informs her, "from the Draginilis."

Anastasia jerks on the floor, her body flopping like a dying fish. Draginilis. Anastasia knows that name. A fatal poison.

"I've heard it makes your insides feel like they are on fire," Ambrosia states, slipping a hand beneath Anastasia's bodice to stroke one of her breasts.

Anastasia gurgles, trying to draw breath into her lungs, but her throat is tight and her stomach, throat, and mouth are burning. Her legs thrash, the fire has reached her skin, her bladder gives way.

Where is Papa?

She is burning.

Why does he not come and tend the flames?

She cannot move.

She cannot breathe.

Papa!

She sees him standing in the doorway but he does not come to her.

Papa!

There is a sad expression on his face. She sees his lips moving, but cannot hear him.

She wants to scream but the fire has lodged in her throat.

"T'is Edward's fault," Ambrosia explains, licking the sweat from Anastasia's brow. "I told him I do not share."

Anastasia tries to break free of Ambrosia's grasp, but the Princess wraps her legs about Anastasia's torso.

Papa!

The fire has fully engulfed her now. Her hair, hands, hips. All aflame.

And then Anastasia no longer convulses. No longer fights. No longer has thoughts. Or feelings. Or emotions.

There is simply one last wheeze.

And the pain disappears along with her soul.

It takes the Princess less time to kill Anastasia than it does to put her shoes on each morning.

CHAPTER
THREE

Wherein rosemary is chosen
for remembrance.

The Sheriff detests the Palace, its long maze of corridors, its slippery occupants, the Princess herself. He stops before the portrait of the King. The man for whom he went to war in the Asiantine. It is hard to believe only six months ago, the man died in his sleep, cut down by assassins who breached the walls of Ferrybone Castle. At the time, there were rumors the Princess may have had her hand in her father's early demise, but the people that spoke those mutterings disappeared and silence soon filled that space.

The Princess strides down the corridor, dressed in a gown made of feathers and what appear to be teeth. She smells of rose water. And there is a wide smile upon her lips. An obese woman trails behind her. The Sheriff doesn't think he has ever seen the Princess genuinely happy before. It completely changes the context of her face; she almost looks beautiful.

"I hear you have caught my murderer," she pronounces, stopping before him.

The Sheriff bows low, "Indeed I have, your Highness. With the knife firm in his hand and his victim's blood upon his fingers."

"Nanny," the Princess says, clapping her hands and the obese woman at her footsteps waddles forth and hands the Sheriff a drawstring bag.

"Ten gold coins for fine work. I trust you will remind my villagers that taxes are due at once."

The Sheriff bows once more.

"Now who is my culprit?" she demands.

"A shoemaker by the name of Edward Cordwainer, your Highness."

The smile disappears from the Princess's face, "I beg your pardon?" she asks. "T'is not possible."

"With much grace, your Highness, I must disagree. I made it known amongst the villagers that he was of interest and when neighbors of the latest victim saw the two enter her home, they fetched me at once. I found him there with the murdered woman."

"And why would this shoe man be killing these women?" she asks, and the Sheriff notes her voice has risen an octave.

"I believe he was sleeping with these women, your Highness. When he was finished with the affair, he would dispose of each."

"I see," she states, and now her voice is as raw as rusted steel. And the smile is completely gone from her face, making the sharp angles and edges of her cheekbones, nose and chin make her appear more malevolent.

"Shall I send for the Executioner?" he asks.

"Nay," she snaps, "It will give me great pleasure to do that myself."

The Sheriff taps his heels together and bows.

"Good day," he says, and strides down the long length of the hall, eager to be rid of this foul place.

The Princess waits until the Sheriff has exited. Then she turns to Nanny.

"Take me to the dungeons."

The Sheriff walks the path back to Houndstooth. Ahead of him, a hunched thin man in a stove pipe hat approaches. As they pass one another, the Sheriff tips his hat but the other man simply brushes by, wiping his hands on his trousers, as though unaware of the Sheriff's presence.

The Sheriff quickens his pace. Anastasia will be waiting for him. He consults his pocket watch. Almost noon. He will cook her lunch and then they can spend the day together. He doesn't want to rush her but he is desperate they leave this town. Find somewhere new. Start afresh. A feeling of warmth settles over him as he recalls last night. The feel of Anastasia's body locked against his. The touch of her skin, her hair. The taste of her breath. The sound of her cries.

A flock of hawks catches his eye over to his right. Nay, not hawks. Vultures. They circle the air before dropping down to the open field that lies beyond the jail.

The Sheriff stops on the path and watches. The vultures remain circling their prize. It could be a dead animal, perhaps the remains of scrywolf prey. But somehow the Sheriff doubts that conclusion.

He changes direction, heading off the path and out into the field. There, a hundred feet beyond lies a figure in a black cloak. Blood staining the ground. A vulture perches, pecking a hand.

The Sheriff takes a deep breath and approaches. Wondering which of the women was discarded by Edward in such an obscene manner.

As he nears, he sees what he mistook for blood is actually hair.

The Sheriff runs.

Recognizes the ribbon that ties the copper tresses.

Christos, no.

He sinks to his knees.

No.

Edward sits in his dungeon cell, his back pressed against the stone wall, his feet flat on the dirt floor. His left foot is chained to the wall, keeping him on a short leash. What in damnation is keeping the Princess? He's been imprisoned here for hours.

He has already decided what he will say. To the Sheriff. To the Princess. To anyone that asks. He heard screams and ran into the shop. Which is when he saw the knife and he just happened to pick it up when the Sheriff and his men broke in. Doesn't matter that he was naked and covered in blood. He'll think of something. He can make any lie convincing. But it won't matter anyway. He'll have the Princess intercede on his behalf. Yes, she'll do that.

And then he will claim his gold from that filthy Sheriff.

Yes, everything will be alright and he will be home come nightfall.

He hears voices and jumps to his feet. He would recognize the cool tones of his lover's voice anywhere. He smooths his hair, shakes out the wool breeches tossed to him by the prison guard upon arrival.

"Ambrosia my love," he calls, "I'm here."

The key rasps in the lock and with a gigantic moan the steel door moves inward.

And there is his lovely Princess. He ignores Nanny with her flat nose and piggy eyes and ridiculous mole with its three wiry hairs.

"You have killed eight women," the Princess hisses.

"I swear to you Ambrosia—"

"Your Highness," she spits.

"Your Highness," he amends, holding out his hands to her, wondering why she is so cold. "T'is not what you think. The Sheriff wants my wife. Will do anything to get her. So he speaks lies."

"I am not stupid," Ambrosia snarls, "I know you have a hand in this mischief."

"I beg you," Edward says, prostrating himself on his knees, "I am innocent." He hides his face in his hands as though he means to cry. But instead he parts his fingers just slightly so he can watch her.

Ambrosia paces the cell, back and forth, back and forth. Until finally she stops before him.

"Nay, you are a liar."

"Please, Ambrosia," he begs, grabbing her delicate ankles with his dirty fingers.

"You are weak, Edward, weak and pathetic. And you betrayed me. Do you know what I do to traitors?"

Edward presses his mouth to her shoe, kissing over and over, wetting the fine leather with his saliva. Digging his fingers into her ankle.

"Mercy, Princess, mercy."

Ambrosia stares down at him with cold eyes and kicks her foot free of his grasp.

"I should have you executed," she says, and a strange keening sound erupts from Edward's throat.

"Silence!" she snaps, and he bites down on his tongue, hoping the pain will distract him from his fear.

"Get up," she orders.

Edward scrambles to his feet and stands before her, his face covered in snot and tears.

"I'm going to let you live," she says, at long last. There is a disapproving tsk from Nanny, but Edward ignores the old bat.

"Thank you, your Highness," he says, his knees shaking with relief, willing himself not to fall to the floor.

"But you will stay here until I can be certain of your loyalty." And she steps back over to the door and calls for the Jailer.

"Wait," Edward cries, his heart thumping madly in his chest, "I do not understand."

"Perhaps the Sheriff is a liar," Ambrosia states, "but perhaps he is not. And the only way to make certain you belong to me is to keep you here."

Edward gapes at her, his jaw flapping, unable to talk.

"I will have Nanny fetch your tools and leather. I know

the light isn't all one hopes for in this cell, but you will continue to make your shoes here."

"Ambrosia."

"Good night, Edward. Sleep well," she says, stepping free of the cell, Nanny trailing behind her.

"Ambrosia!" he screams, yanking on the chain as the Jailer seals him in once more.

He is still screaming long after her footsteps have died away.

The Sheriff sits on a chair next to Anastasia's bed.

He wrapped her in his cloak and carried her back to Houndstooth. Stepping along the cobbled streets, ignoring the stares of the villagers. He knew the shoe shop would be open and so he brought her here. Carrying her upstairs to her bedroom. Fetching a basin of water and a cloth and cleaning the dirt and sick from her skin. And even though she would not rise again, he rubbed soothing cream into the burns that covered her lips and the corners of her mouth. Then he brushed her hair and tied it back with the pink ribbon.

Now that she is tended, he closes the curtains and joins Anastasia on the bed. Holding her in his lap, cradling what is now just bones and flesh.

He kisses her lips one last time, taking his time, hoping to feel breath.

But there is nothing.

He removes the pistol from his coat pocket and taking a deep breath positions the muzzle beneath his chin.

"Goddess, forgive me," he says.

There is a cough behind him and he whirls. Nothing. But something is here. In the room with them.Something dark and nasty. He lays Anastasia back on the bed, and gets to his feet.

The room is small. There are not many places to hide.

Something shuffles behind him and he spins, pointing with the pistol.

"Show yourself," he demands.

From the shadows, steps a creature, child-size in stature, but definitely no youth. It has a bony chin and forehead. A wispy beard.Long clever fingers. It wears a yellow shirt with blackbird buttons. And his eyes are large, focused on Anastasia's body.

"Fie, you foul fiend," the creature growls, spit flying, "I will tear you to shreds with my teeth."

But the Sheriff's hand holds fast to his pistol and he does not waver.

"Be still, creature. I have not caused this horror," he says, resting his hand on Anastasia's forehead. Then he lowers his pistol to look down upon her, "and truth be told, I know not who defouled her in such a manner. I would tear them to pieces myself if I did."

The creature pads over to Anastasia and smells her mouth, "t'is wickedness here. Dragonilis. A most horrendous method of death usually reserved for dispatching Kings."

The Sheriff studies the creature.

"Who are you?" he asks.

"One not worthy to call her friend," the creature says, patting Anastasia's hair with his fingers, "for I could not protect her from this torment."

"Nor I," says the Sheriff.

There is a long moment of silence between the two.

"You mean to join her?" the creature asks at last.

The Sheriff nods.

"She would not want such a fate for you," the creature says.

"That may be true" the Sheriff says, "but if she cannot join me in this life, I will join her in the next."

"There may be a solution," the creature says, and the Sheriff turns his gaze from Anastasia to the creature.

"Speak," he orders.

The creature wrings his hands, looking about the room as though worried they could be overhead.

"It involves magic," he breathes.

"Do it," the Sheriff says, without pause.

"You understand all magic has a price? If it can't be paid in money, it must be extracted by other means."

The Sheriff thinks for a moment, and names the price.

"Agreed," the creature says, and holds out his hand. The Sheriff grips the dry tight skin and they shake.

"Now," the creature says, drawing away to stand once more over Anastasia, "close your eyes and whatever you hear or smell, do not open them until I tell you otherwise."

The Sheriff sets his pistol aside and sits on the bed, taking Anastasia's hand in his own. Then he closes his eyes.

"Now, we begin," says the creature.

And even when the room fills with the most unholiest scream the Sheriff has ever heard, a scream that threatens to split open his skull and rip apart his brain, he still does not open his eyes.

Edward is curled into a ball on the stone floor. He draped some straw over his body for warmth, but still he is cold. And so very, very tired. But he cannot sleep.

"Hello darling, Edward."

Edward glances beside him. A woman sits on the wooden bench, beneath the lantern. She has long blonde hair, large blue eyes, pink cheeks, high pale breasts. She looks as beautiful as that night at the Wolf & Foxtail. All gossamer and gloss, light and shadow, as though she's there and not at all.

"Rosemary," he breathes, sitting and glances towards the door, "does the Jailer know you are here?"

Rosemary laughs, "do not worry about him." She pats the bench beside her, "come, join me."

Edward shakes his head and lifts his left foot, "I cannot. The chain will not permit me."

Rosemary waves her hand as though brushing away a fly, "I think you'll find the chain is quite long enough now."

Edward rises to his feet, and though he feels unsteady, he is able to make the short walk over to the bench. And indeed, Rosemary is quite correct, the chain is no longer as short as it once seemed.

He sits beside her, his senses overwhelmed by her sweet scent.

"What are you doing here?" he asks in wonder.

"I am always here at the end," she says, brushing the hair from his eyes.

As much as it pains him, Edward pulls away from her touch and emits a bark of hoarse laughter. "Well, the wish failed," he snaps, "look at me."

"Oh, Edward," she admonishes, with a kind and loving voice, "the wish has not failed at all. I promise, you are on the cusp of becoming the most famous man in all of the Kingdom."

"How," Edward demands, throwing his arms wide. "What do you think will happen when she realizes I can't make shoes? How long do you think I will last?"

Rosemary turns and takes his face in both her hands. "Darling Edward, I only need you to make one last pair and then this will all be over."

"One last pair?" Edward sniffs.

"One last pair," Rosemary confirms with a smile.

"Without the Elf?"

"On your own."

"And then t'is all done? The killing? The magic? The gold?"

"All done. Can you do that for me, Edward?"

There is a long moment of silence as Edward considers he will have to make the shoes himself. He scrunches his eyes, thinking back to the techniques his father taught him as a boy. Remembering the hog bristle between his fingers as he sewed the leather together.

Finally, he opens his eyes and nods.

"Yes," he says, "I can."

"Good man, Edward," she says.

Edward feels the weight of eight dead women slide from his shoulders. The weight of the gold drop from his fingers. It will be good to be rid of the lies. Of the pretending.Of the Princess. And even the gold. His father's case has become so heavy, it hurts his arms to carry it.

"I am pleased," he says, leaning his head back against the stone wall, "for I have grown quite weary of this whole venture."

"I know," Rosemary says, wrapping an arm around his neck and drawing his head onto her shoulder.

"I've done very well though, haven't I?" Edward asks.

"Very well," Rosemary says, stroking his hair.

Edward is having trouble keeping his eyes open. He feels extremely sleepy.

"How did you find me here?" he asks, glancing down at the swan tattoo on her wrist, thinking he has seen it somewhere before.

"You are very important to me, Edward. As are all my wishers." She places a kiss on his forehead, "Now you must rest as you have a very important day ahead of you."

"Stay," he murmurs, as the lassitude of sleep claims him, "do not leave me alone."

"Of course," she whispers, smoothing her hand over his hair, "I will remain until you wake."

Edward fights to keep his eyes open, but the allure of sleep is too magnetic. But he needs one last glimpse of Rosemary. He peels open his eyes but she no longer resembles Rosemary at all, but rather the Matchmaker.

Who are you? he wonders, but before he can speak the words aloud, he is asleep.

It feels like hours (although the Jailer would most likely say it was mere seconds), before Edward hears a key rasp in the lock of his cell.

Edward shrugs off the last vestiges of sleep, surprised that he feels stronger, more alert than he has felt in months. It's as though the cobwebs have been shaken from his brain.

Nanny enters, a look of grim pleasure upon her lips.

"Well," she states, looking about the cell, "this is where I always told Ambrosia you would land."

Edward smiles at her without malice. He knows that very soon he will be free of both her and her charge.

"You were right to think so," he accedes, rising from the floor and holding out his hands, "now, my tools please. If I am late with her shoes, the Princess will be quite cross."

Anastasia is drowning.

She can think of no other reason why she cannot find her breath.

Her lungs strain for oxygen. She does not want to die. She strikes out with her hands, trying to —

Strong hands grab hold of her.

The Princess.

Anastasia screams, striking out. But she cannot break free of Ambrosia's grip. The Princess means to kill her. She must get away. She must find her Papa.

"Anastasia."

She knows that voice. Her eyes fly open as the man releases her, stepping back. She scrambles away from him and sees that she is no longer at the Palace. This is her bed, her room. She is home. And the man before her.

"Reynard?" she says.

The Sheriff smiles and nods and she reaches out her

hand, grabbing hold of his fingers. And within seconds she is held tight in his arms, her head pressed against his chest, listening to the strong beat of his heart.

"What happened?" she says, touching her mouth, remembering how much it burned.

Reynard sits back from her, brushing the hair away from her face.

"I was dead, was I not?" she asks.

"Yes," he says, his eyes continually drawn to the right side of her face.

She wonders if perhaps the poison ate through her skin and she has been left with fresh damage. She raises her hand to inspect her cheek and freezes.

Her eyes lock with his.

"Hand me the mirror," she whispers, "please."

The Sheriff reaches over to her bureau and selects the small hand mirror that once belonged to her mother. She tips her head to the right, in that old familiar habit, so that her left cheek is on view. That side of her face is as unmarked as it ever has been. Then she takes a deep breath and turns her head, removing her hand from the right side of her face.

A low cry escapes her lips as she stares at her reflection. The skin there is now relatively smooth. Only if one looks close can they see an almost invisible seam along the edges of the new flesh that covers her former scars. And her eyebrow and eyelashes have been restored with delicate thread. Hot tears fill the back of her throat. She lifts her dress, examines the scars on her leg, her arm. They too have been covered with fresh patches of various colored skin.

"I do not understand," she says, looking at him.

"I believe," Reynard says, touching the skin on her face "this was once Sophia. And this," her hip, "Jenny."

"They are a part of me now?" she asks, looking at her face in the mirror. "How is this possible?"

"Your friend. Henry? He —" Reynard shakes his head, "I know not how he accomplished this magic. But whatever it was, it brought you back to me."

"Henry. Where is he?" she asks, looking around.

"He said to tell you it's over. There is no more magic. Not even for the extras."

Anastasia touches the new skin which has been added to her own in such a seamless manner. She is uncertain how she feels about the fact that her friends are now a part of her.

But one thing she does feel certain about.

One life is over. Another can begin.

Ambrosia stands before the fireplace and with every chime of the clock, her shoulders tighten. It has been more than two hours since she sent Nanny to the dungeons to retrieve her shoes from Edward. She hopes Nanny doesn't think Edward is hers to play with simply because she was permitted to punish him once. In fact, it seems to Ambrosia, that as of late, Nanny has been overstepping her bounds as Governess. She may have to have a little chat with the old woman, remind her of her place.

She will not be kept waiting.

The Princess yanks her dressmaker out from beneath her bone skirt and straightens her wig, adjusting the green curls fetchingly over her shoulder. Then she crosses the room and heads down the hallway towards the dungeon.

Ambrosia wishes she had thought of imprisoning Edward far earlier. This way he is far more accessible. Not only can she have her shoes for free, but when she wants to play, he is nearby. She slips a hand beneath her skirt and rubs herself. Perhaps she will have to imprison her dressmaker as well.

Ambrosia withdraws her hand as she approaches the Jailer. She supposes he has been employed here since her father's time but she has had little contact with the man. She watches his thick fingers spin the key in the lock, his muscled arms push open the heavy wooden door. When she grows tired of Edward (as she is most certain she will), then perhaps she will consider this brute. She notices how his eyes focus on her long thin neck as though he would like to snap it between his fingers.

She smiles, pleased. She is not afraid of a fight.

The Jailer bows to her and she enters to find Edward curled up on the floor fast asleep.

"Shoe man," she snaps and stamps her foot.

Edward stirs, stretching his shoulders, sitting up with a yawn and looking at her with bleary eyes.

"Where are my shoes?" she asks, "and why did Nanny not bring them to me?"

Edward rises and points to a shadowy heap, beyond him in the corner.

"Nanny?" Ambrosia calls out, not wanting to approach, as it will bring her nearer to Edward. And right now there is something different about him. He doesn't seem weak at all. He seems strong and sure and there is a wild light in his eyes that frightens her.

"Nanny?" she calls again, but the figure on the floor does not move.

"What have you done to her?" Ambrosia demands. But her voice no longer sounds authoritative; it has taken on a plaintive, child like sound, like a toddler who has had their favorite toy taken away.

Edward smiles at her, and it seems to Ambrosia that his teeth are sharper and his smile wider than any human's ought to be. He takes a step toward her, then bows low, holding out her shoes.

"For you, Princess," he states, and his voice catches somewhat on her title, making him sound like a snake.

Ambrosia doesn't want him to think she's afraid and so she reaches out and grabs the shoes. Jumping back out of his reach once she has claimed them.

Ambrosia now stands in the direct light of the lantern and she glances down at the shoes. They are ugly things. Made of thick brown leather. Stitched together with wiry grey hair. And on the right toe of the right foot sits a large brown mole from which sprouts three course hairs.

Ambrosia screams.

She is still screaming when the Jailer bursts into the cell. Still screaming when the guards arrive and unhook Edward from his leg iron and drag him out of the cell. Still screaming when they lead him into the courtyard to the gallows.

AFTER EVER AFTER

Anastasia stands naked in the small clearing, next to the garden, behind their cottage. It has been six months since she and Reynard left Houndstooth behind them. She listens to her husband shout out a warning. Shortly thereafter comes the sound of a tree crashing to the forest floor.

They had first gone to Ferrybone to be with her family. And it was in her sister's home, that Anastasia and Reynard were wed. They remained in the city for nearly a month, but Reynard was determined to make his own way in the world, and so he and Anastasia found this small cottage on the outskirts of the city and now they make a good living supplying paper to the local newspapiary.

Anastasia places a hand on her belly, imagines the life growing within. Then she touches the patches of skin given to her by Henry. Once a week she slips out of her clothes and stands naked in the clearing so these brave women may feel the warmth of the sun's rays upon their skin. Somehow, when Henry recalled her to life, he restored what little was left of the women as well. And in quiet moments she can hear their voices whispering their secrets; how to cut cloth along the bias (Jenny), how to make drip-less candles (Buttercup), or when Sophia is jostling for position with the others, how best Anastasia can please her husband in bed. There are other voices that belong to women she did not know. But when they speak, Anastasia is careful to listen. For it is only through her that these women now live and Anastasia is determined their wisdom shall not die.

She knows Reynard chose this isolated home so she could be protected from her past. But that time no longer has hold over her. Every now and then she will hear gossip about a shoemaker of great renown who was executed after the Royal House discovered he turned his neighbors into shoes. However, at those times, she thinks on Edward with great sadness and hopes that at last, he has found his peace.

Now, those stories have died away as preparations for the Princess's wedding begin. It is a source of much jocularity for the citizens of the land. For the proposed bridegroom comes no higher than the Princess's knees. Some say it was magic that ensnared the couple. Others say nay, that his great wealth (carried rather eccentrically in a leather shoemaking satchel), is what captured the Princess (for her Kingdom was entirely bankrupted by spending). And even others say that when the intended groom arrived wearing a pair of immaculately constructed leather boots, the right foot embroidered with a dragon, the left with its slayer, for the Princess, well, it was love at first sight.

Coming soon

Bluebeard's Bride

By Roberta Cottam & Kathryn Cottam

The letter from my sister's husband, brief and scrawled in haste, described her death as 'sudden and tragic'. His rough handwriting, smeared where my tears had bled the ink, failed to explain how Helen lost her life five days ago, at twenty-eight years of age.

Enclosed within the envelope, was a photograph of my niece Lucille. As the train rattled towards North Yorkshire, I studied it; although outdated – Lucy appearing no more than four, yet turning six come summer – I was grateful. It was a touchstone of delight folded inside terrible tidings.

In Lucy's complexion, I saw little trace of her father's dark looks, hair and beard so black they shone nearly blue. Looking every bit a descendant of a Jaye, I wondered if Lucy's freckled cheeks had now cleared to ivory, or if her strawberry locks had deepened to auburn like her mother's, or skewed to chestnut as had mine.

It was four years since I had last seen my niece. I recalled Christmas dinner at the Fords' Syndenham townhouse in '89, where Lucy – then not yet two – toddled about in a miniature sailor dress trimmed with gold braid, an homage to her father's naval career. Other officers in epaulettes and their wives toasted Jonathan Ford, and Helen beamed with pride for her husband. Following upon the hard years since we'd lost our father, for the first time in many years I had felt hope for the Jayes that Christmas. Our family, whittled to three orphaned girls, would now strengthen and grow.

As Rosamund, my second eldest sister, and I sipped port and ate brandied cherries, we dreamed of future nieces and nephews. That December, lavishing Rosie and I with expensive gloves and linens, there was no indication that, only a few weeks into the new year, Ford would suddenly leave the fleet and sell his London estate. The following February, he moved our sister and niece to a great house in North Yorkshire, taking with him that which was more precious to us than any brown paper package tied with a branch of holly.

I returned Lucy's photograph to its home, tucked between the pages of Jane Eyre, and slid the book into my carpet bag. I had received no photograph of Helen, and, with a bitter-sweet heart, ached to smell her aroma in the house and touch the trinkets that she called her own.

Seated beside me, Rosamund rested her head against the window as the train thundered north. She also had received a photograph of Lucy (along with her equally abrupt worded letter), which she had trimmed and set into our late mother's locket and hung it about her neck. Fingering the silver locket now, she stared out at fields of meadow foxtail and spear thistle, the passing view blurred by the speed of the engine so that they looked like a bolt of green watered silk, the pigment marbled and bled dry in places. Tightening my travel cloak about my shoulders, I curled into Rosie's side and rested my cheek on the rough tweed of her jacket.

The train carried us closer to Blueford Hall.

in the Cauldron

Coming Soon

A collection of stories from Kathryn Cottam, Roberta Cottam, and Kate Tremills

"In the land of fairy, stories are hidden in the mists. A traveller may catch a glance of one tale, follow its glimmer, and believe he or she understands the whole picture. But there are elements always misunderstood, misread, or simply in disguise.

Ancient tales are tricky creatures. Never wanting to show their whole face. Only trusting the pure of heart with their whispers. Knowing full well that humans have a tendency to steal treasure and use it to their own ends.

Never assume you know the whole truth. For out of the shadows, a new storyteller will rise to reveal their secrets to you…"

Upcoming Releases

To be notified of upcoming releases from FoxTale Press, please send an email with "Book Release" in the subject line to:

Foxtalepress@gmail.com

We will not contact you at any other time, nor share your email with a third party.

www.thefoxtalepress.com

Thank You

Word-of-mouth assists an author to succeed in their chosen field. If you enjoyed this book, please consider leaving a review (even a few words) at Amazon. Your input makes a difference and is received with much gratitude and thanks.

Thank You

To Roberta. Without you, this book would be half of what it is. You will always have my heart for supporting this dream.

To Elizabeth, Andrew, Steve. You are the best cheerleading section ever!

To Mom and Dad. I am truly blessed to be your child. You encouraged my love of literature, my desire to write.

To Kate, for your unwavering support, courage, grace, and fierceness.

To my boys, Andrew and Nathan and my little girl, Analeigh.
The three of you make me a better person.
I will love and cherish you always.

To my Grandma.
Your dying words to me were, "never stop reading."
And I never have.

Without all of you, this book would never have been.

Author Kathryn Cottam
Titles *The Shoemaker, Bluebeard's Bride*

As a child, Kathryn daydreamed her way through school, befriended books as soul-mates and read her way through entire libraries. She loves stories of every shape and style: fairy-tale, mystery, horror, fantasy or non-fiction.
After years of writing screenplays, Kathryn has returned to her first love — novels.

Kathryn is currently working on her next book with her sister Roberta, and is collaborating on a collection of short stories.

If she didn't love her red hair so much, she would probably dye it turquoise.

Illustrator Roberta Cottam
Titles *The Shoemaker, Bluebeard's Bride*

Roberta designs book plates, fashion plates and dinner plates, drawing inspiration from wild mushrooms, wild horses and fairy-tale heroines wild-at-heart.

She believes a woman's greatest accessory is a sense of adventure. Roberta is two countries shy of visiting forty by age forty. Closer to home, Roberta may be found admiring the grizzlies of Bella Coola or tickling the starfish of San Joseph Bay, and has yet to confuse the two.

But she is most at home in her sunny yellow kitchen where her cat sleeps on a ceiling beam, her husband taste-tests the latest creation, and her daughter was born.